Praise

"Carlisle's novel is thoughtful, with well-developed characters who move beyond common small-town girl and big-city boy tropes. Instead, she pulls together two characters who turn out to have far more in common than they think."—***Kirkus Reviews*** on *The Library of Second Chances*

"A Charming second-chance summer love story."—***Kirkus Reviews*** on *The Summer of Starting Over*

"I was completely enchanted by this charmingly sweet beach read and just adored the letters exchanged in the Little Free Library."—**Teri Wilson, *USA Today* bestselling author** on *The Library of Second Chances*

"A charming inspiring and empowering second-chance summer romance that's will make your heart sing!"—**Karen Schaler, Emmy award-winning screenwriter & screenwriter** on *The Summer of Starting Over*

"Fans of *You've Got Mail* will swoon over Lucy and Logan in this charming romance that celebrates the splendor of small-town living."—**KJ Micciche, author of *The Book Proposal*** on *The Library of Second Chances*

"...Savannah Carlisle is now one of my go-to authors for heartwarming, Kleenex-clutching, feel-good romance!"—**Annie Rains, *USA Today* bestselling author**

"...Savannah Carlisle's debut is sure to delight. The author's vivid descriptions put me right in Heron Isle along with the characters and had this city girl longing for the cozy and picturesque small-town life she masterfully depicted."—**Meredith Schorr, author of *As Seen on TV* and *Someone Just Like You*** on *The Library of Second Chances*

"100% recommend this for your summer (or anytime) TBR!" —***The Book Nerd Mama*** on *The Library of Second Chances*

Also by Savannah Carlisle

The Library of Second Chances
The Summer of Starting Over

If I'd Have Known

Meredith —
Hope you enjoy this mental vacation to Big Dune Island!

If I'd Have Known

SAVANNAH CARLISLE

HB
HARPETH ROAD
PRESS
Nashville

HARPETH ROAD PRESS

Published by Harpeth Road Press (USA)
P.O. Box 158184
Nashville, TN 37215

Paperback: 978-1-963483-34-5
eBook: 978-1-963483-33-8
Library of Congress Control Number: 2025942351

If I'd Have Known: A Heartwarming, Charming Romance

Copyright © Savannah Carlisle, 2025

All rights reserved. Except for the use of brief quotations in review of this novel, the reproduction of this work in whole or in part in any format by any electronic, mechanical, or other means, now known or hereinafter invented, including photocopying, recording, scanning, and all other formats, or in any information storage or retrieval or distribution system, is forbidden without the written permission of the publisher, Harpeth Road Press, P.O. Box 158184, Nashville, Tennessee 37215, USA.

This is a work of fiction. Names, characters, places, and incidents are the product of the author's imagination or were used fictitiously, and any resemblance to actual persons, living or dead, business establishments, events, or locales is entirely coincidental.

Cover Design by Kristen Ingebretson
Cover Images © Shutterstock

Harpeth Road Press, August 2025

This one is for Teresa, who started as my law school classmate and then became my family. Thank you for inspiring Gigi's law practice in the book and helping me make it as realistic as possible!

Chapter One

Gigi

"Who's ready to get married?" Gigi Franklin said in a sing-song voice as she slid into a chair across from her best friend, country music superstar Callie Jackson.

Callie beamed. "I still can't believe it's really happening."

"Oh, it's happening," Gigi said as she pulled a three-ring binder out of her oversized purse and plopped it on the table between them for emphasis.

"Omigosh, you still have this," Callie practically shrieked as she pulled the binder across the table for a closer look. She trailed a finger over the puff-paint title on the cover: *The Perfect Wedding*.

"Don't tell Myrtle," Gigi said, referring to her mother, whose only dream for her daughter's life was a husband and children. "I don't want to give her any false hope."

Callie frowned. "You're going to find your Prince Charming one day too."

"No," Gigi said, waving a finger. "I do not need or want a Prince Charming. Do you have any idea how many divorces I did last year? No thanks." Then when she realized Callie was frowning again, she said, "That won't happen with you and Jesse, of course. You found the one man on the planet who actually doesn't mind that you have a career *and* that you make more money than him."

"He might change his mind if I can't get this album recorded before the wedding so we can actually go on a honeymoon." Callie laughed as she picked up her mug to take a sip.

"How's that going?"

"We're a little behind schedule, but I should be able to get caught up. Luckily, Jesse is having to work overtime at the Watson House to get it done before the wedding too, so I don't feel so guilty holing up in the recording studio all the time. Did I tell you Sienna and I are doing a two-part duet? The first one will be on my album, and then the second one will be on hers. I'm the wife in the story, and she's the other woman, and we each get to sort of tell our side of the story."

"Kind of like 'Jolene' and 'That Girl'?" Gigi asked, referring to the Dolly Parton classic that later had the other side of the story told in a Jennifer Nettles song.

"Yes, exactly. The record company thinks it'll help boost sales for Sienna when her debut comes out this winter. I don't think she'll have any trouble—you know how talented she is—but if they think it'll help, I'm happy to shine the spotlight—"

Callie stopped mid-sentence as Gigi practically leaped across the table to grab the binder and flip it over to the nondescript back side. Chloe Beckett, the owner of Island Coffee, was approaching, and she had a bit of a reputation for gossip and the inability to keep a secret.

"Hi, Gigi," Chloe said in her bright, bubbly voice. "Can I get you anything?"

"Two shots of espresso. Thanks."

Chloe glanced down at Gigi's hand still protectively on top of the binder, and it looked like it physically pained her not to ask about it. "Okay, be right back," she finally said after a long pause.

Callie raised an eyebrow after Chloe had left them. "Espresso at four in the afternoon?"

"You're not the only one who's behind schedule." Gigi sighed, sitting back in her chair. "I have a bunch of paperwork to do for the Nickersons to adopt Ty."

Normally, Gigi wouldn't have been able to share privileged legal information, but Big Dune Island was a small town and the Nickersons were high school classmates of Gigi and Callie. Callie knew they'd fostered the five-year-old boy after having two newborn adoptions fall through when birth mothers changed their minds. She also knew they had decided to formally adopt him.

"I'm totally in awe of them," Callie said. "It takes special people to welcome an older child into their lives."

"Right?" Gigi said. "It's actually the first adoption I've done for an older kid. Everyone wants a baby."

Gigi didn't add that she personally felt zero maternal instinct when she saw babies. However, she did find a small part of herself wishing she had the time or energy to help one of the kids she'd met through the local foster care system during her time as an attorney on the island. Although her mother was an overbearing helicopter parent who'd tried to orchestrate her entire life from the day she was born, Gigi knew she was lucky to have grown up with parents who loved each other and provided her with everything she could ever need.

Chloe approached with the espresso, and Gigi thanked her.

"I know this one's your favorite." Chloe winked, referring to the cup and saucer covered in pink peonies.

"It is," Gigi agreed, holding up the tiny espresso cup to admire it.

Chloe was her friend Austin Beckett's younger sister, and she'd opened the town's only Main Street coffee shop a few years prior. One of its most unique features was the china everything was served on, which consisted of pieces donated by women in town who wanted to preserve their formal china, but didn't have children interested in inheriting it. It meant every piece in the cafe had a story to tell and allowed the history of the town's families to be carried into the future.

The cookie Callie had ordered before Gigi arrived sat half eaten on a Noritake plate adorned with pink azaleas that had once been owned by Callie's maternal grandparents. She'd donated pieces of the formal china to the cafe when she'd cleaned out her parents' house last year, opting to only keep her parents' everyday china for her future in the newly renovated family home she would share with Jesse after they were married.

"Back to the task at hand," Gigi said, flipping the binder open between them. "I left all your inspiration photos at the beginning here in case there's something that still catches your eye."

"You mean like those sheer puff sleeves?" Callie said, pointing at a cut-out photo of a bright white wedding dress with the sleeves that were popular in the 1990s.

"Okay, maybe not the dress, but I do still love this cake," Gigi said, flipping the page to a three-tier wedding cake with edible pearls dotting it and a few white roses tucked into the side of the first layer. It was simple. Classic.

"Let them eat cake!" Austin declared as he approached their table with Callie's fiancé, Jesse Thomas.

Austin's trademark was his ability to find a quote or corny saying for every situation. Gigi rolled her eyes, even if it was one of his more endearing qualities.

As he sat in one of the two empty chairs at the round table, Austin motioned for his sister. Jesse leaned over to kiss Callie on the cheek before settling in the chair next to her.

Gigi snapped the binder shut again as Chloe approached. Meeting at the cafe was probably a bad idea for privacy's sake, but it had become a bit of an afternoon habit. It was almost equal distance between Gigi's office in a little historic house one block south of Main and Callie's family home, one block north of it.

Callie steered the conversation to updates on her album after the men ordered their drinks, filling the time until Chloe had delivered their order and was back at the other end of the shotgun-style cafe.

"Is this your wedding-planning bible?" Austin asked, flipping the binder open again on the table.

"Yes, as a matter of fact, it is," Gigi said, attempting to grab it from him.

He was too quick though, and swiped it from her reach.

"Look," he said to Jesse, "it's color-coded and there are even little tabs. Venue. Flowers. Caterers." Austin rattled off each tab as he flicked through them. "Dress. Sorry, dude, you can't see this one," he said, pretending he was peeking at the next page while holding up a hand to block Jesse's view. "No seeing the dress before the wedding. Right, ladies?"

"Give me that before you mess it up," Gigi said, leaning across the arm of her chair to reach for the binder, which he passed to her as he laughed and shook his head.

"Sorry," Callie said, shrugging. Her smile said she wasn't really. "I invited the guys to help us figure out how to pull this off. I want a normal wedding, but I have no idea how we can do that without someone from the media getting wind of it and turning it into a circus."

"You heard her. She doesn't want any media there," Gigi deadpanned in Austin's direction. He'd moved back to town after his brief stint as a Major League Baseball player to host a sports talk-radio show in nearby Jacksonville.

He smirked. "Someone has to make sure this shindig is actually fun. I didn't see a tab for that."

"Children, children," Jesse chided. "There's enough wedding planning to go around. Everyone will get their turn."

"There won't be anything to plan if we can't figure out where to have the wedding and how to keep it a secret," Callie said.

"Yes, that's priority number one," Gigi said, pulling a pen out of her purse and opening the binder in her lap to a blank page.

"Do we need to call the meeting to order before the secretary begins taking notes?" Austin asked her.

"I move we vote Beckett off the committee," Gigi said, looking then to Callie and Jesse, smiling. "Do I have a second?"

"Motion fails to carry," Austin said after their friends only laughed in response. "In new business, we need somewhere these two can get hitched that's worthy of the great Callie Jackson."

Despite the Country Music Awards that confirmed Callie was basically country music royalty, she blushed just like she always did when anyone on the island acknowledged her stardom. The locals had mostly let her live like a normal person since she moved back to town, but tourists still marveled at the sight of her if she ventured into town without a wig. It was why they were sitting in the back corner of Island Coffee, Callie with her back to the door and her trademark blonde curls tucked up into a baseball cap.

"I don't care where it's at or what it looks like. I just want it to be on Big Dune where everyone we love can be there to celebrate with us," Callie said, reaching over to take Jesse's hand.

"What my Cal wants, my Cal gets," Jesse said, leaning over for a quick peck.

The only hitch was they were going to have to put something together quickly if they wanted to fit in a honeymoon before Callie and Sienna had to go on the road to promote albums this winter.

"Well, obviously, I'll draft up NDAs for all the vendors to sign," Gigi said, making a note on the to-do list she'd started.

"Do you think that's enough though?" Callie asked, raising her eyebrows.

"If one of them dares break their nondisclosure agreement, I'll sue their pants right off of them."

"What if they didn't know it was Callie's wedding?" Austin asked.

"If we tell them it's for a secret bride, they'll know it's Callie," Jesse said, shaking his head. "Who else around here would be getting married secretly?"

"Actually, I hate to admit this, but Beckett might be on to something," Gigi said, ignoring the hand Austin held up triumphantly for her to high-five. "I wonder if we could figure out how to book things as if it's a different kind of event, like a surprise birthday party or something."

"Or one of those big events Ms. Myrtle always has," Austin chimed in, referring to Gigi's mother.

"Wait, isn't your parents' wedding anniversary in the fall?" Callie asked, her bright blue eyes lighting up with an idea.

"Yes," Gigi said slowly, hoping she wasn't right about where Callie was going next.

"What if we told people it was a vow renewal for your parents? It's totally something Ms. Myrtle would do, and everyone in town would be sure to show up."

Jesse nodded. "That actually makes a lot of sense. Would your mom go for it?" he asked Gigi.

"Are you kidding me? She loves weddings, and heaven knows she's not going to see me get married anytime soon. The only problem will be keeping her from planning the wedding *she* wants instead of the one *you* want. But I can ask her tomorrow. I need to go over this week to drop off some paperwork for her to sign anyway."

"We have an early morning session tomorrow because Bruce has a flight to catch," Callie said, referring to her producer, "but I could go with you any other time this week."

"Perfect. Then we can figure out if any venues have openings this fall and go from there." It was September already, but surely somewhere would have an off-peak date available. Fall wasn't a busy time on Big Dune Island after school was back in session, and Callie had already said she didn't care what day of the week they held the wedding.

"Now that that's settled, let's talk about the bachelor party," Austin said, wiggling his eyebrows at Jesse. "I'm thinking Vegas. Nothing trashy, of course," he said to Callie. "The showgirls are all true professionals. They really don't get enough credit for their artistry."

Gigi rolled her eyes. "They want a joint bachelor-bachelorette weekend away with just a few close friends. I've already scoped out some vacation rentals up in Savannah and on Tybee Island."

"My apologies. I must have missed that tab," Austin joked, nodding toward the binder. "It's a little different to the vibe I was going for, but I can work with it."

Callie laughed. "I'm not sure I want to be stuck in a house with the two of you after all."

Gigi wasn't sure it was a good idea either. She and Austin had been friends since high school, growing even closer when they both lived in Atlanta during her college and law school years while Austin was playing for the Braves. What rattled her now, however, was that she still remembered how close they'd come to kissing the last time they'd stayed in a house together for a wedding.

Later that evening, Gigi took a glass of wine and her laptop out to the table on her back deck to start researching local wedding venues. She'd renovated a beachfront cottage herself when she'd moved back to Big Dune Island from New York City, where she worked after law school. She spent most of her time at the office, but when she was home, she liked to be on the back deck breathing the salty air and working to the soundtrack of the waves that crashed thirty yards behind her house on the other side of the dunes.

Lighting a citronella candle to keep the mosquitos and no-see-ums away from the glow of the laptop, she opened a browser tab and began looking up the venues she knew off the top of her head. On the fancier end of things, there was the Palm Yacht Club, The Dunes—the only luxury hotel on the island—and Wilson's Landing, a private venue for residents of the island's most exclusive community. All three were on the south end of the island, where Jesse used to help developers build second-home monstrosities that wiped out one-hundred-year-old live oaks and the last of the natural land on the island. Thankfully, he now focused on preserving and renovating historic homes.

She was on the weddings page for the yacht club when she realized it was the location her mother would choose, which made her immediately exit the browser tab. Sure, it might be what people would expect for the Franklins' vow renewal, but the actual event needed to fit Callie and Jesse. And despite the fact that Callie's wealth eclipsed most of the people on the island, a stuffy, white-tablecloth affair with servers in tails and three different kinds of forks at every place setting was about as far from her taste as you could get.

The same went for The Dunes. Too buttoned up for Callie and Jesse. Wilson's Landing might work though. It was a giant wooden pavilion built out over the marsh on the river side of the island. The website showed white twinkle lights and sheer white fabric swagging across the exposed beams. She could picture Callie and Jesse there, so she sent the PDF with more details and contact information to her printer. She'd add it to her binder and give them a call tomorrow to inquire about availability.

The website featured an Instagram feed full of past weddings at the bottom of the page, so she began clicking through for inspiration. As she went down the rabbit hole of one bride's big day, she ended up on the photographer's page, that included photos from other nearby wedding venues. Gigi had been so focused on Big Dune Island that she'd forgotten about the Whispering Palms on Fort George Island just south of them. It was an easy twenty-minute drive.

Fort George Island was largely uninhabited, much of it preserved as a state park. A small portion of the island had been developed in the 1920s, including the historic Whispering Palms estate, once the summer home of a wealthy railroad magnate. It was close enough for everyone to attend, but far enough to give the couple privacy. Gigi printed out their wedding brochure to add to her binder and picked up her wine for a long sip. Something told her she'd already found the venue. Fingers crossed they'd still have an open date.

Whispering Palms had an Instagram feed as well, so she browsed the photos to get a better look at the indoor and outdoor options for the ceremony and reception. One photo in particular caught her attention because it featured the same seafoam-green bridesmaid dress she'd worn to her childhood friend Mary Catherine Morgan's wedding back in college. Apparently, it was one of those bridesmaid dresses that never went out of style—despite the fact it had never actually been in style.

Originally, she'd been planning to go to the wedding on the arm of her longtime boyfriend, Dalton, with a ring on her own finger. But then he'd suddenly broken things off, and she'd been surprised when Austin gave up the opportunity to go to the wedding of their mutual friend as a single man and instead suggested they go together. He had stayed at her side the entire evening, giving up his chance to flirt with the single bridesmaids.

What she remembered most about that weekend, however, was when, after the wedding, they'd ended up being the last two still in the hot tub at the beach house Mary Catherine's mother had rented for the wedding party. Still buzzing from the champagne at the reception, they'd ended up in a deep conversation about their overbearing parents and their impossible expectations. Austin had made it to AAA, the highest level before reaching the majors, and his dad still wasn't happy. It was Major League Baseball or nothing. Meanwhile, Myrtle asked Gigi more about the guys in her classes than her grades. The only degree Myrtle cared about Gigi getting was her "Mrs. degree." College was for finding a husband, not a career.

They'd stayed in the hot tub until their skin was prune-like, and then Austin had exited first and held out his hand to help her up the slippery steps. When she'd reached the top, he'd held her hand a beat longer than was necessary. She remembered looking up at him, water beading down his tan, muscular chest, his green eyes fixed on hers. There had been a moment, hadn't there? Then Carly Lassiter had stumbled out the back door, interrupting them as she shouted Austin's name, still feeling the effects of the shots Gigi had seen her taking in the kitchen when they returned from the wedding.

Gigi shook her head to dislodge the memory, grabbing her wine glass to take a big swig. It didn't matter, anyway, because a week later she wasn't even speaking to Austin anymore. They'd mended fences after they'd both moved back to Big Dune Island, and then Callie had returned to complete their foursome, but Gigi hadn't forgotten. Not about the almost kiss or what happened afterward.

Chapter Two

Austin

The bells above the door jangled as Austin entered Island Coffee the next morning.

"Help yourself," his sister Chloe said as she breezed past him to deliver coffee to a table by the window overlooking Main Street.

Austin stopped by for coffee and a pastry every morning before heading to Jacksonville for work. Some mornings, his sister had it waiting for him on the counter, but she looked harried today. The place was packed with a mix of locals like him who had a daily routine, and tourists getting an early start to their day. He was glad to see business was good. He'd given Chloe the startup capital for the cafe five years ago, thinking maybe he could help her run it following his retirement from baseball. When he'd blown a rotator cuff and then his Achilles, he had an excellent excuse to hang up his cleats and end his career. He'd made enough money to set himself up for life if he invested well, and he had achieved his father's goal, but he was still trying to figure out what he wanted to do with the rest of his life. The radio show was fun for now, and maybe that was enough, but he still felt like something was missing.

"She made the strawberry basil scones again," Iris said, winking at him as she grabbed the coffee pot from the counter before he could reach it and poured him a to-go cup.

"Thanks, Iris. Busy morning, huh?"

"You know it," she said, beaming. She took so much pride in the place you'd think she was the one who co-owned it.

Iris was in her late sixties and had been looking for something to do after her husband passed. She had been the first to respond to Chloe's "help wanted" sign before the cafe opened. She ran the place like a well-oiled machine, freeing his sister to concentrate on the inventive pastries and desserts she liked to make.

After grabbing two scones for the road, Austin set his bakery bag on the counter while he pulled out his wallet and found a five-dollar bill to stuff in the tip jar by the cash register.

"You know you don't have to tip when you own the place and wait on yourself, don't ya?" Iris swatted at him with the dishrag she had begun wiping down the counter with.

"You poured my coffee." He shrugged. "So I didn't actually wait on myself, did I?"

She shook her head and went back to cleaning. She used to take out the money and try to stuff it back in his pocket, but she'd given that up years ago when she learned he gave it to Chloe to sneak back in.

Chloe insisted Iris keep all the tip money at the end of her shifts. Iris's daughter and grandson had moved in with her the past winter, and Austin had heard through the grapevine that the little boy's father hadn't paid child support in a year. Austin couldn't understand how a father could not only abandon his child but also refuse to help take care of him. Sam, Iris's grandson, was on the baseball team Austin coached through the local Little League program, and he was soft-spoken and kind. How anyone could walk out on him was a mystery, but it obviously said more about his dad than it did about Sam.

After stopping to chat with one of his parents' neighbors about the weather and who was taking over the old pharmacy at the end of Main Street, Austin set off for the sports radio station where he co-hosted the midday show. It was nearly an hour's drive each way, but it was worth it to get to live on Big Dune Island. People might always be in your business, but it was because they cared. When one of them needed help, everyone in town stepped up. He'd seen it firsthand last year when Al, who owned the hardware store, needed bypass surgery. Ned, who owned the paint store next door, stepped in to help manage inventory, pay bills and run payroll until Al could get back to work.

Austin had hated living in Atlanta, where he spent more time sitting in traffic than he ever did in his condo and never found out the name of a single neighbor. Not that he'd wanted to spend much time there anyway. It was a soulless square of space with marble, glass, and metal surfaces that were every bit as cold in atmosphere as they were to the touch. His agent had advised him to rent a corporate apartment because he never knew when he might be traded by the Braves to another team. Besides, he was usually only there long enough to sleep between practices, games, and life on the road. He always came home to Big Dune Island in the offseason to recharge before reporting to Spring Training on the other side of Florida.

The radio gig was easy as far as jobs went. He was on air from 11:00 to 1:00 with a retired NFL player who was the yin to his yang. Darold Phillips was grouchy and the tell-it-like-it-is type, while Austin was easygoing and generally optimistic. Austin got into the station an hour early for prep and a chat with their producer, and then he was back on the island by 2:30 after a little chitchat around the station. As long as he watched the big games and caught highlights on Sportscenter every morning, he could easily keep up with Darold and the callers.

Increasingly, what Austin looked forward to each week were the two afternoons he coached Little League. If you'd told him that five years ago, he never would have believed it. He'd burned out on baseball as a teenager but continued to play all the way to the major leagues. All baseball had ever represented for him was discipline, endless practicing, and forever feeling as if he came up short in his father's eyes.

When Austin had made the varsity team as a freshman, his dad had chastised him for not being a starter. Then when he'd been a starter, it had been his fault they hadn't won the state championship his sophomore year. Then when they won the championship senior year, the problem was that his draft projections had him going second round instead of first. Then it had taken him too long to go from A to AA ball, and on and on. Even making a major-league roster hadn't been good enough for Austin's dad because he hadn't been Rookie of the Year or an All-Star selection. It never ended.

Until it did.

Enough years had passed that his dad rarely hounded him about what could have been. Instead, they barely spoke because they had nothing in common. But Austin preferred the silence to the constant pressure that had come before that.

As he pulled into the parking lot next to the field that afternoon for practice, he was singing along to some classic Bruce Springsteen, feeling as if he was winning at the game of life.

"Hey, Coach," Theo Miller's mom, Kelsey, called from the sidewalk as Austin got out of his truck.

"Hey, Kels," he said, nodding at her as he went to the back of the truck to start unloading gear. They'd been classmates in high school. He still found it hard to believe that people his age had kids old enough for him to coach. Sure, they were in their thirties now, but he still believed he wasn't old enough for that yet, despite the fact that he clearly was.

"That was really something else you did for the boys," she said. "Getting them all new gloves. Theo has been oiling his and stuffing a ball in it every night to break it in. I swear, it's his most-prized possession."

"It was no big deal."

She came to stand by him, holding out a hand to take a bag of baseballs he was hauling from the truck. "It's a very big deal to some of these boys, and you know it." When he didn't reply immediately, she said, "I know you did it for Sam and Luke so they wouldn't feel bad that they don't have the same gear the other kids do, but it was nice of you to include them all."

"I didn't want them to feel singled out," he said. "Besides, my sponsor was happy to do it in exchange for a couple of Instagram posts. It really was no sweat."

She reached out with her free hand and rubbed his back in a way that made him feel uncomfortable. She was divorced, but he didn't want her to get the wrong idea.

"You're quite the catch these days, Coach Austin. Who would have known in high school that you'd turn out to be one of the good guys?"

He pulled away from her touch, laughing off her comment and concentrating on a bag of bats that had rolled to the middle of the truck bed and were barely within reach. The only bad thing about moving back to Big Dune Island had been returning to the reputation he'd had as a teenager. Sure, he'd dated a lot of girls back then, but didn't most teenage boys? Well, except Jesse, of course, who'd only ever had eyes for Callie.

Thankfully, Kelsey was spotted by another mom on the team who was crossing the parking lot toward them and ended up getting pulled away for what sounded like local gossip. Hauling bags over both shoulders, he started making his way over to the field.

Austin knew it was partially his fault that the women he'd grown up with, like Kelsey and Gigi, thought he was such a player. He'd, admittedly, been girl crazy as a teen, taking advantage of his good looks and star-athlete reputation to date nearly every girl who showed him any positive attention. But he'd never treated any of them poorly—never been rude, never taken things too far, never even broken their hearts, because he never went on more than a few dates with any of them. Most of the time, he preferred just hanging with Jesse, Callie, and Gigi. They'd all been friends since elementary school, and they were a tight foursome.

And, yes, he perpetuated his reputation a bit with the stupid things he said—like when he'd made the Vegas-bachelor-party quip the day before. He didn't even like Vegas. He was just trying to be funny. He could see it on Gigi's face though. She hadn't thought it was funny; she'd just thought he was a womanizer who only ever considered how to get the next woman undressed. Heck, he hadn't even kissed a woman in over a year, but it's not like he was going to admit that out loud to anyone.

"Coach, Coach," Sam called out from third base. "Watch this!" Then he nodded to Luke, who was holding a bat and ball at home plate.

Luke tossed the ball in the air and then hit a grounder as hard as he could to Sam. The red-haired little boy put his glove to the ground, adjusting it slightly upward as the ball bounced, putting his free hand over the top to secure the ball once it landed in the webbing.

"Thatta boy!" Austin shouted. "That's what I like to see."

Sam had been struggling with hard hit ground balls in the infield. They played against teams with boys who were almost ten and considerably bigger, meaning they hit harder than some of the younger kids—like Sam, who just turned eight—were used to. Ground balls came at you fast at third base, but Sam was insistent he wanted to be a third baseman because he loved Hugo Sanchez, the Braves' third baseman. Austin knew Hugo well enough to know he was an excellent role model, so he'd promised Sam he'd help him get better at the position.

As Sam grinned and rolled the ball back to Luke, Austin wondered what it would have been like to grow up with a coach who told you that you did a good job. Sam might not have a dad who showed up for him, but at least Austin could show up for the kid as his coach.

He watched Luke and Sam repeat their routine as the other kids began to arrive at the field. They were always the first two kids to arrive, and it didn't take a genius to understand that baseball was their happy place, even if it had never been Austin's.

The two boys had more in common than just being the same age and playing on the same team. Like Sam, Luke didn't have a father in the picture, but he also didn't have a mother. Luke was one of the foster kids on the island who lived with the Carsons. Word around town was that his mother died in a car accident two years previously, and the father was unknown. Austin understood how much a father could shape your life, in good ways and in bad. Although he tried not to play favorites openly, he did try to give a little extra time and attention to Sam and Luke.

"Hey, Luke," he called from the dugout as the other boys began filtering onto the field to toss the ball. "Try this bat."

Luke jogged over, accepting the bright blue aluminum bat Austin held out to him. He and Sam had been playing with an old bat of Sam's that both boys had outgrown, but Austin had gotten some new ones for the team from his sporting goods sponsor.

"Thanks, Coach," he said quietly, not meeting Austin's eyes. He was a polite kid but a tad shy.

"Want to work on bunting today?" Austin asked him.

Luke shrugged his shoulders. "Sure."

The boy was the fastest kid on the team, but he didn't always connect with the ball squarely enough to get on base. This was the first league where the boys could bunt, and he thought Luke might have better luck getting on base that way. If Austin lined up a couple of good hitters behind him, he'd probably score more times than not when he got on base.

"All right, everybody in," Austin called out to the boys who were spread over the field warming up.

Once Sam and the others had jogged in, he had them stand in front of home plate so he could show them how to bunt. After explaining the mechanics of squaring off and where to hold the bat, he asked Theo, their best pitcher, to take the mound. Directing the rest of the boys to back up by the dugout, he took his batting stance and told Theo to pitch one to him. As he proceeded to demonstrate a few bunts, he talked the boys through how to squat up and down to match the height of the incoming pitch.

Satisfied he'd shown them as much as he could, he asked who on the team had bunted in the past. Two of the older boys raised their hands, so he had them come give it a try. Then he asked the inexperienced boys who wanted to try it first. He caught Luke looking at the ground, nudging a rock around with the toe of his cleats. Austin could tell he didn't want to go first, so he selected one of the more eager boys with a hand raised.

As the boys lined up to try, Sam and Luke fell to the rear like usual. Not only were they two of the youngest on the team, but both had clear confidence issues Austin never had at their age. In the early years, he'd loved playing baseball. His dad had started throwing with Austin and had him hitting off a tee long before he could even sign up for T-ball, which meant he was the best player on every team those first few years. Eventually, some of the other kids caught up, but Austin had enough natural talent—not to mention extra practices with his dad—to be one of the best on every team he played on through high school.

Austin couldn't help but envy the boys on his team who were just average. The ones whose parents showed up to watch them play and told them they'd done a good job, even when they made a mistake. Sam and Luke's confidence was affected by not having fathers involved, and his own had been affected by having a father who was too involved.

If nothing else, coaching was teaching him a lot about the kind of dad he wanted to be one day. Seeing the joy baseball brought the kids was helping to heal his relationship with the game too, or at least that's what his "mental performance coach," Jed—who was a licensed psychologist who worked with the Braves—told him.

Jed was right though. Seeing the game through the eyes of his team—and, if he was being honest, the way they looked at him because he'd been a Major League Baseball player—had begun to replace some of the bad memories around the game with good ones.

Now, if only he could get his father to look at him the way the kids on his team did.

Chapter Three

Gigi

"A party to celebrate our fortieth wedding anniversary?" Myrtle Franklin's face broke into a wide smile. "I love it. We can book the yacht club. I'll see when it's available." Gigi's mother was already grabbing her cell phone.

"Calm down, Myrtle." Gigi had been calling her mother by her first name since the two weeks they'd spent not speaking to each other after Gigi announced she'd accepted a job offer in New York City after law school instead of leaving with a "Mrs. degree" and returning home to get married and have children. Since Myrtle refused to call her daughter Gigi—opting for her proper name, Georgia—Gigi was sticking with calling her mother by her own first name. "This isn't your actual anniversary party, remember? It's Callie and Jesse's wedding."

Myrtle paused, phone in hand, as if considering what her

daughter had said. "Oh, wait, The Dunes. Yes, The Dunes, for sure. Pierre will make sure we have complete discretion. He owes me for that Junior League luncheon last year when they set the tables with sky-blue tablecloths when he knows *navy* blue is our color."

Gigi shook her head, falling back against the couch and crossing her arms. "See." She turned to Callie seated next to her. "I told you this was a bad idea."

Callie smiled in the kind, patient way she'd always dealt with Myrtle. "It'll be perfect. No one in town would dare miss Ms. Myrtle's anniversary party and, that way, Jesse and I can get married in front of all our friends and family without the press finding out and crashing our wedding."

Piper, Callie's publicist, nodded. "No one outside of this room can know what we're really planning. Even a group this large makes me a little nervous." She glanced around the room as if sizing up who might be the weak link in the group.

Callie, Jesse, Austin, and Piper had all descended on the Franklins' house to discuss how they could turn a fortieth anniversary party into a surprise wedding. Ms. Myrtle had been thrilled to help when asked, though Gigi had her doubts about her mother's ability to not take over.

"You could still elope." Gigi turned to Callie, her eyes pleading.

"No, the whole point in moving back here was to try to live a normal life." Callie's voice was determined.

Just a year ago, Callie would have never stood up for herself and asked for what she wanted. Gigi was missing that Callie right about now. Okay, that wasn't exactly true. She'd been proud of Callie for standing up to her label and leaving them for another that would let her finally call the shots in her career. Gigi just really hated that they had to involve her mother in their big secret wedding plans.

"I want the fancy white dress and dinner and dancing. I

don't want some quickie wedding in a courthouse." Callie scrunched her tiny nose at Jesse, who was sitting on the other side of her on the couch. He grabbed her hand.

"Of course you don't." Myrtle's eyes narrowed in Gigi's direction before turning back to Callie with a wide smile. "You just leave it to me, dear."

"No, no, no." Gigi sat up and cut her hands through the air like a referee at a wrestling match, signaling there had been no hold. "We did not come here to ask you to plan this affair. We only need you on board for the anniversary party idea so you can make sure everyone attends."

"Well," Myrtle huffed, sitting up on the edge of her chair, ready to go to battle. "How exactly do you plan to get the flowers, the food, and the band booked? Callie and Piper can't call around; people would get suspicious. Besides, I can plan these sorts of things in my sleep."

Gigi leaned forward, ready to go toe-to-toe with her mother. "I've got it under control, Myrtle. She's my best friend. I know what she wants."

"Do you? I was at your holiday party." Myrtle shook her head. She was referring to the party Gigi threw annually at her law practice. "The crab cakes were all filler, and the champagne was warm." Her nose wrinkled as her lip turned up.

Gigi's eyes grew wide, her fists clenching at her sides.

"Ladies." Dr. Franklin held up a hand before Gigi could respond. "I'm sure you can find a way to work together on this, for Callie's sake."

Gigi's dad was a soft-spoken man who had spent a lifetime doting on his overindulged wife. Gigi had always been close to her father, but at the end of the day, he always chose Myrtle to her face and then came to Gigi later to tell her he really believed her to be right. It was infuriating that he never stood up for his daughter.

"I thought the crab cakes were some of the best I've had." Austin shrugged.

Myrtle looked as if she'd been slapped in the face. Everyone in the room was frozen in surprise, as Myrtle was rarely challenged by anyone apart from Gigi. She ran every important committee and community organization in Big Dune Island. Her dictator-like reign over the town was tolerated by all because of her superior fundraising skills and the authority she seemed to command simply by the way she strode into a room.

Gigi had forgotten Austin was there until he spoke. He was sitting by himself in a club chair by the bookcases on the other side of the room. He probably didn't know fake crab from lump crab, but Gigi appreciated the show of support. Especially since it *had* been lump crab, and expensive lump crab at that.

"Ms. Myrtle, I was hoping you'd help me design the invitations." Callie expertly changed the subject. "You've always been like a second mom to me and, as we all know, you have impeccable taste."

Myrtle had always doted over Callie, especially since she returned home last year and helped save the town's annual festival, the Beach Bash, by headlining the concert on the final night. While Myrtle had pushed Gigi to marry a wealthy man and pursue a life of philanthropy, she didn't seem to mind that Callie had pursued her music career and been unattached until she returned to Big Dune Island last year and reunited with her childhood sweetheart, Jesse. Maybe it was just that Callie knew how to play to Myrtle's ego, whereas Gigi refused to give her the satisfaction.

Myrtle was beaming back at Callie. "Oh, my sweet girl, of course I will. It would be my honor." She placed a hand over her heart.

"Meanwhile, I will handle the wedding plans." Gigi glanced back at her mother triumphantly. "Callie and Jesse can decide what they want, and I'll just make the calls and attend the appointments."

"Actually . . ." Callie bit her lip as she looked over at Gigi. "I'm not going to have a lot of time to help. I have to get the rest of my album recorded before the wedding so post-production can work on it while we're on our honeymoon, and Jesse has the Watson house to finish up."

"I wish I could promise to pitch in more," Piper said, frowning, "but I have a lot of logistics to handle before the ladies go out on tour."

"So"—Callie glanced nervously at Jesse—"we were thinking Austin could help you, Gigi."

"Austin? What does Austin know about weddings?" Gigi looked at Austin, hoping he would join her protest.

"I've been a groomsman, like, half a dozen times. Nothing to it. You order some food and cake, buy some flowers. Easy peasy." Austin motioned through the air as if he were checking off a to-do list.

"Really, Callie, I'll call Pierre. He can—" Myrtle became distracted. Her brows knitted together as she observed Austin taking a decorative glass ball out of a bowl on the table at his side. He tossed it in the air above his head like a baseball, catching it easily. "Austin, do be a dear and put that back. We don't play in the house." She chastised him like she would a five-year-old.

Placing the ball back in the bowl, he cleared his throat. "Sorry, ma'am."

"Now, as I was saying, I'll make one call to Pierre and get this all taken care of."

"Thank you, Ms. Myrtle, we really do appreciate the offer." Callie looked to Jesse. "But Gigi and Austin know us best. We know they'll make our special day absolutely perfect."

"We know you have so many other obligations with the hospital gala and the tour of homes coming up, and those things would all fall apart without you." Jesse expertly stroked her ego, just as Callie had. "You've taught Gigi well. I'm sure she'll make certain our wedding is everything we want it to be."

"Yes, dear, but it must also be believable as *my* anniversary party," Myrtle pointed out.

"Actually, it just has to be believable as the surprise anniversary party *I* would throw you." Gigi smirked at her mother.

Myrtle huffed in reply.

"Won't it be weird that I'm involved?" Austin asked. "I mean, why would I help Gigi throw her parents' anniversary party?"

Gigi seized on the opportunity to boot Austin from the planning. "Good point, Beckett. I think this is a one-woman job."

"You and I both know planning a wedding isn't a one-woman job, especially a secret wedding." Callie's eyes twinkled as she mentioned her upcoming nuptials. "Everyone knows how much you adore your father. If anyone asks, just tell them you wanted to make sure you had a male's point of view so your dad would be happy. It's not like it's unusual for you two to spend time together. Didn't you just help Austin buy the Bailey Building for the coffee shop so Chloe wouldn't have to keep leasing?"

"Oh, fine, he can help." Gigi frowned as she slumped down on the couch, admitting defeat. She just didn't want Austin getting in the way or distracting her. She wanted Callie and Jesse's wedding day to be perfect. They both deserved it after all they'd been through, personally and professionally.

Callie had left Jesse behind on Big Dune Island when she was signed to a record deal at sixteen and moved to Nashville. Sure, she'd done it for a good reason. His uncle had embezzled from his family's construction company and she'd thought he should stay behind to help his dad. But it had taken them thirteen years to find their way back to one another, when Callie had come to town to deal with the sale of her family home.

After Callie's parents died in a car accident, her uncle inherited the family home and then had secretly sold it to Jesse to help him with his business. When Callie returned, she fell for Jesse again before finding out he was the secret buyer of the house. But they'd laid all their cards on the table, and when Callie got the opportunity to sign with a new label and return to live in Big Dune Island, she'd jumped at the chance. A few short months later, they were engaged and they wanted a secret wedding right here on Big Dune Island that the whole town could attend without the media catching wind of the plan. Which reminded Gigi of something.

She turned to Callie and Jesse. "Beckett does know he can't tell Chloe, right?" Austin's sister had spilled the beans last year about Jesse buying Callie's childhood home before her uncle and Jesse had been ready to reveal the truth.

"Umm, I'm right here." Austin waved. "And of course I'm not telling my sister."

"Although I would like her to do the cake." Callie bit her lip as she turned to Austin.

"You mean the anniversary cake, right?" Austin smiled back at Callie.

"Exactly." Gigi and Callie said in unison.

"Piece of cake. Pun intended." Austin chuckled.

"Come on, honey. Let's leave the kids to it." Gigi's father rose from his chair and offered a hand to Myrtle to help her out of hers.

"At least let me give you Pierre's number." Myrtle directed this at Callie, rightly assuming Gigi wouldn't take it from her.

"I think The Dunes is a little too public of a venue for us." This came from Piper, who was no doubt adept at handling big egos in her line of work. "But perhaps you could suggest some florists and caterers. I remember your garden party last month for the Tree Conservancy. It was worthy of the cover of *Southern Living*."

Myrtle blushed, holding a hand over her heart. "Come with me, and I'll make you a list of all the right people."

As Piper followed Myrtle to her study on the other side of the foyer from the living room, Callie turned to Gigi and Austin.

"Thank you, guys." She reached over to squeeze Gigi's hand. "I know this is a lot to try to pull off in a short amount of time, but it means more to me than you'll ever know."

Seeing the tears shining in Callie's eyes, Gigi vowed to do whatever she had to in order to make her best friend's wedding dreams come true. Even if it meant babysitting Austin and pretending he was being helpful.

THE GROUP WAS HELPING CLEAR PLATES FROM THE dining room table when Ms. Myrtle took a call on her cell phone. Almost immediately she gave a dramatic gasp, and her hand flew over her mouth. "That poor woman," Gigi heard her mother say. "She never talked about any family after Ron passed. Who do you think will plan the funeral?"

Gigi stopped by her mother, still holding the plates she'd been taking to the kitchen. "Who died?" she whispered, but her mother waved a hand at her and kept talking to whoever was on the other end of the call.

"See what you can find out, and I'll mobilize the League," her mother said, referring to the Junior League she'd led for the past two decades.

When she finally ended the call, Callie, Jesse, and Austin had gathered around, Gigi having whispered to them that someone had passed.

"It's Margaret Cunningham," Ms. Myrtle said, shaking her head. "She had a heart attack last night, and they couldn't revive her. So sad. She was never the same after Ron passed a few years ago."

Gigi placed a hand over her heart. "Oh, no. She was such a sweet woman."

The Cunninghams had moved to town fifteen years previously when they purchased the Salty Breeze B&B from its original owner. It was the only bed and breakfast on the beach side of the island and it was on the National Register of Historic Places. The whole town had been relieved when the sweet couple bought it to run in their retirement years, saving it from the corporate hotels that wanted to buy it only to bring in bulldozers and rebuild on the prime real estate. Unfortunately, National Register status didn't prevent private property owners from doing what they wanted with the building and the property, but the Cunninghams had had no interest in demolishing it to develop something new. After purchasing it, they'd become an integral part of the community.

Gigi always suggested the B&B to friends from Atlanta and New York who came to visit, though, so she'd spent enough time at the Salty Breeze over the years to have grown a relationship with Margaret. Although Margaret—she'd told Gigi not to call her Mrs. Cunningham because it reminded her of Ron's mother and made her feel old—had become more withdrawn after Ron's death.

"Someone else was helping her run the B&B, right?" Callie asked.

"Yeah, her front-desk manager, Rebecca, has been running the day-to-day since Mrs. Cunningham had a stroke last year," Gigi supplied.

"They didn't have any kids, right?" Jesse asked.

Gigi shook her head. She'd tried to get Mrs. Cunningham

to draft a will after Mr. Cunningham passed, because neither of them had one. She'd gone out to the inn and went over everything with her, but Mrs. Cunningham kept putting her off. Gigi could only hope she'd gone to see another attorney to draw it up.

"She must have some family though," Jesse said. "Siblings or nieces and nephews? Someone will inherit it."

Gigi couldn't reveal anything from her interactions with Mrs. Cunningham because of attorney-client privilege, but the truth was she didn't know much more than the others. She could only explain to them how Florida law worked. "If she doesn't have children, and assuming her parents are long since deceased, her assets would first go to any siblings and then to their children if none of her siblings are still alive."

"Georgia, why don't you go see Rebecca and offer your legal assistance in sorting out the inn? I'll talk to the League ladies and see what we can do to help with the funeral."

Gigi was a little surprised by the request. Her mother usually tried to pretend she didn't know her daughter was an attorney. She preferred to focus on her embarrassment over her thirty-one-year-old daughter still being single. Gigi searched for a retort, but for once she had none. Going to see Rebecca was exactly what she should do to ensure there weren't any problems now the inn's ownership was in question.

Luckily, her mother was already saying hurried goodbyes to the others so she could move to her study to make calls. At least Gigi wouldn't have to acknowledge publicly that she was taking direction from Myrtle.

Chapter Four

Austin

Austin followed Gigi, Callie, and Piper out front while Jesse was out back talking to Dr. Franklin about a screened-in porch addition. He stood waiting after they'd all said their goodbyes and watched as Gigi climbed into her little red convertible while she waited for Callie and Piper to pull out from behind her. Her red-and-white dress was a perfect match to the candy-apple red of the car. He wondered if red was Gigi's favorite color. When she'd pulled her mouth into a thin line every time her mother spoke, he'd noticed that her lipstick was the same shade as her dress, a stark contrast against her pale skin and dark hair. Did stores sell things like that together?

He shook his head as she backed out of the drive. What did he care about lipstick and dresses anyway? Nothing, except he hadn't been able to stop noticing things like that about Gigi since that night of Mary Catherine's wedding six years earlier. He'd had a crush on Gigi back in high school, but then she'd friend-zoned him, and he'd settled for that. Until the night in the hot tub.

Since then, it had been hard to deny his attraction to her, but he knew she'd only agreed to go to the wedding together because Dalton had just broken up with her. It's why he hadn't kissed her that night, because he knew she was too vulnerable. And now he knew he'd probably never have that chance again after she'd learned about his role in the whole Dalton debacle and practically cut him out of her life until Callie moved back to town.

"The ladies gone already?"

Jesse came up behind where Austin stood with his elbows on the porch railing. Window boxes full of flowers were secured to the railing at perfect intervals across the full width of the porch, blooms falling toward the ground as if trying to escape the Franklins. Austin could understand why, at least when it came to Ms. Myrtle.

"Yeah, they said they'd meet us later at Mack's," he said, referencing their favorite diner. Austin followed Jesse down the porch stairs to Jesse's truck. There was no sense in fighting the old familiar pattern the four of them had fallen back into, so all he could do was fight his attraction to Gigi.

As soon as the truck doors closed and he knew their conversation couldn't be overheard, Austin let out a long sigh. "Man, she's intense."

"Ms. Myrtle?" Jesse laughed. "Yeah, she likes things a certain way, that's for sure."

"I'd forgotten what she was like. No wonder Gigi ran off to New York after law school." Austin shook his head. "Makes you wonder why on earth she came back."

"You know how this place is." Jesse shrugged. "It's got a magnetic pull. Everyone comes back eventually."

It was true. Jesse had been the only one in their group

who'd never left. Austin had been drafted by the Atlanta Braves right out of high school, reporting to minor league training camp that summer. Callie had left for Nashville at about the same time, finishing high school with a tutor. Gigi had gone off to college and law school at Emory in Atlanta before heading to New York to practice.

They'd all found their way back though. He had returned four years prior after an injury ended his career and Gigi had appeared a year later, followed by Callie last year. Since Gigi moved back, he'd been impressed as he'd watched her hang out her shingle and take on the biggest developers on the island. Today he'd been reminded that her family home had been the perfect training ground upon which to hone her battle skills.

"Did I ever tell you about that time Ms. Myrtle and Dr. Franklin came to visit Gigi in Atlanta, and I opened the door to her apartment in nothing but a towel?" When Jesse shook his head, Austin laughed. "I thought Ms. Myrtle's eyes were going to pop right out."

"Why were you at Gigi's in nothing but a towel?"

"The water main broke at my place, and I needed a shower. Gigi had gone to class, and I thought it was just her coming back because she'd left me the key. Ms. Myrtle immediately jumped to conclusions and totally chewed me out. She said she wouldn't have me 'sullying her daughter's good name.'" Austin put Ms. Myrtle's words in air quotes.

"No offense meant, I'm sure." Jesse laughed.

"Oh, I'm pretty sure she meant it. You should have seen how relieved she was to learn Gigi wasn't home and my story checked out."

In fact, it was Ms. Myrtle and Austin's dad who'd bonded Austin and Gigi as much as their respective friendships with Jesse and Callie growing up. Both parents had operated out of the same playbook, dictating the exact paths their children would pursue. Then, when they'd both wound up in Atlanta after high school, it had been nice to have a familiar face in the big city.

"I forgot you guys were so close all those years in Atlanta."

Jesse hadn't meant anything by it, but the comment made Austin wince. He and Gigi had gotten close in Atlanta. But then he'd done something that forever changed their friendship. It was another reason he could never be with Gigi, no matter how fast his heart raced when she was nearby.

Thankfully they pulled into the driveway at the Watson House before Jesse dug up any more of the past. After a successful renovation of Callie's historic home last year, Jesse had taken on a steady stream of clients looking for a builder who could preserve their home or business within the historic district of Big Dune Island. Jesse was under a tight deadline on this one though, so Austin was pitching in a little.

They worked at the house for a few hours before grabbing showers at Jesse's so they could meet the ladies for dinner.

"Have you decided what you're going to do with this place yet?" Austin was drying off his hair with a towel when he joined Jesse in the living room of Jesse's small two-bedroom, one-bathroom cottage. Jesse would be moving into the Lyman House, Callie's family home he'd restored, to live with Callie once they were married.

"Yeah, I'm going to list it after the wedding. We decided if I did it before, people would be tipped off that the wedding was getting near."

"Ahh, smart. Boy, keeping this thing secret sure has a lot of moving parts."

Jesse shrugged. "Yeah, Callie's life is kind of like that."

Austin slapped him on the back. "Man, did you ever think you'd be marrying a celebrity?"

"Of course I did." Jesse smiled broadly.

Austin hadn't ever really believed in anything like destiny or the idea of "The One," but watching Jesse and Callie come back to one another after so many years apart had warmed him to the idea. It was clear they'd never really stopped loving each other, and it made Austin wonder if everyone got someone they could call their person.

His thoughts instantly shifted to Gigi. She had been the one female who'd been a constant in his life. She'd been like a kid sister until his senior year, when he'd noticed she was kind of cute. She was crazy smart too, and she was the first to call him on his nonsense, which he secretly loved. He still remembered seeing her in the stands at one of his games after she moved to Atlanta, and his breath had caught in his throat. The woman sitting in the family section with the other players' wives looked nothing like the teenager he'd left behind on Big Dune Island. She'd turned into a total knockout.

"You about ready?" Jesse's voice broke into his thoughts.

"Can I borrow your hair dryer?"

"Can't help you there, sorry." Jesse ran his hand through his short-cropped, dark blond hair. "Before you ask, I don't have any face cream either." Jesse loved to tease Austin about his "products," as Jesse called them.

"Hey, one day you'll take skin care seriously too. Just you wait. I think I see sun spots forming already right there." Austin pointed at Jesse's forehead, squinting as he examined the fictional problem.

Jesse swatted his hand away. "You take longer to get ready than a girl, Beckett. Comb that mop and let's get out of here."

Entering Mack's, they joined the ladies at their usual table by the window.

"Hello, beautiful." Jesse slid into the worn red-leather booth next to Callie, kissing her on the cheek.

This left Austin to slide in across the table from Jesse next to Gigi. As Jesse and Callie nuzzled into each other on the other side of the booth, Austin tried not to be so aware of Gigi's leg so close to his and picked at the edge of the paper placemat in front of him.

"How did the wedding planning go?" Jesse looked from Callie to Gigi and back to his bride.

"We jotted down some ideas. You know the only thing that's important to me is having everyone I care about there. And marrying the love of my life." Callie leaned in to kiss Jesse, and the two of them continued to gaze dreamily into each other's eyes in that way the chronically in love tended to do.

"Do you guys remember the first time we came back here last year? You two have sure come a long way since then." Gigi motioned a finger at Jesse and Callie.

"Yes, if I remember, you ladies were sporting some different hairstyles that evening." Jesse laughed.

Austin and Jesse had run into Callie and Gigi outside Breakwaters, the local watering hole. The women had been barely recognizable, each sporting a wig. Callie had covered her blonde curls with short red hair, and Gigi's long dark hair was tucked up into a short, icy-blonde wig. Austin hadn't recognized them, but Jesse had spotted Callie's charm bracelet and outed them. The four of them had ended up at Mack's for dinner, reunited all together for the first time in nearly a decade.

"It feels like old times," Callie said, snuggling closer to Jesse, who wrapped an arm around her.

"Except in high school, Beckett here would have had some chick with him and forced me to sit at the end of the table in a chair." Gigi raised an eyebrow in his direction.

"We can't all meet our soul mate in high school," Jesse said before Austin could formulate a reply.

"Yeah, some of us are still striking out in our thirties." Gigi nodded in Austin's direction to indicate she didn't only mean herself.

"Nice baseball analogy." Austin's lip curled up on one side in a half smile. He was still thinking about what Jesse had said about meeting the right girl in high school.

"This one acted like he had one of his lady friends coming tonight." Jesse smiled in Austin's direction. "He must have fixed his hair in the visor mirror a half dozen times on the way over here."

"At least I put in some effort." Austin tossed a balled-up straw wrapper at Jesse. "The only effort you make to have a hairstyle is taking the clippers to your hair any time it grows longer than the spikes on a porcupine."

"Hey, I like his porcupine look." Callie laughed, rubbing her hand back and forth on Jesse's head.

"Didn't you win 'Best Hair' in the yearbook?" Gigi asked Austin. "You always did have great hair."

Austin felt heat flicker across his face. Had she just paid him a compliment?

"Yes, thank you for remembering." He ran a hand slowly through his floppy blond hair for dramatic effect.

"Okay, back to the wedding," Gigi said as she pulled the official wedding binder from her gigantic purse. Was it possible the binder was even thicker today?

"I think the first thing we need to do is figure out the venue. So much of the rest depends on that. Callie said she's open to inside or outside, and I think I've found some contenders. What about you, Thomas?" Gigi looked up at Jesse, pen poised above a fresh piece of paper in the binder.

Jesse shrugged. "I thought Lonnie and Jacqueline's wedding out on the beach was nice." He referred to Callie's uncle and her record label president, who had wed last summer after Jacqueline came to town to try to sign Callie and managed to fall in love along the way.

"That was a second wedding for sixty-five-year-olds. I think we can do a little better than that." Gigi frowned.

"He's right though," Callie said. "We both love the water so much; it'd be nice to have it as a backdrop somehow. I don't think I want to be out in the sand for the ceremony, but maybe something that overlooks the water?"

"I don't want to get married in some stuffy ballroom though. So, what are our options?" Jesse posed this question to Gigi, who had become the official wedding planner.

"The Dunes does have a lawn that overlooks the ocean where they host weddings, but that would just make Myrtle too happy, so it's out." Gigi crossed through "The Dunes" on her list with her pen, which, by the smile on her face, gave her a sense of satisfaction.

"Wilson's Landing is an option," she said, going to the next venue on her list. "You haven't ever seen it, have you, Callie? I think it was built while you were living in Nashville." To this, Callie shook her head. "I also love Whispering Palms down on Fort George Island. I've never been, but I've seen photos of weddings there. The lawn has these one-hundred-year-old oak trees you can get married under with the marsh right behind you."

Callie shrugged. "I can look on their website, but maybe you can go look in person? You know how it is. Anything can look good in a photo online."

"I've been to weddings at Wilson's Landing and Whispering Palms," Jesse offered. "I'm fine with either of them."

"Great, I'll go scout them out this week and see what offers us the most privacy and is worthy of Callie Jackson's wedding." Gigi winked at Callie just as Mack arrived with their order.

As Mack walked away from the table, a brunette in a short skirt sidled up. "You're Austin Beckett, right?" The woman batted her eyelashes in his direction.

"Uh, yeah." He looked around the table to see if anyone else knew the woman. They all stared back with great interest, but no sign of recognition.

"Omigosh, you're just my favorite baseball player of all time." She reached down to touch his arm. "I grew up just a few towns over in Cedar Bluff, but you guys used to come play us in high school. Then I saw you playing with the Braves one day, and I said to myself, 'Alyssa, you knew him when.'"

Austin shifted uncomfortably in his seat. Sure, he'd once relished this kind of attention from women, but it had been years since it had happened. Once he stopped playing, the ladies stopped following him. Which had been perfectly fine by him. The game on and off the field had gotten old.

"Hey, well uh, thanks." He gave a perfunctory smile. "Nice to meet you, Alyssa."

"My friends are never going to believe I met *the* Austin Beckett. Can I take a selfie?" She was already wrapping one arm around his shoulder, leaning her head next to his and holding her phone out in front of them before he could respond.

Trying not to cough from the overpowering scent of her perfume, Austin pulled away as soon as the photo was snapped.

"Holy cow, I can't believe I didn't notice it. You're Callie Jackson!" Alyssa's attention turned to the other side of the booth. "Which must make you Jesse." She pointed at Jesse. "And . . ." She paused as she turned to Gigi before frowning. "Is this your girlfriend?" she asked Austin.

Gigi chortled. "He wishes."

At this, Alyssa perked up and started digging around in her purse. She extended a pink business card in his direction. "Call me sometime."

Gigi grabbed the card from Austin's hand as soon as

Alyssa was out of earshot. "Alyssa Johnson, Beauty Blogger. I think she's perfect for you." She handed the card back.

"You could have at least pretended to be my girlfriend to save me from a potential crazy stalker," he grumbled, shoving the card under his plate, where he planned to leave it.

"Your girlfriend?" she shot back. "In your dreams."

Yes, in fact, sometimes Gigi was his girlfriend in his dreams. More nights than he'd ever admit.

Chapter Five

Gigi

Gigi navigated to the south end of Big Dune Island the next day after lunch, taking A1A until just before the bridge that would take her off the island. She needed to make a pit stop on her way to look at Whispering Palms for Callie and Jesse's wedding.

There wasn't really a road to where she was going so much as a path off A1A, but she turned on her blinker and crossed the road so she could park her BMW Z4 convertible on the side of the road. She felt the tires slip slightly as they made contact with the sand that lurked just below the thin grassy layer. She wondered, not for the first time, if an SUV might be a better choice for someone who often had to do site checks on undeveloped land.

Slipping off her heels, Gigi put on the tennis shoes she kept in her car for just this purpose. This morning, a resident on the south end of the island had called to tip her off that someone was on an undeveloped twenty-acre parcel they'd all been watching for years and appeared to be surveying it. The Big Dune Island Tree Conservancy had hired Gigi to attempt to purchase the land the year prior, but the out-of-town owner had refused, while also providing assurances that he had no intention of developing the land. Even Callie had expressed interest in buying the land to preserve it, but to no avail. Recently, rumors had swirled that the owner was in poor health and his children, who might not feel the same way about preserving the land, were managing his affairs.

It was on her way to Whispering Palms, so she decided to stop and see for herself what was going on. It was doubly concerning because it sat right next to the Salty Breeze B&B. If the inn came up for grabs too, whoever wanted to develop this piece might try to scoop it up, since the B&B had the ocean frontage the twenty acres lacked.

After cutting through the ancient oaks that created a natural border between the road and the parcel of land, she spotted a neon-pink ribbon floating just above the top of the marsh grasses up ahead. Her heart sank the instant she saw the unnatural color against the deep green and golden hues of the native grass. Sure enough, when she got to the ribbon, she saw it was attached to a short wooden stake. The parcel was being surveyed. You only did that if you were selling or developing it.

Gigi considered plucking the stake from the ground and searching for others. At least she could make their work a little more difficult and buy herself some time to figure out what was happening, but she was afraid a strategically placed trail camera might catch her act of sabotage. More and more of the developers she knew were using trail cams to keep an eye on their property. Sometimes, being a rule follower was a real hindrance to her objectives.

As she furiously stomped back to her car, she quickly dialed her assistant, Reagan.

"Do a records request," she said after filling in Reagan on the situation. "See if they've filed for a rezoning."

"Sure thing, boss." Reagan was nothing if not polite and efficient. She was only a few years younger than Gigi and had grown up on the island as well. As sweet as a glass of fresh-squeezed lemonade, clients loved Reagan and often hung around the office long after their appointments to show her photos of their grandchildren or chat about the upcoming bake sale.

"I doubt there's anything to be found yet. If they had already filed, everyone on the island would be talking about it, but we have to cover all our bases." Another baseball analogy. Gigi shook her head. She'd been spending way too much time with Austin lately.

Thinking about him and all his sports analogies and corny quotes off bottle caps made her smile in spite of the discovery that had ruined her morning. Although feigning annoyance at each other was part of their schtick, she actually found it tough to be in a bad mood when he was around. He was always happy and, admittedly, a lot of fun. But that was also his problem. He was Mr. Fun Times, who never had a care in the world. She wasn't sure he'd ever taken anything seriously in his whole life. And although she had forgiven him for meddling in her relationship with Dalton, she hadn't forgotten it either.

"Anything else?" Reagan's chipper voice broke into her thoughts.

"No, sorry. I got distracted. I'm out the rest of the afternoon. Call me if you get anything, otherwise I'll see you tomorrow."

Back at her car, Gigi removed her tennis shoes to slide back into her heels. One thing she could agree with Myrtle on is that heels made you feel more like a woman. Gigi liked the way heels made her feel taller, more confident. Of course, she'd never admit to Myrtle that she was right about anything.

Checking the road before pulling out, Gigi pressed the toe of her black patent-leather Louboutin heel on the gas pedal, but nothing happened. Then she heard it. The telltale whirling of a tire stuck in the sand. She opened her door and looked back. Everything seemed fine, and the ground had felt firm when she'd walked on it.

Throwing her heels into the passenger seat, she donned the tennis shoes again to get out and walk around her car. There it was. Her back passenger-side tire was squarely in a patch of sand she hadn't noticed when she was parking. That was the danger of parking anywhere but asphalt on this island; the rest was all sand underneath, even if it looked like grass on nice, firm earth.

"Great. Just great." She threw up her hands at the sky as if someone there was responsible for her bad day and trudged back to the driver's seat. Glancing at her watch, she wondered who she could call to come rescue her in the middle of the day. She hated to bother Callie or Jesse. Callie had to get an album recorded before the wedding, and Jesse had to finish the Watson House. She was supposed to be making their lives easier, not more difficult. She couldn't pull Reagan away from the office because she knew a client was coming by to get some documents notarized.

Just then, a honk from a passing car startled her. She looked up to see a familiar truck pulling over on the shoulder in front of her. It was Austin. Stepping out of her car, she shielded her eyes from the sun and waited for him to get out.

"Well, well," Austin said as he approached, "what do we have here?"

"I appear to be stuck." She led him around the passenger side of the car and pointed at her back tire, which was entrenched in the sand, having spun itself into a rut.

"Lucky for you, I specialize in damsels in distress."

"Yes, I'm aware." Gigi rolled her eyes, hands on her hips. "I, however, am no damsel in distress."

"Oh, so you have a plan for getting out of here?" Austin crossed his arms over his chest, waiting for her answer.

"Under any other circumstances, I'd just call AAA, but I'm supposed to be at Whispering Palms in twenty minutes. They only have one date left when Callie and Jesse could get married there, so I really need to look at it today."

"Come on." Austin started back toward his truck. "I'll take you."

"You want to go along to look at a wedding venue?"

He turned back to her and shrugged. "Sure, why not? I'm done with work for the day."

"I forgot you only work three hours a day." Gigi rolled her eyes.

"Plus the five or six hours a night I have to watch games to be able to talk about them on the show." Austin winked at her.

"Oh, I'm sorry. Forgive me for not realizing how demanding your job must be." She put her hands together as if praying for his forgiveness.

"You're forgiven." He gave her a smirk. "Now, let's hit the road."

"Fine, let me grab my purse." Gigi opened the passenger door and grabbed her heels as well.

"What did you pull over for anyway?" Austin asked as he did a U-turn with the truck to head back south, off the island.

Gigi ran a hand through her hair, her curls from earlier now barely a wave. She'd expertly sprayed them into place this morning, but she'd gotten hot traipsing around outside and they had quickly wilted. "You know about the twenty acres everyone was upset over last summer, right?"

"The hotel and condo project? I thought that was dead."

"More like it took a long winter's nap, I suppose. Someone's going to want to develop that property one day. It's too valuable not to for most people." Gigi propped up her elbow on the ledge of the truck's window and cradled her head with her hand. "I got a call this morning that someone was out there poking around, so I stopped to look on my way out to Whispering Palms. Sure enough, I found some early surveying stakes."

Austin shook his head, blowing out a long breath. "Man, that sucks."

"Yeah. Reagan is looking to see if they've pulled permits yet. I doubt it though. They won't want to alert anyone to what they're doing any earlier than necessary."

They rode in silence for the next few miles, and Gigi's nerves were soothed as they glided along mere feet above the water down Tidal Creek Road, crossing small bridges every mile or so. To their right, tidal creeks snaked across the gold-and-green landscape of marsh grass before feeding into the Atlantic to their left. The sun reflected off the water, creating a mirror of the cotton-candy clouds that billowed against a bluebird sky.

"Turn here." Gigi pointed to her right at a nondescript road just as they crossed onto Fort George Island. The truck bounced as they made their way down the curvy, unpaved road.

"You were going to drive your car back here?" Austin turned to ask just before having to jerk the truck over to hug the side of the road to let pass a delivery truck coming from the other direction. The road wasn't really wide enough for two vehicles, especially when they were both large trucks. Dust billowed as the other truck sped past them, clearly more familiar with the road and all its twists and turns.

Gigi shrugged. "My car needs to be washed anyway." It was the second time today she'd been reminded how impractical her car was, but she didn't care. She loved the way she felt when she lowered herself onto the leather seats that were as soft as buttercream icing and hugged her hips as if she was sitting in a cloud. The car practically purred when she started its engine, and she felt powerful behind the wheel.

She might have moved back to Big Dune Island from the Big Apple, but everything from her car to her shoes reminded her that it was a choice. She knew what people thought when you moved back, that you couldn't hack it somewhere else. But she hadn't come back with her tail between her legs. She'd come back because she wanted to make a difference. She wanted to preserve their little slice of paradise, not bow to the pressure of the almighty dollar the way they always seemed to in her BigLaw job.

"Hold on," Austin said, laughing as they bounced over a pothole.

Gigi shrieked out in surprise. "Good grief." She straightened her dress and smoothed down her hair. "How are we even supposed to get guests back here? We can't ask people to drive this road, especially not at night after they've hit the open bar at the wedding. Maybe this one is already a no."

Austin looked at her, his eyes twinkling.

"What?" she asked.

"You know who would really hate this?"

"Myrtle!" they said in unison before bursting into laughter.

"You're right, let's keep going." Gigi pointed ahead, smiling as Whispering Palms quickly became a frontrunner. Austin was the only person in her life who really understood what it was like to have a parent like Myrtle because Mr. Beckett could give her a run for her money when it came to overbearing parents.

The road straightened out and then they were under a canopy of oak trees, their branches stretching out from either side of the road to create a tunnel of green leaves and long, wispy Spanish moss. Canopy roads were common in this area of Florida and were protected by state and local law. The canopy led directly to the entrance to Whispering Palms, and as the trees parted Gigi's eyes got wider.

"Wow. It's beautiful," she said. "Have you been here before?"

"No, don't think so."

"It's really not that far from the island. We could rent the island trolleys to bring people out here."

Locals on Big Dune Island hated going "off island" for anything, which was why no one Gigi or Austin knew had ever gotten married here before. The venue catered more to destination weddings, and people from Jacksonville probably thought it was no big deal to drive up here. Islanders acted as if they'd turn into Cinderella after the ball if they left the island, although Gigi had found Manhattanites to be the same.

Austin pulled into a small parking lot to the left of the building and they both walked to the front of the truck before they stopped and stared at the grand home in front of them. The main house was a two-story white structure flanked on either side by what looked to be additions that extended toward the backyard. A circular drive led up to the front door with oaks billowing overhead, and varying shades of pink azaleas dotting the landscape. The green shutters on the windows helped the house blend into its surroundings in a way that made it seem like it had been there forever, born from the earth just like everything else around them.

Gigi spotted the "National Register of Historic Places" gold plaque by the front door as they approached. Austin opened the door for her as she tapped the plaque with a red manicured nail. "Jesse will like that."

It had been Jesse's dream to restore historic homes and buildings, and he'd finally convinced the investors in his family's business to start doing more restoring and less new development. Gigi knew Callie had been offering to buy out the investors so Jesse and his dad could have the company back and call their own shots. Jesse was proud of what he'd been able to accomplish on his own, however, and the investors had started to come around. Gigi definitely liked being on the same side as Jesse these days when it came to preservation and conservation—it hadn't always been the case when he was working on so many new developments—so much so that she even handled legal for his company now.

As they waited for the venue's wedding coordinator to meet them, Austin and Gigi were shown to a small room off the front entryway that had been set up as a museum of sorts for the house. As Gigi wandered around and read the placards next to the historic photos on the wall, she kept catching Austin staring at her.

"What? Why do you keep looking at me like that?"

"Me? Nothing. I'm just looking at the pictures." He pointed to one in front of him of a grand party at the house back in the 1920s when it had been a private club for the wealthy.

Unconvinced, Gigi ran a hand along each side of her skirt, making sure it hadn't inadvertently hiked up to reveal anything it shouldn't, but everything seemed to be in place. She'd passed a mirror in the hall and her hair and makeup seemed to have survived her trek into nature earlier. So what was he looking at? Austin had been acting really squirrelly lately. Something was up with him, but she wasn't sure what. She'd get it out of him on the way back to the island.

Chapter Six

Austin

Gigi had caught him looking at her at least twice while they walked through the room with all the history about the house. He'd played it off like she was being paranoid, but he wasn't sure she'd bought it.

You'd have to be blind not to notice how beautiful Gigi was, her ivory skin highlighted by her dark brown hair and the red lipstick she so often wore. And she was completely brilliant. She'd gone to an elite college, graduated law school with honors, and then gone to work for one of the country's biggest firms in New York. Living there had made her street-smart too.

He followed behind Gigi and Hannah, the young red-headed event planner, out the back door of the house, where the lawn opened into a flat area encircled by towering oaks dripping with Spanish moss. Hannah was explaining that they might want to give out personal-size insect repellent if they planned to host the party under the old oak trees.

"Omigosh, Myrtle will hate this." Gigi turned to snicker at him, her eyes twinkling with mischief.

"I'm sorry." Hannah turned back to them, her brows furrowing with concern. "We do get it sprayed regularly, but mosquitos are tough this time of year. Many of our parties give out insect repellent just in case. Guests are usually pretty understanding."

"No." Gigi waved a hand as if swatting away the pesky insect. "It's perfect. We want the party under the oak trees."

Gigi and Austin exchanged smiles, and Austin shook his head as Gigi continued to push forward a confused Hannah to show her where they could lay out a dance floor.

Gigi was completely fearless. That was probably what drew him in the most. Her dogged determination to get what she wanted and the way she blazed into every situation fully confident, with no reservations. She was a force of nature, just like her mother—though he certainly knew better than to ever share that comparison with Gigi. He understood why Myrtle rankled her; it was the same for him with his dad. Whereas he had cowered and followed the path laid out by his overbearing parent, Gigi had forged her own path without worrying what Myrtle thought. He admired that about her.

And that was it. He admired her. He wasn't attracted to her in *that* way. Or at least not any more than any man would be attracted to any woman who looked like her. The way her laugh made his heart skip a beat was irrelevant. And he certainly wasn't watching her from behind as she strutted across the lawn in that black skirt that hit just above her well-toned calves, which were highlighted by the tall heels she'd changed into in his truck. Not that he had been watching.

"What do you think?"

Gigi's question interrupted his thoughts, and he saw that she and Hannah were both waiting for a response.

Gigi turned to Hannah. "Don't mind him. He's easily distracted." Looking back at him, she motioned around the yard. "Wouldn't this be a nice spot for their vow renewal? Hannah says we can set up the dance floor back there," she said, pointing to a spot immediately behind the house, "and we can serve dinner inside so there won't be any turnover time between dinner and dancing."

He shrugged, not knowing the first thing about planning an anniversary party, especially one that was really a wedding for a celebrity bride. "Sounds good to me."

"Don't worry." Hannah placed a hand on Gigi's arm. "My boyfriend doesn't even understand what I do for a living. He hears me talking about table linens and flatware and thinks I'm part of the waitstaff or something."

Gigi frowned. "Oh, Beckett's not my boyfriend." She laughed as if it were an absurd notion. "We're just old friends. I had some car trouble on the way over, and he was kind enough to give me a lift."

Austin felt himself wince and immediately hoped neither of the women had noticed. Was it that ridiculous of an idea that he might date Gigi? After all, it was the second time in as many days someone had asked if they were a couple.

"What about dinner?" Gigi changed the subject. "Where would you serve that?"

"Come on, I'll show you where we can set up the dinner service." Hannah motioned for them to follow her.

Inside, they entered the room off the right side of the back of the house. Featuring windows on three sides, it was made even brighter by the pale yellow on the walls.

"How many can this seat?" Gigi asked.

"You can get around one hundred and twenty-five in here, and then there's a matching room on the other side of the house if you need to split the group up for dinner." Hannah pointed across the backyard to the extension that jutted out in a mirror image of the one they stood in now.

"They're completely identical?" Gigi looked out a window across the yard.

"Yes. I'd recommend putting your closest friends and family in this room and then everyone else in the other room if you need to use both. Do you know how many you're expecting?"

"I'm thinking in the one hundred and seventy-five to two hundred and twenty-five range, so we'd probably need both rooms."

The women continued to chat about table linens, chargers, and flatware, and Austin felt like Hannah's boyfriend must. It was like a foreign language. When they'd mentioned chargers, he'd initially thought they meant in case people's cell phones were dying. But then they'd launched into a lengthy discussion about the colors the chargers came in, and he got the feeling they must be talking about something else entirely. By the time Hannah showed them to the front door, and promised to email more information and save the available date for forty-eight hours, Austin was barely holding his eyes open.

"Someone have a late night?" Gigi asked after catching him yawning on the walk back to his truck.

"Braves are playing on the West Coast right now, so it was after midnight before the game was over."

"Did they win?"

"Yep. Manny leaped over the fence to catch what would have been a walk-off home run." Manny had been Austin's roommate in AAA ball, and then they'd been called up to Atlanta within weeks of each other.

"That's a home run that ends the game, right?"

Austin smiled at her as they reached the truck. "That's right."

"Why do you look so surprised? I've watched like a million of your games over the years. It's impossible not to pick up a thing or two."

Austin stepped around her to open her door.

"Well, wasn't that gentlemanly?" It was Gigi's turn to look surprised.

"At your service," he bowed.

"Now I like the sound of that."

As her light laughter filled the air, he tried not to stare at her toned calves flexing as she stepped onto the running board and hoisted herself up into his truck. Closing her door, he crossed behind the truck and tried to clear the sound of her laughter out of his head, but the melody stuck with him.

Why didn't she have a boyfriend? Sure, it was slim pickings on the island, but he was sure there were plenty of successful men in Jacksonville who'd be happy to drive out to the island for her. Austin hadn't really seen her date anyone since she moved back though. From what it sounded like from Jesse, she hadn't dated anyone seriously since Dalton Hennings back in law school.

"So Manny's still with the Braves?" Gigi asked when he joined her inside the truck's cab.

"Yeah, he won a Gold Glove last year and got a contract extension. He's actually one of the highest paid guys on the team now."

"That's great. He was always such a nice guy." She paused, looking at him with a more serious expression on her face. Austin caught the look when he turned to check behind him as he backed the truck out of the parking spot.

"What?"

"Is it hard? Watching him play . . ."

Her voice had trailed off, but he knew what she meant. Was it hard to watch Manny play when he wasn't anymore?

Austin shrugged, pulling back onto the canopy road. "Not really. I never loved it anyway. I always felt kind of guilty taking a roster spot from someone who wanted it more than I did."

"I know it was more what your dad wanted than you," she said, pausing as if choosing her next words carefully. "But it had to have felt good to make it to the big leagues, right?"

"Sure, there was a piece of me that knew I was doing what little boys all over the country dream of doing one day. When I got called up or got my first big league win, I kept waiting to feel like I had accomplished something, but I never really did. I was only ever just going through the motions." Austin swallowed hard. He wasn't sure he'd ever said that out loud to anyone.

Gigi was silent, but he could feel her eyes on him.

Uncomfortable with the silence, he cleared his throat. "That probably doesn't make much sense to someone like you, huh?"

"What do you mean? 'Someone like me'?" She tilted her head to the side like Jesse's dog Fenway did when he heard something he didn't understand.

"Someone who's so accomplished. Someone who's done exactly what she wanted how she wanted to do it." He stole a glance in her direction as he reached a straighter stretch in the curvy dirt road. He couldn't read her face.

"Spite." She said the single word as if it were a full sentence that explained everything.

"Spite?"

"In the beginning, I did it all out of spite. To spite my mother. To spite Dalton. To prove to them that I could be more than a wife and a mother. Not that there's anything wrong with those things; they're just not me." Her voice was devoid of emotion, her face still unreadable.

Austin hadn't heard Gigi mention Dalton in years. He'd always wondered if she was more sad or mad about the breakup and the direction it had taken her life. Sure, Gigi seemed happy with her career, but did she wish she had more than that? Did she wonder what could have been with Dalton?

After the initial shock of the breakup had worn off, it had seemed as if she was angrier with Austin than Dalton. But, then again, she didn't exactly know the whole story. She'd known enough though, and their friendship hadn't been the same since. But then Callie came home last year, and their old foursome was back together again. Still, Gigi rarely spent time with him unless the other two were present. First, he'd been stuck in the friend zone, now he was stuck in some sort of limbo between that and persona non grata.

And, really, that was his lot in life: stuck. He'd spent too many years chasing things he didn't really want, and now he had no idea how to figure out what it was he wanted. Except that Austin had a sneaky suspicion it involved Gigi. And that wasn't going to happen. See? Stuck.

Chapter Seven

Gigi

"You're happy with your career now, right?" Gigi aimlessly turned dials on Callie's recording equipment in her home studio the next day while she waited for Callie to finish so they could eat lunch.

Sitting next to her, Callie was emailing her producer a rough cut of a new song she'd recorded that morning. The room had been Callie's childhood bedroom, but Jesse had transformed it into a home studio as a surprise to try to soften the blow of her finding out he'd been the secret buyer of her family's home.

"Would you please stop playing with the equipment?" Callie swatted Gigi's hand. "Yes, I'm deliriously happy. Being able to move back and focus on writing the kind of songs I want to be singing is like a dream come true."

"Do you think some of us get more of our wishes granted than others? I mean, your first dream of becoming a famous recording artist came true when you were only sixteen. When that became a nightmare, you got handed a second chance at a dream career. Same for me. I landed that BigLaw job in NYC that set me up for anything I wanted to do, and now I'm here doing exactly what I want."

Callie spun the chair around until she was facing Gigi at the mixing desk. "First, it was never my dream to be famous. I just wanted to make a career doing what I loved. And second, what are you even talking about? Like you said, we're both in a great place in our careers right now. What gives?"

Gigi reached to fiddle with one of the knobs on Callie's mixing board again, but she stopped midair, remembering what Callie had said about not playing with the equipment. "Just something Austin said to me yesterday. Do you think he's happy with what he's doing now?"

Callie shrugged. "I think so. You know he never liked living in Atlanta. I know Jesse is glad to have him back." Callie paused, probably thinking about how the three of them had left Jesse back here for all those years they were off going to school and starting their careers. "I know baseball was more his dad's dream than his, but I think he likes sports and has fun talking about them on the radio. Why, what did he say?"

Gigi waved her hand through the air as if shooing away the thoughts. "It was nothing. We were just talking on our way back from Whispering Palms."

"Austin went with you?" Gigi started to open her mouth to explain, but Callie stopped her. "I want to hear all about it. Want to go out back?"

Gigi nodded, grabbing the bag with their sandwiches and following Callie downstairs and through the house to the kitchen that lined the back side. Grabbing a pitcher of sweet tea from the fridge, Callie poured them each a glass. Although Callie often mentioned she was jealous of Gigi's back deck that overlooked the beach, last year she'd realized how much keeping the Lyman House, right in the middle of Big Dune Island's historic district on the river side of the island, in her family meant to her last year when her mother's brother, Uncle Lonnie, sold the house to Jesse.

As part of the renovation since then, Jesse had turned the formerly flat backyard covered in patchy grass into a tropical oasis. Bougainvillea climbed the fences that lined the property, and Callie said its bright pink blooms reminded her of concerts she'd played in places in the Mediterranean, where it filled trellises. Large palms and other dense tropical plants formed another perimeter. Callie's neighbors were all people she'd known since she was a kid, who would never invade her privacy, but Gigi knew it was still nice for her to be able to go out back and feel as if she was in a world of her own.

Sitting down at the table and unwrapping their sandwiches, Callie prompted Gigi to spill the details of her day with Austin.

"You know that twenty acres you tried to buy to conserve?" When Callie nodded, Gigi continued. "Well, one of my clients owns the house immediately to the north of the property, and he spotted someone on it yesterday morning and called me. He was afraid they were surveying it, a sure sign they're getting ready to develop."

"Were they?"

Gigi's expression was grim. "I think so. They were gone by the time I got out there, but I found some preliminary stakes in the ground."

"Can you find out what they're planning?"

"Reagan checked to see if they'd filed for a rezoning, but there's nothing yet. Gail over in the planning office will call me the second she hears something though. It worries me that it's right next to the Salty Breeze, now its ownership is in question. The only thing the twenty acres are missing is ocean frontage, but they'd have that with the Salty Breeze. I have a meeting with Rebecca after she serves the guests happy hour today."

"I wish I could just buy the land," Callie said between bites of her sandwich. "Could we make them another offer?"

"Doesn't hurt to try. You miss one hundred percent of the shots you don't take."

"Geez, you have been spending too much time with Austin if you're saying things like that." Callie laughed. "Speaking of which, why did he go to Whispering Palms with you? Did Jesse ask him to?"

"No, my stupid car got stuck in some sand on the side of the road when I pulled over to check out the twenty acres."

"I told you to get an SUV instead of a convertible." Callie shrugged.

"You have a convertible," Gigi defended herself.

"Yes, but I'm not a land use attorney." Callie smiled back at her. "Besides, I'm going to get an SUV once we start trying for a baby. That car is from the old Callie's life." She waved dismissively in the direction of the garage.

Gigi rolled her eyes. "You're not even married yet and you're already talking about a baby."

"Yes, I know, kids aren't your thing, but you'll love mine." Callie winked at her. "Auntie Gigi."

"I was born to be an aunt," she said. "I'll spoil them rotten and then send them home when they start crying or need a diaper change." Gigi refused to perpetuate her family's cycle of mothers trying to live out their dreams through their children the way her mother and grandmother had. She was going to concentrate on her career and live her own dream.

Callie shook her head, laughing. "Anyway, so Austin rolled in and saved the day and got your car unstuck?"

"Sort of," Gigi said, taking a swig of her tea to help wash down her chicken salad sandwich. "He happened to be passing by and saw me stuck. I was going to be late for the appointment, and they only have that one date left. So he offered to take me over there and drove me back."

"How'd you get your car out? Did you have to call for a tow?"

"No, he had some plywood in the back of his truck from working with Jesse over at the Watson House. He wedged a piece under my back tire, and I was able to drive right over it and get out."

"Mmm," Callie said, her mouth full of sandwich.

"It's good, right? I wish Chloe had added sandwiches to the coffee shop a long time ago."

Callie wiped her mouth with a napkin. "Oh, I'm not talking about the sandwich—although it is really good—I'm talking about you and Austin."

"What about us?"

"Oh, come on. You have to see how he looks at you."

"I have no idea what you're talking about." Okay, she did have an idea. The night after Mary Catherine's wedding flashed through her mind. She balled up her sandwich wrapper and tossed it in the bag from Island Coffee, pushing away the image of Austin nearly kissing her back then.

"That man looks at you like someone lost in the desert who just spotted a water fountain."

Gigi rolled her eyes. "That is the most absurd thing I've ever heard."

Callie raised an eyebrow, holding up her hands. "Okay, if you say so."

"We're friends. Always have been. Can we please talk about Whispering Palms now? We only have another twenty-four hours to secure the date before it's up for grabs."

Gigi regaled Callie with all the details about Whispering Palms. She left out the part about how much Myrtle was going to hate it. That would just be her little secret. Well, her and Austin's.

By the time she left, Callie was pretty sold on Whispering Palms, but Gigi still had Wilson's Landing to see after lunch. She promised to call Callie after her meeting at the Salty Breeze and update her on both appointments.

Popping back into her office to sign a few things Reagan had finished while Gigi was at lunch, Gigi could overhear enough of her assistant's call to know she was speaking to Gail in the planning department.

"Thanks, Gail," Reagan confirmed as she ended the call. "Appreciate the heads up."

"They have filed something, haven't they?" Gigi said, putting a hand on her hip. She was ready to go to battle.

Reagan shook her head. "No, but they did call Phil about listing it. His assistant told Gail when she came in to check the zoning on another property today."

Phil Sanders had moved to Big Dune Island ten years ago and quickly became one of the most successful real estate brokers in town. He specialized in representing second-home buyers on the south end of the island and developers. No doubt, he'd help a developer purchase the land, sneakily try to rezone it without anyone noticing, and then serve as the agent for the developer when they were ready to sell whatever homes or condos they put on it. News traveled fast on Big Dune Island, and no doubt he knew by now that Mrs. Cunningham had passed.

He wasn't going to catch Gigi Franklin off guard though. She was on to him.

Her meeting with Rebecca tonight couldn't come fast enough.

WILSON'S LANDING WAS A BEAUTIFUL SPOT, BUT IT lacked the indoor options of Whispering Palms should the weather not cooperate with their plans for an outdoor ceremony and reception. Although the pavilion was covered, it was open on all sides, so there was still the risk of rain blowing in. There was also no air conditioning one could escape to if needed, so Gigi would tell Callie that Whispering Palms was the obvious choice when she called her after meeting with Rebecca.

As Gigi pulled into the crushed seashell driveway of the Salty Breeze, she noticed how weathered the exterior appeared. It had obviously been like that for a while, but she was seeing it with new eyes now that its ownership was uncertain. The white railings on the wraparound porch that encircled the entire two-story structure were gray, even from a distance, and the gray paint on the cedar-shingled siding was peeling and splotched with mildew. Luckily, the land itself didn't require much maintenance. The lot stretched from the ocean to the main road, with everything except the inn, drive, and parking lot left to its natural beauty. The drive and parking area were made from crushed seashells, an alternative to gravel that was used for most of the older homes on the island.

As Gigi made her way up the front stairs, she noted a wobbly board and more peeling paint on the once-white rocking chairs that lined the porch. She wasn't sure if Mrs. Cunningham hadn't had the funds to keep it up or had simply gotten behind on maintenance since her stroke. Gigi felt bad she hadn't been out to visit in a while, but work had been keeping her incredibly busy.

The brass plaque by the front door identifying the property as being on the National Register of Historic Places reminded Gigi why she was here. She wanted to see the Salty Breeze end up in the hands of someone who would give it a facelift, returning it to its former glory. Not someone who saw prime oceanfront property and wanted to turn it into firewood.

Pushing open the heavy wooden front door that had swollen in the humid air and stuck slightly, Gigi immediately noticed the smell of fresh-baked cookies as she entered the foyer. Two couples sat in the living room off the entryway, drinking wine and chatting. She nodded with a smile when they looked in her direction.

"Gigi," Rebecca said, coming down the hallway from the kitchen at the back. "Perfect timing. I think everyone has settled in with their drinks and snacks, and I can finally sit down for a few minutes."

Rebecca smiled, but it didn't reach her eyes. The woman looked exhausted. She was only ten years older than Gigi, but she'd aged at least another ten since the last time Gigi had seen her just a month earlier in the grocery store.

Gigi hugged Rebecca as they met in the hallway. "So good to see you, Rebecca. I only wish it were under different circumstances."

"Speaking of which, I'm off the clock. Let's grab some wine and go see if we can find somewhere private out back." Rebecca steered Gigi over to the sideboard in the dining room where bottles of white and rosé sat in a bucket of ice, a bottle of red next to it along with several empty glasses.

After they both poured themselves glasses of cold sauvignon blanc, Gigi followed Rebecca out to the back porch, which overlooked the dunes, with the ocean crashing onto the shore just beyond it. The view was nearly identical to the one at Gigi's house, but she never got tired of it.

They spotted two rocking chairs on the far-right of the porch, which would put them at enough distance from the guests sitting on the left side. The sound of the waves would drown out their conversation and provide privacy.

Rebecca sighed as she eased into her rocking chair. "It's been a long couple of days. This might be the first time I've been off my feet other than to sleep."

Gigi reached over and patted the woman's hand that rested on the arm of the chair. "I'm so sorry, Rebecca. I know you loved her like family."

Rebecca's eyes shimmered with unshed tears. "I really did. She would have done anything for me, and I for her. My mother passed when I was a teenager, so she's been like a mom to me for the past decade. It's such a shame she and Mr. Cunningham never had children of their own. They were such lovely people. I know kids aren't for everyone, but I always got the sense it hadn't been their choice. They loved when families came to stay, and they doted over the children like they were their grandparents, sneaking them an extra cookie and giving them little presents like sand toys and kites."

"I've only ever heard wonderful things about them, and they were always kind to me when I ran into them," Gigi said. "I only wish I'd had time to get to know them both better."

Rebecca frowned. "I wish Margaret would have taken you up on your offer to draft her will after Ron passed. Gigi, I don't think she ever got one done. I never saw her meet with another attorney, and she rarely left the property after her stroke. I've already been through her office files, and she didn't keep any kind of paperwork in the owner's quarters that I could find. What's going to happen to this place?" She looked up at the roof covering the porch, biting her lip.

"I was really hoping she had seen someone else," Gigi said. "I'll make some calls. There are only a couple of other attorneys in town who do wills. We'll keep our fingers crossed."

"Do you even know who she was planning to leave it to?" Rebecca asked. "She never wanted to talk about what would happen once she was gone, and she only ever mentioned one sister, who had passed some years back. I got the feeling there was a story there, but she didn't ever share it with me."

Gigi shook her head. "No, I'm sorry. She didn't give me much to go on the one time we met either. She said she didn't have any family to leave it to. I don't know if that meant she literally had no family or simply didn't have any family she *wanted* to leave it to. We might be able to get what we need from public records. I also have a private investigator who specializes in finding people who I've used in a couple of other probate matters. There has to be an heir out there somewhere, even if it's a second cousin twice removed. The law basically has us keep looking for an heir as far out in the family tree as it takes, but if she truly didn't have a living family member, it would eventually go to the state."

Rebecca had sat her wine on the table next to her and was wringing her hands. "Oh, Gigi, what if whoever inherits the inn wants to close it down? Or even worse, what if they want to tear it down? They can do that, can't they?"

Gigi wasn't ready to go there yet, but she didn't want to give the woman false hope either. "Yes, it's possible, but let's not stress about something that hasn't happened yet. Maybe there's a niece or nephew or a cousin or someone out there who would be delighted to keep this place running. After all, you're already running things, and business is good, right?" The parking lot had been practically full when Gigi pulled in.

Rebecca ran her hand over the peeling white paint on the arm of her chair. "Yeah, despite the fact that she could use some sprucing up, most of our reservations are return guests who've been coming for years. Margaret would send them birthday cards and holiday cards, and then she spoiled them while they were here. They're all very loyal. We even get people who've been coming since they were kids and now bring their own families. Did you see those two couples in the living room when you came in?"

Gigi nodded in reply, taking a sip from her wine glass.

"The two men are brothers, and one of them met his wife here as a teenager when she was visiting with her family. Can you believe that? It's so sweet. Anyway, Mark, the younger brother, is a contractor, and he asked if he and his brother could do any projects while they're here this week. It's their vacation, and they're volunteering to work because this place means so much to them."

"That really is touching," Gigi said.

"Many of the guests were here the night it happened, and they want to plan a little tribute to Margaret this weekend. You should come. The one thing I did know was that she didn't want a funeral. She said they were too morbid. She wanted a celebration of life here at the B&B like she had for Ron. Your mother already called and said the Junior League ladies would help me pull it together."

Gigi's eyes stung with tears as she thought about what the inn meant to people, and she never cried. One thing Myrtle had taught her that was ingrained in the fiber of her physical being was that you never cried in front of anyone. Tears were for private only. It made your face puffy, and public displays of emotion were messy and made others uncomfortable. You plastered on a smile and pushed through until you were home alone.

Clearing her throat, Gigi said, "I'd love to attend. Keep me posted on the details, and I'll let you know what I find out when I call around to the other firms." She decided not to mention the surveying stakes on the property next to the Salty Breeze. Trees and other foliage created a natural barrier between the inn and the property next door, so Rebecca probably hadn't seen any activity over there yet. No sense in giving her one more thing to worry about.

The two women fell into a companionable silence, rocking to the rhythm of the waves lapping at the shore. The sea oats that crowned the dunes in front of them swayed in the early-evening breeze, and the heat of the day had receded as the sun began its descent on the other side of the inn. The stress left Gigi's body little by little with each rock of the chair. She thought of the colorful signs sold to tourists in the stores downtown that said, "The cure for anything is salt water: tears, sweat, or the sea." Gigi might not be willing to cry over the Salty Breeze, but she'd put in all the sweat necessary to save this little piece of heaven by the sea.

Chapter Eight

Austin

"Thank you, Austin," Katie Carson said. "You're a lifesaver. Let Luke know I'll be home as soon as I can. I'll call you from the hospital when I know more."

Liam, the other foster child currently living with the Carsons, had been rushed from school to the emergency room with suspected appendicitis, and Katie's husband, Jared, was out of town visiting his sick mother. Her normal babysitter was a high school student still in class, so Katie hadn't been able to reach her to ask her to pick up Luke after school. Knowing Austin got home early in the afternoons from his radio job, she'd asked if he'd mind meeting Luke at the bus stop and occupying him for a few hours until she sorted things out at the hospital.

"Happy to help, Katie. He can stay over at my house tonight. You should stay with Liam."

"I might take you up on that. I just got to the hospital. I'll update you in a little bit."

Austin had half an hour before Luke was due to get home from school, so he tidied up his place in case the boy really did need to spend the night. He had a spare bedroom and a PS5 gaming system, so as long as they got takeout or ordered in, he was as ready as he could be for an unexpected eight-year-old guest.

The Carsons lived less than five minutes inland from Austin's house, which sat across the street from the beach. The island was only thirteen square miles, so it didn't take long to get anywhere. He left in plenty of time to beat the bus so Luke wouldn't get home and wonder why the house was empty.

Sitting on the front steps of the Carsons' modest ranch, he watched the giant yellow bus pull up a few doors down and open its doors to allow a handful of children to spill out. Luke was the first one off, which must mean he sat at the front of the bus. That didn't surprise Austin. He seemed like a studious, front-of-the-bus kind of kid.

Lifting a hand to wave as Luke started down the drive, the boy's face registered surprise and then panic. He slowed his walk as if he was afraid to get all the way down the driveway and learn why Austin was greeting him at his door.

"Everything's okay," Austin said, standing up and moving toward Luke. "Liam got sick at school, and Mrs. Carson had to go help him. So now you and I get to hang out for the night."

Luke's face only showed slight relief. "For the whole night? What's wrong with Liam?"

"Do you know what an appendix is?"

Luke shook his head as he reached Austin.

"It's part of your body you don't really need. Sometimes it stops working, and it has to be removed." Seeing the boy tense up again in fear, Austin hurried to give a better explanation of what was happening. "Liam is going to be just fine. I promise. I got my appendix out when I was playing minor league ball. And look," he said, holding out his arms, "you'd never even know."

The boy's face finally relaxed. "Is he going to have to stay at the hospital tonight?"

"Afraid so. He'll probably have surgery tonight, and he should be able to come home tomorrow. But that means we get to hang out. Mrs. Carson said you knew the code for the door. We'll get you a bag packed, and then we can decide what we want to do."

"Can we work on bunting again?" Luke asked as he moved to the door to enter a code on the keypad for the deadbolt.

"Sure, pal," Austin said, ruffling the little boy's brown hair. "You were doing pretty good with it the other day."

"I'll get my baseball stuff," Luke said, dropping his bookbag in the hallway as they entered before running toward the kitchen and out into the garage. He returned with his glove and a ball to where Austin waited in the foyer. Luke didn't have his own bat, but Austin had some gear he kept in his truck.

"Got it," the boy said, holding up his glove.

"How about some clothes for tomorrow? You'll need pajamas too and your toothbrush."

Luke nodded, handing his glove and the ball to Austin to hold. Austin followed him down another hall to his bedroom, which had a twin bed decked out in a baseball-themed bedspread. You'd never know Luke didn't live there permanently with his biological family. His dresser held two photo frames, one of him and Liam at the beach, and another of both boys with the Carsons at what looked like an amusement park.

Austin knew the Carsons had fostered quite a few children over the years, but both Liam and Luke had been with them for longer periods. They tended to get children who only needed temporary housing and eventually went back to a biological parent, grandparent, aunt, or uncle when court proceedings were complete. He didn't know Liam's situation, but Katie had told him Luke didn't have any biological family left.

He'd wanted to ask Katie if they might adopt Luke, but he didn't feel comfortable asking. He didn't want to imply he thought they should or make them feel guilty if that wasn't a decision they were able to make.

"I'm ready," Luke said as he shoved what looked like pajamas, a pair of shorts, and a T-shirt in his bag.

"Did you pack underwear and socks?"

Luke frowned. "No." He went to his dresser and opened the top drawer, pulling out both items. "Now I'm done." He hauled the strap of the bag onto his small shoulder.

"Toothbrush?"

"Bathroom." Luke pointed into the hall.

Austin followed him to the doorway of the bathroom, watching as Luke carefully wrapped his toothbrush in toilet paper before putting it down in his bag.

"Okay, I think I have everything else you need at my house," Austin said. "Do you have homework?"

Luke groaned. "Spelling. I hate spelling."

"I think I'm supposed to make you do your homework before we go play ball, but why don't we go hit the field first? And then I'll help you with your spelling while we wait on pizza for dinner. If you get it done with your homework before we eat, then we can play some PS5 before bed."

"Do you have Minecraft?" Luke asked, beaming. When Austin nodded, Luke's smile grew even bigger. "This is going to be the best night ever."

"It's still a school night though, okay? We can't stay up too late. What time do you normally go to bed?"

Luke's eyebrows drew together like he was struggling to remember. "Ten?"

Austin raised an eyebrow at him in response.

"Nine?"

Austin nodded. "That sounds more like it."

"Let's go," Luke said, walking past Austin toward the front door. "We've got a lot to do."

Austin laughed, shaking his head as Luke flung open the door and bounded down the stairs. The boy's excitement was contagious, and Austin was surprised at how much he was looking forward to it too.

AFTER HITTING LUKE SOME GROUND BALLS IN THE infield, Austin asked if Luke was ready to practice bunting. The boy nodded enthusiastically and ran to the dugout to deposit his glove and pick up a helmet and bat. Austin grabbed his bucket of baseballs and set up a few feet in front of the mound so he could pitch.

Luke missed the first few Austin tossed in, but he told the boy it was his fault, blaming it on bad pitching. It was difficult to pitch to someone half your height, and he didn't want to toss it underhand and have the ball rising on its way to the plate instead of falling like it should in overhand pitching. The pitches actually hadn't been bad, but he wanted to build up the boy's confidence. If Luke could get this down, he'd get on base more times than not. The eight- to ten-year-olds in this league usually weren't experienced enough with bunts to get to the ball in time and make the play at first.

"Don't forget to bend your knees. You want to move your body up and down, keeping the bat level, instead of moving the bat to meet the ball." Austin demonstrated, squatting up and down while he held an invisible bat parallel to the field.

Luke practiced with his bat and then nodded. "I'm ready." The boy's eyebrows were furrowed in intense concentration.

Austin could feel how badly Luke wanted to connect with the ball, so he did everything he could to place the pitch in the perfect spot over the plate.

The bat connected with the ball, and it bounced off only to die in the dirt a couple of feet in front of the plate. Luke jumped in excitement at the same moment Austin pumped a fist in the air.

"You did it," Austin said, running up to high-five the boy. "That's a perfect bunt. Think you can do it again?"

"Definitely," Luke said, looking more excited and confident than he did when the rest of the team was around.

Austin went back by the bucket and pitched in a few more, celebrating each time Luke connected and laid down the perfect bunt.

"Okay, now that you've got the hang of that, let's practice running. The minute you connect with the ball, you want to quickly toss the bat behind you as you take off for first. Then I want you to run as fast and as hard as you can all the way through the bag. Bunting is really just a race to see whether you can get to first base faster than one of the fielders can get to the ball. If it's close enough to the plate, the catcher will take it, but hopefully you'll catch them by surprise, and that'll buy you a couple of seconds. If you bunt it too far in front of you, the pitcher might be able to get to it fast enough to throw you out. There are situations where the first or third baseman might field it, but they probably won't have been taught that at this age, so don't worry about it."

Luke listened intently, nodding along, before setting up in the batter's box to try it. Austin pitched a few more in, giving Luke small adjustments to make so he could take off as fast as possible after connecting with the ball. He was so focused on Luke that he didn't know someone had approached the field until he heard a familiar voice.

"You could just teach him to drag from the left side. It's easier to learn when you're young." It was Austin's father, Dan Beckett. He was referring to what was known as a "drag bunt," where a player batted left-handed—even if they weren't left-handed—so they were closer to first and could poke it down the third baseline and take off faster.

Austin frowned. "He's just a kid. Let him master batting right-handed before you try to make him a switch hitter."

"How old are you, son?" the elder Beckett asked Luke.

Luke looked to Austin, clearly confused about the strange man weighing in on his batting.

"Luke, this is my dad, Mr. Beckett. Dad, this is Luke, one of the kids on my team. He's eight."

"Nice to meet you, Mr. Beckett," Luke said.

"Luke, have you ever tried batting left-handed?"

"Dad, seriously. He's too young to be trying to learn how to hit both ways. He's the fastest kid on my team. We're just working on bunting so he can get on base more often."

"You have to develop a switch hitter between the ages of eight and twelve," his dad said. "That's when your muscle and nerve connections are forming. Once they're set, you might as well forget it."

Austin rolled his eyes. Only around ten percent of professional baseball players could switch hit. He'd been one of them though, and no doubt it had not only improved his batting average, but also made him more attractive in the draft.

Austin's dad had entered the dugout, exiting onto the field and striding toward Luke. Austin threw his glove in the bucket of baseballs, meeting his father beside Luke. It would only take a few critical words from his father to undo the progress they'd made today on Luke's confidence.

"Do you want to play in the big leagues one day?" his dad asked Luke.

Austin broke in before Luke could answer. "You can't help yourself, can you? Let the kid just enjoy the game."

His dad frowned. "Every little boy wants to play in the majors one day. You did too at this age."

"Yeah, that was before—" Austin stopped himself from rehashing the same old argument with his father. He had dreamed of being a professional baseball player when he was young. That was until his dad sucked all the fun out of it and made it a chore. Luke was too young to understand all that, and he certainly didn't need to be a witness to their argument. Austin took a deep breath before addressing his father again. "What are you even doing here?"

"I like to walk the path when your mother kicks me out of the house for her book club," he said, nodding toward the paved walking trail that led from downtown over to the city park and ball fields.

"Well, we don't want to keep you from your walk," Austin said. "Luke has homework, so we need to get going anyway."

"Aww, already?" Luke asked. "I was just getting the hang of it."

"You had some good form out there," his dad said. "I saw how fast you caught on. Do you want to try a few left-handed? I'm a lefty myself, so I'll show you how." He reached out for the bat.

Luke was already handing him the bat, and Austin decided it would be worse to make a scene and refuse to let his father demonstrate. There were other people on the walking path that snaked between the two ball fields and tennis courts next door.

"Did you play baseball like Coach?" Luke asked as he followed Mr. Beckett to the plate.

"I did," Mr. Beckett said. "I made it to the minor leagues,

but I never made it to the majors. Maybe if my dad had taken more of an interest in practicing with me, I might have made it too." He said the last part while shooting a disapproving glance in Austin's direction.

Austin was all too aware of why his dad was the way he was. His own father had been of the old-school belief that women raised the children, and men worked and provided for their families. When he got home from the mill every day, his wife had his paper and a stiff drink waiting for him, and he had no time for tossing a baseball in the backyard. Even so, Austin's dad had made it further than most people ever did. But he hadn't achieved his dream of making it to the majors, and he was convinced if he just invested enough time in practicing with Austin, he could see his dream realized through him. And although he'd been the proud father in the stands for Austin's MLB debut in Atlanta, he'd been the same old drill sergeant after the game, rattling off everything Austin could have done better when they were supposed to be grabbing a celebratory dinner with Austin's mother.

Austin dismissed the memory, trying to focus on what his father was saying to Luke in case he needed to intervene. Luke was hanging on his every word though, dreams of the big leagues dancing in his eyes.

"Toss me one so I can show him how it's done," his dad said, nodding toward the bucket of balls in front of the mound.

Giving in, Austin grabbed the bucket and moved it back onto the mound. Resisting the urge to try to breeze one past his old man, he threw in a strike for him to bunt.

His dad perfectly executed three bunts in a row down the third baseline, explaining to Luke how he could already be moving forward and toward first in the batter's box as he bunted, taking off the instant after the ball hit the bat so he'd already be several steps toward first before the ball even hit the ground.

Austin had to admit that his dad not only had perfect form, he was also adept at breaking everything down in a way that was easy to understand. He'd always been better at working with the other boys on Austin's teams. Heck, Jesse had loved going to the fields with him back when they both played high school ball. But then his dad hadn't had the same expectations for the other boys as he'd had for Austin.

"All right, toss one in for the kid," his dad said, moving a few steps behind the plate after he helped the boy get his hands on the bat correctly.

Luke missed the first ball Austin tossed in. "That's okay," Austin reassured him. "That time you—"

"—angled the top of the bat too high when you started to move," his dad finished his sentence.

Austin frowned at his dad, determined not to let him take over his coaching. "Remember, keep the bat parallel with the ground as you move forward in the box."

His dad held up his hands as if in surrender, backing up behind the plate as Austin threw in another pitch. This time, Luke made contact, but he got under it and popped it up behind him. Mr. Beckett was able to grab it barehanded.

"There you go. You made contact that time," the older man said, smiling at Luke before throwing the ball to Austin.

"I know what happened," Luke said. "I got too far under it, didn't I?"

"That's right," Mr. Beckett said. "But now that you know, you can fix it next time."

Luke did fix it on the next pitch, tapping a bunt directly in front of him that rolled toward Austin.

"I did it!" Luke said, jumping up. "I can bunt left-handed." He looked to Austin and then Mr. Beckett for their approval.

"You did. Good job," Austin said, smiling at him before trying to silently telegraph a message to his father to say something nice. He braced instead for his father to tell Luke he needed to aim toward third, that hitting it as hard as he had toward the pitcher would be a sure out. It was true, but now wasn't the time for that lesson. Let the kid make contact a few times and get his confidence up.

Mr. Beckett had stepped forward to Luke and was patting him on the back. "Thatta boy. Want to try another one and work in the steps toward first so you can make a break for it when you connect?"

Relief and surprise washed over Austin. His father had actually managed to control himself. Maybe he was getting soft in his old age.

Austin let Luke bunt another dozen balls, running to first after each one, before he noted the boy's pink cheeks and increased breathlessness.

"I think that's enough for today," Austin said. "You've got homework to do before dinner. Grab some water and cool down while I get the gear together."

Luke nodded, walking back to the dugout where Austin had left a water bottle for each of them.

"Where's the rest of the team?" Mr. Beckett asked, walking over to Austin.

Austin turned so his back was to Luke, speaking quietly. "Luke's one of the Carsons' foster kids. Their other foster had appendicitis and was rushed to the hospital, and Jared is out of town, so Katie asked if I could grab Luke after school."

His dad glanced in Luke's direction. "How long has he been in foster care? Seems like a nice kid."

"He is. One of the most polite and well-behaved kids on the team. I don't know much, just that his dad was never in the picture, and his mom died in a car accident a couple of years ago."

"Good that he's got baseball," his dad said.

"What does baseball have to do with him being a foster kid?" Austin asked as he tossed the glove he was still holding into the bucket of balls.

"You never learned this lesson, Austin. Never had to. Baseball isn't just a game. It's a constant, something he can hold on to when everything else feels uncertain." His father's gray eyes clouded over as he looked off in the distance.

He was right. Austin had never understood why his father was so obsessed with baseball. It was just a game. Sure, you learned important life skills like teamwork, patience, and discipline, but at the end of the day, it was just a game. Everyone struck out. Everyone lost. It said nothing about your worth, and it wasn't the only worthy pursuit in life. He'd never understand the weight his father placed on it.

Not knowing what else to say, he began gathering the rest of the gear scattered on the field. Luke ran out to help, and they said their goodbyes to his father as they exited the dugout to head to Austin's truck in the parking lot.

"Thanks, Mr. Beckett," Luke said. "I'm going to work on my left-handed bunt."

"You do that, son. Practice makes perfect."

Austin winced. How many times had he heard that phrase? He'd never said it to his team. Sure, you need to practice to improve, but you shouldn't be so focused on perfection. Then you'd only be disappointed when you fell short.

"Are you coming to our first game next week?" Luke asked Mr. Beckett.

Austin was surprised Luke had become so enamored with his father so quickly.

But he was even more surprised when his dad said, "I'll be there. When is it?"

His father had never come to a game he'd coached, and Austin wasn't sure he wanted him to start.

Chapter Nine

Gigi

Gigi had called the other attorneys in town who did wills, but none had done Mrs. Cunningham's. A call to the funeral home where Mrs. Cunningham had been taken revealed that she had signed a contract and prepaid to be cremated back when her husband died. It made Gigi sad to think of the newly widowed woman planning for her own death. And she had been so diligent about that and yet put off getting a will. Unfortunately, a lot of people did, especially if they weren't sure who they wanted to inherit their assets.

Cathy, the funeral director's wife, said they'd been instructed to deliver her remains to Rebecca at the B&B and that Mrs. Cunningham had made it clear she didn't want a ceremony at the funeral home.

"Did the poor woman really have no family?" Cathy asked.

"It doesn't seem like it," Gigi said. "At least not any she was close to."

"Thank heaven for Rebecca. She'll see to it that Margaret gets the tribute she deserves."

Gigi agreed, but she couldn't help the gnawing feeling that somewhere out there Mrs. Cunningham had family who needed to know she had passed.

After telling Cathy she'd see her at the Salty Breeze for the memorial, Gigi decided to call her private investigator, Mitch. He owed her a favor, and he was a good tracker. He'd found fathers who had skipped out on child support and developers trying to hide their identity by buying land through shell companies. Rebecca already had access to everything she needed to keep the inn running in the meantime.

Gigi had just hung up with Mitch on her office phone when her cell lit up on the desk. She let out an exasperated sigh when she saw it was Myrtle.

"Hello, Myrtle," she said, making no effort to hide her annoyance at being interrupted in the middle of the workday.

"I hope you don't answer client calls like that, Georgia," her mother said with a harrumph. "I taught you better."

"Good afternoon, Myrtle. How may I help you?" she said in a sickly sweet tone.

"I just paid a visit to Rebecca over at the Salty Breeze, and she said you'd already been by. Any luck finding the poor woman's family?"

"Not yet, but I just got off the phone with my investigator. He's going to work on it as soon as he can."

"That probably won't give them time to get here for the service on Saturday," her mother said, "but the woman deserves a proper send-off. I spoke with the ladies at the League, and we've voted to approve paying the expenses for the celebration of life. I've already called the caterer, the florist, and booked a harpist, and we'll all be there early to help set up.

Wear blue. Rebecca said it was Margaret's favorite color, so we're all wearing blue."

Gigi had always found the Junior League to be a frivolous organization more interested in throwing parties and making themselves feel important by handpicking who could join them than in any of the philanthropies they purported to support. She wondered if perhaps she'd been too quick to judge, however. What they were doing for Mrs. Cunningham was lovely.

Before she could decide how to express this without admitting anything of the sort to her mother, Myrtle was speaking again.

"Don't wear light blue though. It washes you out. Remember how ghostly you looked in those prom photos your junior year? I told you not to wear that dress, but you just had to make your own choice. Do you have something in a royal blue? Or a navy perhaps?"

And there was the Myrtle she knew. More worried about appearances than what was important here.

"I'll make sure I wear something blue," Gigi said, refusing to acknowledge her mother's warning.

"The League ladies are making calls to all the people we think would want to be there. I'm sure Mrs. Thomas will tell Callie and Jesse, and Mrs. Beckett will tell Austin and Chloe," she said, referring to Jesse and Austin's mothers, who were also members of the Junior League. "You'll make sure they all wear blue?"

"Yes," Gigi said dutifully. She almost asked sarcastically if she should pass along shade suggestions to them as well, but stopped when she realized her mother would gladly give her opinion.

After successfully ending the call without taking any additional shots, Gigi told Reagan that she was leaving for lunch and would be out for the afternoon. It was time to switch gears from a funeral to a wedding, and today was wedding dress day.

"I FEEL LIKE I HAVE EMOTIONAL WHIPLASH," GIGI said, sighing as she unzipped a dress bag from the top of a pile on Callie's bed.

"We don't have to do this today," Callie called out from the giant closet off her master bedroom. "I know you probably have a lot to do for Mrs. Cunningham's celebration of life."

"No, this is exactly what I need," Gigi said. "Myrtle and the League ladies have that under control. All we have to do is show up and wear blue. This, however," she said, pulling a bodice covered in rhinestones out of the dress bag, "is not what *you* need."

Callie scrunched her nose as she joined Gigi. "No, hard pass. Too much bling."

"This is the last of them," Piper said, entering the room with an armful of dress bags stacked so high she had to peek around the side to see where she was walking. She made it to the other side of the bed, where Gigi and Callie had started unzipping bags, and unloaded them on top of the duvet with an oof.

"It was so nice of your friend to ship me all these dresses," Callie said. "And for you to lug them all over here. Thank you."

"Of course." Piper waved a hand. "Now we don't have to close down a store and make everyone sign an NDA to keep your wedding dress shopping a secret."

"I cleared a rack in my closet so we can hang them all in there," Callie said, grabbing a few from the top of the pile and starting toward the closet that was the size of a bedroom itself.

"Perfect," Gigi said. "You two get those hung up, and I'll

go downstairs and get us some champagne. You can't try on wedding dresses without champagne."

By the time Gigi opened the champagne, grabbed three glasses, and returned to Callie's bedroom, the dresses had all been moved into the closet. She could hear Callie grunting as Piper helped her get into a dress. She poured the champagne and waited for the two women to emerge.

"Wow," she said when Callie swished into the bedroom wearing a giant satin ballgown, part of the voluminous skirt catching on the doorframe on the way out of the closet. "I don't know if you look like a bride or a princess, but that's quite a dress."

"Way too much poof for me," Callie said, "but it's kind of fun. I definitely feel like a princess." She twirled in a circle, satin swirling around her.

Gigi brought two glasses of champagne across the room to Callie and Piper before returning to grab her own from the nightstand.

"To feeling like a princess," Gigi said, holding up her glass.

"To feeling like a princess," the other two repeated as they clinked with her.

"Maybe something that will fit through doorways would be a little better." Callie laughed.

"I saw just the thing," Piper said, retreating into the closet. The laughter that trailed behind her, however, said the next dress was probably ridiculous in some other way.

Gigi unzipped Callie and then sat in an oversized ivory-colored wingback chair in the bedroom to wait for the next dress reveal. She nearly spit out her champagne when Callie waddled through the door in the next selection. The mermaid dress was so tight through the hips and legs that Callie couldn't take an actual step.

"Well, that does fit through the doorway better," she said.

"Right?" Piper giggled from behind Callie. "You wanted slimmer; you got slimmer."

"*The Little Mermaid* was my favorite movie as a kid." Callie shrugged. "But maybe something more befitting the human version of Ariel?"

"So somewhere between a formal ballgown and a mermaid tail? You're so high maintenance," Gigi teased.

"Well, I am a bride. We're supposed to be high maintenance," Callie said, sticking her nose in the air.

"You're the least high-maintenance client I've ever had," Piper said. "Did I tell you about Britt's wedding?" she asked, referring to a pop star she used to represent. "She changed dresses four times. Four times! She spent more time changing clothes than she did dancing with her husband."

"I saw the *People* magazine spread," Gigi said. "There wasn't one flattering gown in the bunch. You'd think out of four options she could have found one good one."

"Gigi already has the perfect dress," Callie said. "Her mother's dress is a timeless classic. We used to try it on as kids when she wasn't home."

"What's it like?" Piper asked.

"Did you ever see Jackie O's wedding dress?" Gigi asked, and Piper nodded. "It's an off-the-shoulder number like that, but with a simpler satin skirt. My mother wore hers with a crown and white gloves, but that's a little dramatic for me."

Myrtle had looked like an epic mix of Jackie O and Audrey Hepburn, but Gigi would never tell her that. Her head was big enough as it was.

"It has the most beautiful little pearl buttons down the back too," Callie added.

"Do you really think it's what you'd want to wear for your own wedding one day?" Piper asked.

Gigi shrugged as if she hadn't given it much thought. As if she hadn't pictured herself walking down the aisle in that dress her entire childhood. Being a lawyer, however, had taught her that marriage wasn't all it was cracked up to be.

"Moot point. I haven't even been on a date in, like, a year. Speaking of which," she said, turning to Callie, "please tell me there are going to be hot men at this wedding. Ooh, what about that Chris guy who won all those CMAs last year? You know him, right?"

Callie laughed. "Chris Colt? Yes, I know him and his lovely girlfriend, Anna. And, no, they're not coming to the wedding. I don't want a bunch of industry people there. I'd never be able to keep it a secret that way."

Gigi groaned. "So it's just going to be the same old lame guys I see here every day?"

"Afraid so," Callie said.

"That Aiden guy is cute," Piper offered, referring to the architect Jesse worked with on his historic rehab projects.

"She already dated him," Callie said. "Apparently she was a little much for him."

"If by 'a little much' you mean that he didn't like it when he found out I make more money than him, then yes. I was a little much for him."

"What about Austin?" Piper asked. "Did you ever date him? You two kind of have that enemies-to-lovers thing going on."

Callie gave Gigi an I-told-you-so look, mouth pursed to the side, an eyebrow raised.

"No, I have not dated Beckett. He was too busy dating everyone else in our class in high school, and then he had his pick of the cleat chasers in Atlanta," she said, referring to what the wives of the players had called the women who waited for Austin and the other single guys after games.

"He does have ladies' man kind of vibes," Piper said.

"He's a big old mush ball under all that bravado," Callie defended him. "Admittedly, he loved the attention a little too much at times, but he was always a gentleman. Seriously, have you ever heard a woman say anything bad about dating him?" She looked pointedly at Gigi.

"Well, it's not like I know *all* the women he's dated," Gigi said. "I mean, who could? There are so many."

"So you wouldn't mind if I flirted with him a little?" Piper asked.

Gigi could tell Piper was baiting her more than showing any genuine interest, but she refused to bite.

"Not at all. Go right ahead." She didn't like the image of the two of them together that popped into her head though. Piper was all wrong for Austin. She was constantly jetting off to New York and Los Angeles to take care of clients. And although she seemed to enjoy spending time on Big Dune Island with Callie, she'd never settle down here, and Austin had hated living in a big city.

"Oh, well." Gigi sighed. "I'll be too busy with my maid-of-honor duties to entertain a date anyway."

Callie and Piper retreated into the closet again to find another dress to try on. When Callie exited this time, there were tears in her eyes.

"I think I found my dress," she said, smiling as a tear rolled down her cheek.

"I think maybe you did. It's perfect," Gigi said, taking in the vintage-inspired A-line dress covered in delicate lace with a sweetheart neckline and sheer-lace cap sleeves. It was elegant and just a little bit country, just like Callie.

Piper nodded as she followed Callie out into the middle of the room. "Show her the back."

Callie spun around to reveal that the sheer lace of the cap sleeves extended to cover the open back of the dress, small pearl buttons dotting the back from the waist up. It was both sexy and sweet. It struck the perfect balance.

Piper fanned out the lace train, and Gigi told Callie she'd

snap a few pictures so she could see the full effect from behind.

When she showed the photos on her phone to Callie, her friend smiled through the tears now streaming freely down her face.

"Your mother's dress was lace, wasn't it?" Gigi asked, remembering the wedding photo of Callie's parents that still hung on the wall lining the staircase.

Callie nodded and Gigi put an arm around her and squeezed. She was never good at what to say in moments like this, so she just wanted her friend to know she was there for her.

Piper sniffed, a tear streaking down her cheek. "Well, I think we have the dress. I'll let Sophie know," she said, referring to her designer friend who'd sent the gowns. "I don't think it even needs any alterations. We just need to find a veil and some shoes."

"I have the perfect shoes," Gigi said. "It can be your something borrowed."

"I don't know if I even want a veil," Callie said. "I want all the attention on this gorgeous dress. Maybe just a flower in my hair?"

The women were interrupted by the sound of the front door and male voices downstairs.

"Jesse," Callie gasped. "He can't see me in this. Shut the door."

"I'll go run interference," Gigi said, closing the door behind her on her way downstairs.

She found Jesse and Austin in the kitchen debating whether *Seinfeld* or *Friends* was the better show as they peered into the refrigerator.

"Can I help you two?"

They spun around like kids who'd been caught with their hands in a cookie jar.

"Geez, Gigi, you scared the crap out of me. I thought Callie was going out shopping with you somewhere today," Jesse said.

"She's trying on wedding dresses upstairs. We didn't actually go anywhere. Piper brought the dresses here."

Guys. They were never great with details. She was sure Callie had told him they weren't going to just waltz into a bridal store to look for a dress.

Jesse looked up like he had X-ray vision and might be able to see through the ceiling to Callie's bedroom. "Sorry, I guess that means I can't go upstairs and look for my sunglasses. I think I left them in her studio this morning."

"I'll get them," Gigi offered. "You two stay down here."

"Yeah, man. You can't see the bride in her dress before the big day. It's bad luck," Austin said in a serious tone. No one believed in superstitions more than a pro athlete.

Austin looked like a ball player today too. He was wearing one of those baseball shirts with blue three-quarter sleeves and the white body, and a pair of athletic shorts. Gigi had always thought that any man looked hotter in one of those shirts. It stretched across his chest and around his arms just enough to show off his well-defined muscles. He was still in just as good shape as he had been during his playing days.

"Is that seriously how you get to dress for work?" Gigi asked him. Although she only had to wear suits on days she was in court, and business casual was very casual on Big Dune Island compared to New York, she still couldn't get away with workout attire and sneakers in the office. People liked to just stop by and chat or ask questions since her office was so close to Main Street.

Austin shrugged. "No one can see me on the radio. Everyone at the station dresses like this. Besides, I have practice this afternoon."

"Practice? Like you're playing again?"

"No, he's coaching Little League," Jesse said, slapping Austin on the shoulder like a proud dad. "That's why I came by. I'm going to help him today, but I need my sunglasses."

Gigi forgot she was supposed to be getting his sunglasses. Seeing Austin in that shirt had stopped her in her tracks. "Uh, yeah. I'll go get them."

Austin was coaching Little League? He'd been very clear how happy he'd been to close the baseball chapter of his life. Jacksonville didn't have an MLB team, so he didn't even have to talk about baseball on his show very often.

When she returned with the sunglasses, Austin was telling Jesse about some of the kids on the team.

"How old are these kids?" Gigi asked, handing Jesse the sunglasses.

"Eight- to ten-year-olds," Austin said.

"Oh, so they're on your level?" Gigi retorted.

"Can't even keep up with them some days," Austin replied with a smile. "But they think I've got mad rizz."

"Rizz?" Gigi asked. "Is that some sort of new slang?"

Austin winked, patting Gigi on the shoulder as he walked past her toward the front door. "You're so cheugy."

"Do you have any idea what he's saying?" she asked Jesse as he followed.

"Not a clue," he said, laughing. "But that's nothing new." Everyone was always trying to decode Austin's mantras, proverbs, and just plain made-up sayings.

Gigi stopped at the window by the front door to watch the two men climb into Austin's truck. Not for the first time, she thought how happy she was that all four of them were back home together again on Big Dune Island. It felt like the way things were supposed to be.

Chapter Ten

Austin

For the second time in as many days, Austin was pretty sure he'd caught Gigi checking him out. He'd met her and Jesse at Callie's before the celebration of life so they could all ride together, and her eyes had lingered over his slim-cut suit for an extra beat.

"Do we clean up nice, or what?" he'd quipped, holding his dark gray jacket open and doing a little twirl in the foyer. He'd always had a habit of joking when he was nervous. But why was he nervous? It was just Gigi. He'd known her when she had braces and chipmunk cheeks in ninth grade.

Luckily, Jesse had taken his cue and struck a pose, dusting off the shoulder of his jacket with flair.

"Very nice," Callie said, walking up to kiss Jesse on the cheek.

"That's a nice cut," Gigi said, nodding at Austin's suit. "You should wear that to the wedding. It'll go nicely with what I ordered. We'll just have to match your tie and pocket square to my blue dress."

Ahh, she was just considering the aesthetics for the wedding. Austin had let his imagination get away from him.

"Is it blue like the one you're wearing?" he asked, pointing to the sky-blue knee-length dress that hugged her curves in all the right places while still looking appropriate for today's event. "I might have something."

"This?" Gigi asked, looking down. "No, it's too daytime. I bought a darker one for the wedding. It should be here in a few days. I'll bring it over and we can try to match it."

"I can't believe we have a venue and dresses already," Callie said, grabbing Jesse's hand and grinning. "It's all feeling really real."

"It'll be more fun than today, that's for sure," Jesse said, tugging at his tie to loosen it.

"At least it's not one of those long church funerals," Gigi said. "This is what I want when I go. Food and drinks and an ocean view. Toast me with champagne and remember me fondly."

"You just can't leave me anytime soon," Callie said, dropping Jesse's hand to embrace her friend.

"I'm not going anywhere. Promise," Gigi vowed, hugging her back.

"I don't mean to break up this lovely moment, but we all need to get going," Jesse said, ushering the women toward the door.

"Is there a ladder to help me get up in this thing," Gigi asked once they were standing next to Austin's four-door pickup truck in the driveway.

Austin stepped in front of her and opened the driver's side rear door. "Madam," he said, holding out a hand to help her up.

She hiked up her skirt a little so she could get a foot on the running board, and he tried not to let his gaze linger on her exposed thigh.

"Did you have to buy the biggest truck on the lot?" she asked.

"In fact, I didn't have to buy it at all." He smirked. "The dealership gave it to me."

She rolled her eyes as she sat and smoothed out her dress. "I forgot about those terrible commercials," she said, referring to the ads he did for the dealership in exchange for the leased truck.

"No curveballs here, just straight-up steals. Knock it out of the park with our wheel deals!" the two women in the back of the truck sang the jingle.

Feeling his face flush, Austin shut the door on Gigi as she and Callie howled with laughter.

On the way to the Salty Breeze, the women played around with additional baseball-themed lines to the jingle.

"Don't let these offers fly right by. Catch a great deal, don't be shy!" Callie sang.

"Wait, I've gone one," Gigi said. "Don't let high prices throw you a curve. We've got the trucks and cars you deserve!"

Austin had to admit they were coming up with some funny lines.

"Don't mind them," Jesse said. "I'd sing on TV for a free truck too."

"I'm not even the one singing." Austin laughed. Although he probably would have done it. He didn't take himself that seriously.

As they pulled into the lot at the Salty Breeze, which was already filling up, Callie asked Gigi if her investigator had had any luck locating Mrs. Cunningham's family.

"I haven't heard anything. It feels kind of wrong not to have anyone here, but she considered these people her family —Rebecca and all the rest of the staff. Most of them have been here since she bought the place, and some of her regular guests stayed or made the trip."

The group made their way into the Salty Breeze, where people gathered in the living room and spilled into the dining room and out onto the porch. Everyone wore varying shades of blue and white, and blue flower arrangements were placed on the tables with thick white candles flickering. As they greeted friends and neighbors and walked past the French doors that led out back, Austin could see a tent had been set up between the stairs from the back porch and the dunes that separated the lawn from the ocean.

Rebecca came over to greet them and introduced the group to a few of the regular guests who lived within driving distance, as well as a few who had been staying at the inn and helped with the planning. After they got over their initial shock of meeting country superstar Callie Jackson, Austin was relieved to find they treated her like a normal person. Callie would hate if people tried to make this about her.

As Austin listened to two brothers and their wives share stories about Mrs. Cunningham and her generosity, he noticed Phil Sanders across the room talking to a man he didn't recognize. Phil was like a vulture circling its prey. The real estate broker would salivate over the chance to sell the Salty Breeze to some big developer.

The man Phil was with had thick black hair and a slim-cut black suit similar to Austin's gray one. Something about the guy felt off, but Austin couldn't say what. It was probably just his proximity to Phil.

Ms. Myrtle came in from the back porch with a woman holding a clipboard, speaking in hushed tones. He couldn't make out what she was saying, but she was definitely giving orders. Austin buttoned his suit jacket and stood up taller. He wasn't afraid to admit he was afraid of Ms. Myrtle and her discerning taste. Why he cared about her approval, he didn't have the slightest clue. She just had that commanding sort of presence that made you snap to attention.

"Callie, darling," she said, approaching their circle and kissing Callie on the cheek. "You look lovely. That color really suits you."

"Thank you, Ms. Myrtle," Callie said. "You look beautiful too, like always."

"Thank you, dear. Jesse, Austin." She nodded at the men. "Don't you both look dashing."

Whew. He'd passed.

Then she turned her attention to Gigi. She leaned in to hug her daughter, who stood next to Austin, and he could hear her when she whispered, "Didn't we talk about that color blue? You look like a ghost."

Austin hated it when Ms. Myrtle criticized Gigi. He couldn't resist the urge to come to her defense.

"Doesn't Gigi look great in that dress?" he asked Ms. Myrtle.

The older woman raised an eyebrow at Austin, as if perhaps she hadn't heard him correctly.

"I really like that color blue on you, G," he said, smiling at Gigi.

Her eyes twinkled back at his with a mix of mischief and satisfaction. "Why thank you, Beckett. And that blue tie really brings out your eyes."

Ms. Myrtle squinted, looking back and forth between them as if she was trying to solve a puzzle. Austin didn't think he'd ever seen her rendered speechless, and silently congratulated himself.

Before Ms. Myrtle had a chance to respond, the woman with the clipboard tapped her on the shoulder and said the caterer needed her in the kitchen. She left without further commentary on the group's attire.

As Callie's uncle Lonnie and his wife, Jacqueline, who ran

Callie's label, walked up to her and Jesse, Gigi turned to Austin and silently mouthed, "Thank you."

He nodded, smiling, before greeting Uncle Lonnie and Jacqueline.

"Hey," his sister said as she tapped him on the shoulder from behind. "Could you give me a hand unloading the desserts?"

"Sure," he said, following Chloe to the front door, which had been propped open. "Anything good? I'm starving."

She turned and gave him a look of mock horror. "Everything I make is good. And I'll pay you in petit fours after we get all this inside."

"Are those the tiny little cakes? I'd need about twenty of those to tell I'd even had one."

"They're bite-sized and perfect for nibbling while standing around talking to everyone. I've got pies too, but we're not cutting into those until after the ceremony." She stopped at the back of her SUV and opened the door to the cargo area.

"Strawberry rhubarb?" he asked, reaching in to grab a stack of pink bakery boxes.

"Blueberry. Ms. Myrtle wanted everything to be blue."

"And you're sending me in there with a stack of pink boxes." He looked down at the offending items, half joking and half terrified of the woman's wrath.

Chloe shrugged as she grabbed a smaller stack. "There wasn't time to order blue boxes just for this, so we'll get everything out as fast as we can and hide them." She laughed.

Thankfully, Ms. Myrtle wasn't still in the kitchen when they walked in with the piles of pink boxes. The kitchen staff helped remove everything and placed them on crystal and silver serving trays and pie stands.

By the time they left the kitchen, the woman with the clipboard was ushering everyone out to the tent on the lawn. Austin and Chloe joined Jesse, Callie, Uncle Lonnie, and Jacqueline a few rows from the front. If Austin hadn't known better, he would have thought it was a wedding, not a funeral. Rows of white chairs sat on either side of an aisle, facing the ocean. Arrangements of blue hydrangeas sat at the end of each aisle. There was a white podium where a bride and groom would have stood, a large photo of Mr. and Mrs. Cunningham on an easel to the right.

In the photo, the Cunninghams were on the porch of the inn, looking out toward the ocean. The picture had been taken from the side, showing them in profile as they held hands on top of the porch railing. They were both smiling out at the ocean as if waiting for their ship to come in. He hadn't known them well, but they looked happy and still very much in love. Wasn't that what everyone wanted? Someone they could grow old with?

Once everyone was seated, Rebecca walked to the podium. She waited for everyone to fall quiet, the crashing of the ocean waves behind her and a gull calling overhead were the only sounds.

"Thank you, everyone, for being here today." She put a hand over her heart. "Margaret would have never let us make such a fuss over her if she'd been here, but I can't help but think it's a shame she can't see how many of you came to honor her. As you know, she lost her dear husband, Ron, a few years ago. She considered everyone here at the inn her family, both those who were here every day and those who only got to join us once or twice a year.

"Margaret didn't want a formal funeral, but some of our regulars who were here this week thought a celebration of her life was in order. I want to thank Myrtle Franklin and the ladies of the Junior League for giving generously of their time and money to make this an event fit for a woman who always gave more to others than she asked for herself. Thank you, ladies," she said, making eye contact with Ms. Myrtle and several others in the crowd, nodding to them each.

"I don't have a speech prepared. I just wanted to thank you all for being here and open the floor for those who want to share memories of Margaret." She looked out at the crowd expectantly, waiting for someone to volunteer to go first.

Josephine, who'd run the kitchen at the inn since before the Cunninghams bought it, was the first to step up to the podium. She talked about all the times Mrs. Cunningham had sent her home early when her grandkids were in town and how she'd insisted on paying her regular salary when Josephine had to take off two months to recover from a broken hip.

Mark and Jack, the two brothers who had been staying at the inn when Mrs. Cunningham passed, went up to the podium together next. They explained how their mother insisted on having a picnic by a beach bonfire on their final night of vacation every year. They'd eat dinner, cook s'mores, and then everyone in the family would write on a piece of paper something that had been frustrating them or making them unhappy and then throw it in the fire to symbolize letting it go. Mark remembered his one year was not making the high school track team, and Jack remembered when he'd been upset about not getting into Duke, his top choice. The first summer without their mother, after she lost her fight with breast cancer, Mrs. Cunningham had surprised the men, their father, and girlfriends with a bonfire and a picnic, even though their mother hadn't been there to arrange it.

"Remember, your mother is one thing you never have to let go, because she's always right here with you," Mrs. Cunningham had said when she'd brought out pens and paper for them. "I can feel her, can't you?" And they could.

By the time they finished the story, both men had wiped tears from their faces. Austin swiped at one with his own knuckle, glancing around him to see if anyone had noticed.

Everyone around him was crying except Gigi. She sat with her back rigid and lips pursed, as if actively fighting not to show any emotion. She'd always been like that though. She hadn't even cried the night she came to him about Dalton breaking up with her instead of proposing as she'd expected.

Austin thought about his mother, who'd always been his safe harbor, and had to swallow hard to keep from releasing a flood of tears. She and his father had gone up to Savannah for the weekend, two hours north of Big Dune Island, for a couples' trip they had planned with her best friend from college months before. Now he wished she was there in the crowd so he could see her and know she was okay.

It was silly. There was nothing wrong with his mother, but seeing Mark and Jack break down made him wish he spent more time with her. He hadn't realized until now that avoiding extra time with his father had also led to less time with his mother, since the two were always together. He'd change that. Maybe he could take his mom to breakfast or dinner one day next week, just the two of them.

After about a dozen people got up to tell similarly touching stories of Mrs. Cunningham's generosity and sincerity, Rebecca invited everyone into the house for food and drinks. Gigi had been right behind him as they walked up the aisle toward the back deck, but when Austin turned around to say something to her, she was gone. Glancing around, he saw she'd stopped to talk to the man with the black hair who'd been inside with Phil earlier. She seemed very interested in whatever he was saying. Did she know him?

"Hey, who's that guy?" he asked Jesse as his friend extracted himself from a nearby conversation and came over.

"No idea. Cal, you know who that is?" Jesse asked his fiancée as she joined them.

She shook her head. "Nope, never seen him."

The guy reached out and touched Gigi's arm as he spoke.

Was this guy flirting with her at a funeral? He had that sort of big-city shiny quality to him. His shoes were too polished, and his black suit had a skinny white pinstripe.

Austin wanted to stay and continue observing them, but it was their turn to funnel up the stairs to the back porch. His stomach growled again, and he followed Jesse and Callie into the inn. After they'd all piled their plates high with finger food, they went back onto the porch to stand at one of the high-top tables that had been brought in for the event.

Gigi strode up the stairs toward them, the black-haired guy keeping pace at her side.

"Guys, meet Simon Frazier, Mrs. Cunningham's long-lost first cousin once removed," she said, presenting Simon as if he were a prize on a game show.

Simon gave a tight smile and nodded. "Nice to meet you all, although I wish it were under better circumstances."

"Wow," Callie said, "I'm so glad she had some family here. She was such a lovely woman."

"You're Callie Jackson, right?" he asked.

Callie blushed. "Yes." She extended a hand across the table to shake his. "And this is my fiancé, Jesse Thomas."

Jesse shook Simon's hand, and then the man's cool blue eyes turned to Austin.

"This is Beckett," Gigi said, motioning toward him.

"Austin Beckett," he said, reaching out an obligatory hand.

Simon's grip was a little tighter than necessary. Austin knew the type. Alpha males who wanted you to know who was in charge.

"So you're Mrs. Cunningham's cousin?" Austin asked.

Simon nodded, his expression unreadable. "Well, her first cousin once removed. Unfortunately, my mother, her cousin, passed when I was young, so I never really knew her family. Did you know my aunt well?"

Austin engaged in the staring contest Simon had initiated

with him. "Well enough," he said, even though it wasn't really true. He felt protective over Mrs. Cunningham though. Gigi had told him even Rebecca wasn't aware of any family the woman had. No one had shown up when Mr. Cunningham had passed.

"I'm glad she had so many people here who looked out for her," Simon said, gesturing around. "My mother passed when I was a small child, and my father quickly remarried, so I only ever really knew my father and stepmother's families. I only wish I'd had the chance to meet her."

What a prince. Swooping into town on his white horse as soon as he heard he might inherit an inn on prime ocean frontage.

Chapter Eleven

Gigi

Gigi was finishing up a breakfast meeting with her client, Mr. Prescott, at Island Coffee when she spotted her mother entering the restaurant. Mr. Prescott had been in a rush, so he was already on the way out the door as she waited for the server to return with her credit card.

"Good morning, darling," her mother said, occupying the vacated seat across from Gigi. "Are you helping Mr. Prescott with something?"

"Yes, but you know I can't discuss client matters. Who are you meeting?"

Her mother waved a hand. "Just a few of the League ladies. We have some logistics to finalize for the tour of homes."

She was referring to the annual event that raised money for the local preservation society by selling tickets to see inside some of the historic homes that lined the downtown streets of Big Dune Island. The Victorian homes, like Callie's family home, had been built in the mid- to late-1800s, with many featuring wraparound porches and gingerbread detailing.

"Morning, Myrtle," Iris said as she returned Gigi's credit card. "Can I get you a cup of coffee, or are you having tea this morning?"

"I need to get to the office," Gigi said before her mother could answer. "So I'll leave you to your League business."

Myrtle pouted. "You can keep your mother company for a few minutes, can't you? I wanted to talk to you about the Salty Breeze."

"I heard the service was lovely," Iris said. "I wish I could have made it, but I had to go visit my sister this weekend in Daytona."

"I don't know why we couldn't have a proper funeral," Myrtle said, "but we did the best we could under the circumstances."

Gigi suppressed the need to roll her eyes. Myrtle wanted all the pomp and circumstance of a royal processional for her funeral when the time came.

"We didn't have a traditional funeral because it's not what Margaret wanted," Gigi reminded her.

"I'll have an Earl Grey," Myrtle told Iris. "I'll just sit with my daughter until my friends arrive." As soon as Iris left the table, Myrtle turned back to Gigi. "There was gossip at church yesterday that some relation of Margaret's was at the celebration of life on Saturday. Does that mean your investigator found someone?"

Gigi frowned. "Unfortunately, no. Mitch is still working on it, but there was a man named Simon who showed up and claimed to be the only son of her cousin on her mother's side."

"So Margaret dies, and some cousin suddenly materializes out of thin air?" Myrtle asked.

"Technically, her first cousin once removed. But yes. Funny how that happens, huh?" Gigi agreed. "He told me his mother died when he was very young and his father quickly remarried, so he never got to know his mother's side of the family."

"Well, it is distasteful to remarry so quickly, but some men are just like that. He probably had no idea what to do alone with a small child to raise. But how did he find out Margaret had passed? I thought you said your investigator hadn't found anything yet."

"He hasn't, but I suspect someone else was looking for an heir, and my money is on Phil or one of the developers. I've gotten several calls from developers in the past trying to find out if someone who just passed had a will so they can find out who's inheriting and make them an offer. It's disgusting. And I know Phil is sniffing around that piece of land next door because I already got a heads up from Gail over in the planning department."

"Phil had some nerve to show up at Margaret's funeral," Ms. Myrtle said, shaking her head. "I almost kicked him out when I saw him. Phil Sanders is nothing but a weasel. He no more wanted to pay his respects to Margaret than I want to join the circus."

Picturing her mother as a circus performer brightened Gigi's mood momentarily before she remembered the fate of the Salty Breeze.

"They were both pretty tight-lipped about the whole thing," Gigi said, "but I saw them talking before the service. I'm pretty sure that wasn't a coincidence. And when I asked Simon how he found out about Margaret's passing, he just said someone had called his dad to tell him and that he couldn't remember who it was."

"Well, you can't keep a secret around here long," Myrtle said. "Is there any way to find out if he is who he says he is?"

"Yeah, I let Mitch know about him. He'll do a more thorough search and make sure he's legit and that he's the only heir with a claim to the estate. If she didn't have any living parents or siblings, then it goes to nieces or nephews or their children, or then cousins, like Simon."

"So there might still be others out there who would inherit before him or alongside him?

"Yes," Gigi said. "It'll take time to sort out if we have to start branching that far into her family tree. Birth records aren't public, so it's not a fast and easy process. Mitch is the best though."

"Did this Simon fellow tell you anything else about himself or what he would do with the inn?"

"I doubt he's had time to think through all that. It sounds like he didn't even know Margaret existed, much less the inn. He actually lives in Manhattan, right around the corner from that apartment I had in Hell's Kitchen. Small world."

Myrtle's distaste for Manhattan showed on her face. "I thank the good Lord in heaven every day that you're no longer up there in that terrible city."

This time, Gigi didn't hold back her eye roll. Her mother was one of those southerners who still called people from New York "Yankees." She'd hated when Gigi took a job there after law school instead of staying in Atlanta and trying to win back Dalton. He came from a prominent family who belonged to the city's most prestigious country club and was in line to take over his father's law firm one day. He was exactly the kind of man Myrtle expected her to marry and, despite that, Gigi had fallen head over heels for him. Until the night she thought he was going to propose, but broke her heart instead. She'd jumped on the offer to move to New York, ready to put distance between herself, Dalton, and the life she was supposed to lead in Atlanta.

"Georgia, you must do everything in your power to ensure

the Salty Breeze ends up in the right hands. That inn is an important part of Big Dune Island. Didn't you hear all those people who got up to speak on Saturday?"

"Obviously, that's what I want too, but there's only so much I can do. Technically, I'm not even legally involved in this matter. No one has hired me to do anything here."

Myrtle harrumphed. "Well, if you go in with an attitude like that, we might as well kiss it goodbye."

"Stop being dramatic. I'm just being realistic. Simon was there on Saturday too. He heard what it meant to everyone. I'm sure he's not an unfeeling monster. Hopefully he'll do the right thing if it is indeed all his."

"I'm just saying you could turn on the charm a little, darling. You can talk anybody into anything. You learned that from me." She winked.

It was true, although Gigi wouldn't admit to being anything like her mother, especially not to her mother.

"I'll do my best," Gigi said, "but I really do have to get going. I have a call in twenty minutes, and I just saw Lorraine come in." She nodded to her mother's friend, who'd just pushed open the door.

"Put some lipstick on," her mother said as Gigi stood to leave. "You're looking pasty."

"Goodbye, Myrtle," Gigi said, ignoring her comment and waving to Lorraine so she could be her mother's next victim. There was no way Myrtle wasn't going to comment on the hideous floral skirt Lorraine was wearing that looked like it belonged on someone from *Little House on the Prairie*.

As she strode to the front door, Gigi glanced to her left and caught her reflection in the mirror that hung above the booths lining the wall. She really did look pasty this morning. She hadn't put on enough blush in her rush to get out the door, and her trademark red lipstick had worn off over the course of breakfast.

She hated it when her mother was right.

After she finished her afternoon client meeting, Gigi drove over to the Salty Breeze. Her conversation with her mother that morning had given her an idea. Rebecca ran the day-to-day operations of the B&B, so she had the legal authority to hire Gigi to represent the inn. That would allow Gigi to watch out for the inn's interests, at least up to a point. Rebecca had agreed it was a great idea, so Gigi prepared an engagement letter to take over for her signature. That would at least protect their conversations as attorney-client privileged and give Gigi a valid reason to be involved in the search for an heir. Rebecca told her that Mrs. Cunningham kept the inn's office very organized, and that Gigi could go through it and look for anything that might help.

Gigi climbed the steps at the inn and noticed the brothers must have repaired the loose stair that had been there on her first visit after Mrs. Cunningham's death. There was still plenty to do, but it was a start.

Rebecca was cleaning up plates in the dining room when Gigi found her.

"Here, let me help you," Gigi said, holding out a hand to take a stack of plates.

"Thanks," Rebecca said, handing them off before grabbing two bowls and various utensils from the table. "We had a baking class this afternoon, and everyone got to eat their creations afterward."

Gigi followed Rebecca into the kitchen, placing the dirty dishes in the sink while Rebecca put the leftovers on the counter.

"Josephine will take care of the rest," Rebecca said. "Come with me."

They went down the hall to the small office, and Rebecca unlocked the door to let them inside. The small room held a desk with drawers on either side. An old metal filing cabinet stood in the corner of the room, and a credenza under the windows held two neat piles of paperwork. Once they were in the office, Rebecca closed the door behind them.

"I brought the engagement letter for you to sign," Gigi said, pulling it from her large purse.

"This was such a good idea," Rebecca said. "I feel better already just knowing you're on my side." She signed the letter, handing it back to Gigi.

"Reagan will scan this in and email you a copy for your records," Gigi said as she put the letter back into her bag.

"You met Simon the other day, right?" Rebecca asked. When Gigi nodded, she continued. "Well, we had an open room, so I offered it to him. I've tried to talk to him the past couple of days, and I just don't think Simon is who Margaret would have left the Salty Breeze."

"Well, she didn't have a will, so I'm not sure how much she really thought through who she'd leave it to. Trust me, I wish she had. But why do you say that about Simon?" Gigi was naturally distrustful of people, especially when it came to matters of inheritance, but she was curious about what was setting off red flags for Rebecca.

"Call it a sixth sense, but something about him just feels off. Every time he gets a phone call, he runs back to his room to take it. And when I've tried to talk to him about how I could continue to run the inn if he does indeed inherit it, he always puts me off."

"I think maybe we're just all on edge because of the unknowns," Gigi assured her. "I'm sure it's been a lot for him to digest."

"Maybe," Rebecca said, but it was clear from the concern on her face that she was unconvinced.

"My investigator should have more soon," Gigi assured her. "I'll keep you posted."

"Thank you," Rebecca said, reaching out to hug Gigi. "I don't know what I'd do without you. This whole thing is so stressful. It's nice not to have to face it alone."

"Of course," Gigi said, hugging her back. "I'm happy to help. This inn is important to a lot of people."

Rebecca wiped her eyes, which were filling with tears. "I have to go get ready for happy hour, but feel free to look through anything. Aside from the usual office supplies, the desk is mostly personal documents, medical records, and that sort of thing," she said, gesturing at the dark cherry piece of furniture. "I didn't feel right going through them all other than to look for a folder that might contain her will, but I guess someone will have to at some point just to determine what can be tossed and what should be shredded, or if there's anything we need for the inn."

She turned toward the cabinet in the corner. "That has all the records for the inn. The folders are labeled. The papers on the credenza were just bills to be paid, which I've taken care of, and paperwork she hadn't filed away yet."

"You said you found the survey she had done a few years ago?"

"Yeah, she was thinking about taking out an equity line for some improvements, but the rates back then were terrible and she decided to hold off. It's here," she said, grabbing a folded paper from the top of a pile on the credenza.

"Thanks." Gigi took it from her. She wanted to review it on the off chance she might spot something useful, either in staving off a developer or convincing an heir to keep it.

When Rebecca left the office, Gigi unfolded the survey and spread it out on the desk, but she didn't find any surprises. The B&B had two fifty-foot lots that had been combined decades previously, before the town code forbade merging lots in an effort to prevent mega mansions from taking over the beachfront. It was part of what made it so desirable to developers, because it was grandfathered in. Although it couldn't be combined with the lot next door that was already being surveyed by developers, there were other creative ways to build out a massive residential or hotel complex on the two side-by-side lots.

Folding it back up, Gigi moved on to the filing cabinet. It was mostly years' worth of old utility bills, equipment leases, and ledgers full of information on guest stays. She pulled some files with financial documents so she could get a better feel for the health of the inn. The first thing you learned in law school was not to ask a question you didn't already know the answer to, and she wanted to know everything there was to know about the Salty Breeze.

Gigi moved over to the desk and sat in the chair, reaching first to her right to open the bottom drawer. There were neatly labeled files about health insurance, medical bills, credit cards, and loans. She leafed through them quickly, but nothing caught her eye. She took the files on the Cunninghams' personal finances, because she'd have to ensure all the creditors were paid and bank accounts located for probating the estate.

Opening the drawer on the left side of the desk, Gigi noticed several files without labels. Her curiosity piqued, she pulled out the fat folders and laid them on the desk. She flipped through the pages at random, but they appeared to all be the kind of miscellaneous stuff people couldn't let go of: a get-well card from a friend; a recipe for pumpkin bread with a handwritten note that said, "This one is my favorite"; there was a program from a funeral a decade earlier; Christmas cards with photographs of happy families standing in front of fireplaces and decorated trees. Once Gigi was satisfied that the three folders held personal mementos of no relevance to Mrs. Cunningham's assets, she turned to flip through the remaining files and noticed a folder lying in the bottom of the drawer. She couldn't see it under the hanging files, but her removal of the three fatter personal files had revealed nearly half of the bottom of the drawer and the folder that seemed purposely hidden there.

Pulling out the folder, she laid it on the desk and flipped it open. The first piece of paper was one of those drawings of a turkey children made using an outline of their hand and then coloring it in. Large block letters at the bottom read, GRACE.

Gigi flipped to the next page. It was another drawing, this time of three stick figures, two larger and one smaller. It was clearly meant to be two parents and a child. The same name appeared at the bottom, printed in a child's scrawl: GRACE.

Who was Grace? Gigi flipped through more pages. It was all artwork. It advanced from misshapen and brightly colored animals and figures to pencil sketchings that became increasingly lifelike and realistic.

And that was it. The whole folder was just artwork. Gigi didn't know what it meant. Maybe it was a goddaughter or a friend's child from before the Cunninghams came to Big Dune Island, because the pages were yellowed and looked as if they were old. After all, they'd had a whole life before moving here that no one seemed to know much about.

Something about it gnawed at Gigi though, so she decided to tuck it into the box Rebecca had left her along with the financial files she'd pulled from both the business and personal drawers. She'd ask Rebecca if she knew anything about it on her way out.

Rebecca, however, was just as surprised as Gigi by the drawings. She'd never heard Mrs. Cunningham mention anyone named Grace. Like Gigi, she thought perhaps it was from someone the Cunninghams had known in the past.

So why hide it at the bottom of a drawer?

Chapter Twelve

Austin

After work on Tuesday, Austin ran by the coffee shop to grab a cold brew for him and a coconut iced latte for Gigi on the way to her office to talk about the joint bachelor-bachelorette party. As he rounded the corner from Main Street to the side street that led to her office, he practically ran into a man on the sidewalk.

"Sorry, man," Austin said before registering who it was he'd nearly plowed into. "Simon, right?"

The man furrowed his brows before responding. "Have we met?"

Seriously? It had only been a few days since the celebration of life, and this guy didn't even register him looking familiar? Austin hadn't expected him to remember his name or anything, but he had to remember they'd met and talked with Gigi, Callie, and Jesse for a solid ten minutes.

"Yeah, at the celebration of life."

"Oh, the football player, right?"

Austin frowned. "Baseball."

Simon was holding a folder in one hand but gestured with the other. "My bad. Baseball. Remind me of your name again."

"Austin Beckett," he said, reaching out a hand. When Simon shook it, Austin made sure he applied just enough pressure to send a message.

"Good to meet you again." Simon met Austin's eyes and gave him a phony smile.

Austin glanced down at the folder and recognized the silver embossed logo on the front: *Law Office of Neville Long*.

Simon's cell phone began vibrating in his hand. "I have to take this," he said. "See you around." He sidestepped Austin to continue down the sidewalk in the opposite direction. Simon was a few strides away already when Austin heard him say, "It's two hundred feet of frontage."

He had to be referring to the B&B's oceanfront lot. Austin couldn't make out anything after that, but he didn't like the guy's tone. The Salty Breeze wasn't safe. Austin could feel it in his bones.

Once he was inside Gigi's building, he greeted Reagan and showed himself into Gigi's office. He plopped down in a chair across from her desk as she finished up a phone call, placing the iced latte he'd grabbed for her on a coaster.

"Thanks for the latte," Gigi said after she ended the call. "I could use some caffeine today. The city council meeting went past nine last night. Huge debate over the heritage oak over on 8th Street that's pulling up the sidewalk and street with its root system."

"What'd they decide?"

"To defer it until more studies can be conducted to see if there are any alternatives to removing it."

"That sounds like a win," he said, knowing she was on the side of preserving the tree.

"Short term, perhaps, but it buys us some time." She relaxed back in her chair, drinking her latte.

"So I ran into that Simon guy outside," Austin said.

"Oh, yeah? I went over to the Salty Breeze yesterday to look at something Rebecca found, and she said he's staying at the inn. I'm sure he's going to meet with someone to try and open probate while he's here."

"I think you're right. He was carrying a folder from Neville's office."

"Ugh," she said. "Figures. Neville does all of Phil's closings. Phil probably referred him there."

"You think that's who tracked him down? Phil?"

"Probably. Phil's assistant told Gail over in the planning office that the kids of the guy who owns the twenty acres next door called about listing the property."

"And if he could get his hands on the inn's property too, it would all be worth more."

"Bingo," Gigi said, pointing at him.

"Is there any way to stop it at this point?"

"Only if we find more heirs. But even then, they might want to do the same thing. It would be a big pay day, and it's not like anyone in Margaret's family is going to have any sentimental attachment. It doesn't seem like she kept in touch with any of them."

"Man," Austin said, running his hand through his hair, "that sucks. That place has been there our whole lives."

"Yeah, and just think about all the people who work there, and all the families who have made memories there over the years."

"Didn't Callie want to buy the twenty acres at some point? She could probably afford to buy both pieces of property, right?"

Gigi shook her head. "I don't think even Callie has that kind of money. We're talking tens of millions of dollars if you could get both properties together."

"Well, that's depressing."

"Agreed. But let's not give up until we hear back from my investigator about the potential for other heirs. Besides, we don't even know for sure what Simon would do with the inn if he got it. I have to prep for an HOA meeting tonight for a client though, so let's talk about something more fun, like this joint bachelor-bachelorette party," Gigi said, pulling the wedding binder from a giant tote she'd slid out from under her desk.

Jesse and Callie had contacted them the previous day to let them know there was only one weekend they both had free before the wedding. They'd left it to Austin and Gigi to decide on the details.

"I've got it all under control—" Austin started, but before he could continue, Gigi cut in.

"We're not going to Vegas," she deadpanned.

He frowned at her. "What is your problem with Vegas? What did it ever do to you?"

She straightened in her seat. "I've never been, nor do I want to go."

"So you hate a place you've never even been? That's rational."

"It doesn't take a genius to know it's a place men go to get drunk and make bad decisions."

"Women too." He shrugged, getting that little thrill he always had when he got under her skin.

"Can you be serious for ten minutes? I really do have to get ready for the meeting."

He sat up in his seat, straightening an imaginary tie and clearing his throat. "I called my uncle Tommy this morning, and he said we can use his lake house. He's got canoes and kayaks and jet skis we can take out, there's a fire pit out back, a home theater and pool table downstairs, and it's totally secluded so we don't have to worry about anyone seeing Callie."

Gigi sat back in her chair. "That doesn't sound half bad."

"Did that hurt?"

Confusion furrowed her brow. "Did what hurt?"

"Admitting I did something right." He smiled.

"Even a blind squirrel gets a nut every once in a while." She sipped the water bottle she'd grabbed off her desk.

He laughed. "Why don't you just leave the party to me? That way you can concentrate on the wedding plans."

She narrowed her eyes at him across the desk. "Fine, but keep it classy, Beckett. It's just supposed to be a chill weekend away with a few friends."

"Speaking of which," he said, "who's coming? I know Jesse wants to invite Teddy and Wyatt." Teddy was Jesse's second in command at Thomas Construction, and Wyatt was another close friend from childhood. They could both be trusted to keep the wedding a secret.

"Callie said just Sienna and Piper on her side. Does this lake house have enough bedrooms for everyone? I'm not sleeping on a couch."

"There's four bedrooms plus a bunk room with another four beds. Plenty of room for everyone, princess."

"Perfect. Callie and I will take the master," she said.

"I figured as much. There's a room with two doubles Jesse and I can take, and the rest of them can duke it out over what's left."

"Works for me. You'll figure out food and firewood and all the other provisions?"

He saluted her. "Aye, aye, Captain."

"Great," she said, putting the unopened wedding binder back in her bag. "I think we're done here."

Some people might have called her bossy, but her confidence and command of every situation were what he most admired about Gigi.

"Pleasure doing business with you," he said, standing to leave, giving a small bow in her direction.

Gigi laughed, and the real pleasure was in making her smile. She might think he was never serious, but in his estimation she was serious too much of the time.

"See you later, Beckett," she said, waving him off as she turned back to her computer.

The first game of the season was getting ready to start the next night when Austin realized Luke kept looking into the stands. Austin had already seen the Carsons arrive, and when he looked into the metal bleachers, he saw they were still sitting there waiting for the game to begin.

"You ready?" Austin asked the boy, placing a hand on his shoulder. "First game of the season is always exciting."

"He said he'd be here." Luke frowned.

"Who?"

"Your dad. He said he'd come to our first game. I wanted to show him I've been practicing that left-handed bunt."

Austin was so surprised he didn't know what to say at first. He'd forgotten his father had told Luke he'd come to the game. And as much as Austin wasn't particularly excited about his dad's critical eye watching him coach, it was unlike him to not show up. He hadn't missed a single game Austin had played from T-ball through high school.

"He'll be here," Austin said. "He's a man of his word. You know what probably happened? My mom probably needed him to get something out of the attic or to carry something heavy up the stairs and he's just running late." He glanced at his watch. "He's still got three minutes until game time. Why don't you go run our lineup to the ump." He pulled the paper out of his back pocket and handed it to Luke. Then he pulled his phone out of his other pocket, typing out a text to his dad.

> Are you coming to the game? Luke is asking.

He watched for the dots on the screen to dance, indicating his father was typing a reply, but there was nothing.

Luke was trotting back to the dugout from the field when his face lit up, and he waved wildly in Austin's direction. He wasn't looking at Austin though, but someone behind him. Austin turned to see his father walking down the path toward the field. That was one thing you could say about Dan Beckett. He never missed a baseball game.

As Luke ran to the fence to tell the elder Beckett about how he'd practiced his bunts at home with Liam, Austin hovered nearby, hoping his father would give a suitable reply.

"Can't wait to see it, son," his father said to the boy. "Don't forget to keep your bat level, and don't go to the ball; let it come to you."

Luke nodded dutifully. "Yes, sir."

His dad assumed his usual position, arms crossed over his chest, feet planted wide, directly behind home plate on the spectator side of the fence. He'd keep the ump honest and analyze every pitch, every at bat. Austin was just glad he was old enough to drive his truck back to his own house afterward so he wouldn't have to listen to his father break down every mistake made by each player on his team after the game.

Austin's team jumped out to an early lead in the first inning, putting up two runs on the scoreboard and then getting three consecutive outs in the field. Luke had been walked his first time up at bat. It hadn't been the right situation for a bunt, and he'd only swung at one pitch, barely missing it when it curved a little inside on him.

"Shortstop is playing too shallow." His father's voice from behind made Austin jump from where he leaned against the fence at the edge of the dugout.

Austin frowned at him. "He's fine, Dad. This isn't the majors. These kids are far more likely to hit a dribbler up the middle than hit it over his head."

"Easier to run up on the ball than back, and the left fielder is too deep. Can't have a gap like that."

Austin pretended not to hear him, concentrating on his pitcher, who was getting flustered now that he was behind on the batter 3–1. "You've got this, Owen," he said loud enough for the kid to hear, clapping his hands a couple of times for emphasis.

Then, as if the baseball gods wanted to punish him, the batter hit a pop-up that sailed right over the shortstop's head and landed squarely in the grass between him and the left fielder as they both ran to get it and nearly collided with one another.

Austin heard his father harrumph and walk off, but refused to acknowledge him, gritting his teeth.

"That's okay, guys. Shake it off," he told his players. "Two down, just need one more out."

Unfortunately, the final out was elusive. The pitcher got more and more rattled, and his pitches became wild and unpredictable. Austin called time and trotted out to the mound to give him a pep talk. He just needed to calm down. The other team had gotten two more on base, driving in the base runner who'd hit into the gap. They were still up 2–1 though.

After telling the pitcher to take some deep breaths and focus on the batter, ignoring the base runners, Austin turned to go back to the dugout. His father was behind home plate on the other side of the fence again. He held up his hand and demonstrated the motion of a pitcher letting go of a ball with his hand tilted to the side instead of over top of the ball like it should be. He was telling Austin that Owen was letting go of the ball wrong.

Austin knew he was probably correct—his father's vantage point was better than Austin's in the dugout—and that he should turn around and mention it to Owen, but Austin hesitated, not wanting to admit his father was right. This was his team to coach, and for once he just wanted to be on a baseball field making his own judgment calls.

But he couldn't stand the thought of Owen walking the batter or giving up another hit and losing his confidence completely. So he turned around and took the two steps back to his pitcher and relayed the information, reminding him to make sure he released with his hand on top of the ball instead of letting it rotate to the side.

When Owen struck out the batter he was facing, Austin refused to let his eyes wander over to his father. He'd corrected the pitcher, and that was as close as his dad was going to get to hearing Austin say he was right.

Sam was up first the following inning, and Austin heard both Iris and Sam's mother cheering him on from the stands. The boy ignored them, at the age when parents and grandparents yelling out your name is embarrassing. His face was serious as he approached the plate, and on the first pitch he lined one up the third baseline. Sam wound up on second base with a double, grinning ear to ear as everyone on their side of the stands cheered and whistled.

Luke was on deck and headed to the plate when Austin gave him the sign from where he was coaching first base. Now was the time to try a bunt. First base was open, and even if the ball were fielded, the fielder would have to decide between holding Sam at second or getting Luke out at first. Hopefully their indecision would give Luke plenty of time to get on base.

Luke glanced back at Austin's father, nodding at him. Austin wished he could tell the boy what happens when you start seeking out Dan Beckett's approval, but for now all he could do was cross his fingers that the boy could lay down a bunt and get on base. He knew it would do wonders for the boy's confidence, but he also feared the blow his father's disappointment would do if Luke failed.

Luke put the bat out to show he was bunting earlier than he'd be able to get away with as he got older and the fielders got better, but at this age it only rattled the pitcher and confused the fielders. This team may not have even practiced for this situation yet, and Austin made a mental note to do some drills with his own fielders next week.

The first pitch was high, and Luke pulled the bat back in time to get the ball called by the ump. As he squared to bunt during the pitcher's windup for the second pitch, Austin couldn't remember the last time his nerves were so on edge. It was definitely harder to sit back and watch these boys than it was to go up there and bat himself. There was a heavy weight of responsibility to build them up and make them not only better ball players but stronger mentally too.

The second ball was high as well. The pitcher was so worried about the bunt and running up to field after he pitched that he was letting go too soon. A walk was just as good as a hit in this situation, so Austin clapped and said to Luke, "Good eye."

When the ball connected with the bat on the third pitch, Luke hesitated for a second as if surprised at the result. It was a nearly perfect bunt that died in the dirt two feet in front of him. Although he'd batted left-handed, he hadn't dragged and taken off for first in the fluid movement older players had perfected. Still, he was such a fast runner that he made it to first base well ahead of the catcher's throw, and Sam was around on third.

Austin walked over and gave Luke a high five after the ump called him safe. "Nice bunt, buddy."

"I did it," Luke said, beaming. "I really did it."

"You sure did," Austin said, patting his helmet. "Now, let's get us some more runs. Remember, you've gotta take off when the ball hits the bat. If it's on the ground, go as hard as you can, and if it's in the air, make sure you can get back to first if they catch it."

"Got it," Luke said, flashing a thumbs up.

By the time the inning was over, Austin's team was up 5–1 on their way to a 7–2 win.

Austin huddled the team together outside the dugout and talked through all the positives from the game. He congratulated Owen on recovering from a tough inning pitching, Sam for three big hits, and pointed out a few key fielding plays from other boys. As the group broke up and he reminded them about the next practice, Austin noticed his father was waiting to the side. Luke ran straight to Dan, excitedly talking about his bunt. Austin excused himself from a parent who'd stopped to thank him, feeling the need to oversee any interactions between his father and the young boy.

"It was really nice placement," his father was saying as he joined them. "But remember what we practiced with the drag." He held an invisible bat and demonstrated the fluid movement from bunt to taking off for first. "You should already be a couple of steps down the line by the time the ball hits the dirt."

"It was a great bunt," Austin assured the boy. "Most of the catchers we face won't be faster than you anyway."

"It was good," his dad corrected. "Practice makes perfect. You need to keep practicing the drag so you're ready when you do face a better catcher."

"Dad," Austin said sternly, "let's not ruin what was a very effective bunt. He's eight. He got on base." He patted Luke on the shoulder. "You did great."

"But you can always get better," Dan Beckett said to Luke. "Don't ever settle for good enough. There's always someone out there working harder, getting better."

Austin could feel his jaw twitching. Before he could respond and assure the boy he was on the right track and should be proud of his performance in the game, the Carsons came over to collect Luke, congratulating him on the win.

"Thanks again for picking him up last week, Austin," Katie said. "I didn't realize he'd get a private lesson in, but that was a pretty cool bunt, kiddo." She ruffled Luke's hair.

Luke blushed at the attention, but his wide smile showed Austin's father hadn't dented his pride. "I'm going to practice more and hit an even better one next game," he said.

"I bet you will, but for now we have to get home, eat some dinner, and get your homework done. Tell Coach Austin 'thank you' and go with Mr. Carson to the car. I'll be right there." Katie turned to Austin. "Can I have a minute?"

"Thanks, Coach Austin," Luke yelled over his shoulder as he took off.

Austin moved away from his father, who was now caught in conversation with another parent he knew, to give him and Katie some privacy.

Katie's face was suddenly drawn, disappointment painted all over it. "I'm afraid I have some potentially bad news."

Austin shifted his weight, knowing it had to be about Luke's placement with the Carsons. He didn't know much about the foster system, but he knew most kids didn't end up in one place for very long. Was he being adopted? That wasn't bad news, was it? As wonderful as the Carsons were, it would be even better if Luke had a permanent home and a family of his own.

"I got a call from Child and Family Services yesterday. Liam's half sister was originally placed with a grandparent on her mother's side when their father was incarcerated. Unfortunately, her grandmother has passed, and now she's being placed in foster care. State policy dictates that siblings be placed together when possible, which, of course, I wholeheartedly support. Because we're the closest placement to where their father is incarcerated, that means they'll be placing her with us."

"Oh, wow," Austin said. "So what's the bad news?" He couldn't imagine that Katie would consider taking in another child as bad news, even if it meant her house was a little more crowded. Luke would probably have to move into Liam's room so the young girl could have her own.

Katie sighed. "Unfortunately, I'm only licensed for two foster children at a time. That means they'll move Luke." Tears shone in her eyes. "We're going to apply to increase our license to three, but even if we get approved, I'm not sure it'll happen in time. I'm just devastated. I know it's the right thing for Liam and his sister, but it's not fair to Luke. He's so happy here. He'd likely end up somewhere else, because there are only a few foster families here on Big Dune Island, and we're all at capacity."

Austin removed his baseball cap and ran a hand through his hair before placing the hat back on his head. His mind was racing. How soon would they relocate Luke? How far away would he be? Did he know anyone who could help get the license approved? Gigi. She'd know what to do.

"Have you called Gigi? Maybe she can help expedite the license."

"We just found out right before the game, but I'm going to call her first thing. I'm just not very optimistic. There's so much red tape with these state agencies. Things move at a glacial pace."

"But surely they'd rather have him stay in an environment that's working for him, right? If you're willing to have three, why would they go to the trouble of moving him?"

"I wish they were that logical," she said, shaking her head. "His social worker will go to bat for him to stay with us, but the agency has all these policies and procedures, and they don't bend the rules for anyone."

"Remember, the game's not over until the last out," he said, reaching over to hug Katie. "I bet Gigi can figure it out."

When Katie pulled back, she was smiling through the tears still threatening to escape. "Thanks, Coach. I'll keep you posted."

Austin was relieved to see his father had already taken off. He wasn't in the mood to get his feedback on the game. All he could think about was how to make sure Luke stayed on Big Dune Island. Could he foster Luke? What did you have to do to get approved to foster? Gigi would know.

He didn't want to act impulsively though. It was a big decision, and it might not even be necessary. Surely, Gigi could find a way for the Carsons to keep Luke. Gigi never took no for an answer.

Chapter Thirteen

Gigi

After a particularly adversarial HOA meeting where Gigi had to play referee between warring neighbors, all she wanted was a giant cheeseburger and a plate full of fries. Stress eating at its finest. She decided to stop at Mack's Diner on her way home, taking in a file so she could mark up a contract while she ate. She'd placed her order and was two pages into the contract when Austin startled her as he slid into her booth across from her.

"Mind if I eat with you?" he asked.

He was wearing a baseball hat and a T-shirt that clung to his chest and arms in all the right places. Not that she noticed.

"Twice in one day. To what do I owe the pleasure?" She put the cap back on her pen and closed the file.

"Just grabbing a bite after the game. You?"

"City council meeting ran late, and I have no food at home."

Mack came over to greet Austin. "The usual?"

"Yes, sir," Austin said. "How's business?"

"Can't complain," the older gentleman said. Mack's was an institution on Big Dune Island that dated back to the 1970s. It was the first Black-owned business in town, and no one had a better burger, fries, or milkshake for at least one hundred miles. He'd even been featured in an episode of the popular television show *Diners, Drive-Ins and Dives*.

"How's your sister doing?" Mack asked Austin. "I hear she bought her building."

Austin smiled proudly. "She did, and she's started baking wedding cakes in her spare time."

Gigi noticed he didn't take credit for helping Chloe buy the building. He'd given her the startup capital when she opened the coffee shop, and Gigi knew he'd invested alongside her in the building when it went up for sale. Austin would say he did it because he felt guilty that their father's attention had always been on him and baseball, not leaving much time or energy to be interested in Chloe as a child, but Gigi knew it was more than that. Austin had always been generous. She remembered a game she'd gone to in Atlanta where he'd hosted a child from Make-A-Wish, spending time with the little girl before and after the game, and showering her with jerseys, signed balls, and more.

"Spare time?" Mack laughed. "What's that?"

Austin gave him a knowing look. "She's learned how to delegate. Iris is the one who keeps all the plates in the air so Chloe can focus on baking. Maybe if you ever let someone help you around here, you'd have some spare time too."

Mack was not only the owner but usually waited on at least half the tables and ran the cash register too. He prided himself on not needing help, but it was starting to make him look much older than his years.

The man shrugged. "I don't know how to bake cakes

anyway, so I guess things can just stay the way they are." He smiled before leaving the table to put in Austin's order.

"Did you guys get a win tonight?" Gigi asked.

"We did. Speaking of the team though, you're going to get a call tomorrow morning from Katie Carson. She thinks they're going to move Luke to make room for Liam's half sister. Something about her only having a license for two kids at a time. There must be a way to get it increased to three, right? It doesn't make sense to move Luke from a situation that's working for him."

Gigi frowned. "I wish it were that simple, but the number of kids you're allowed under your foster license is based on a formula that takes all kinds of things into consideration, from how big your house is to your resources, the needs of each individual kid, how much you work outside the home, how many years you've been fostering, a whole list of factors. The biggest problem is the amount of time it takes to apply for an amendment to your license. It's usually an annual assessment, so getting them to look at it between those is a challenge."

"You love a challenge," Austin said, lifting an eyebrow.

"It's true," she said, pausing the conversation to take her food from Mack and thank him. "I'll make some calls in the morning and see what I can do. It would be easier if Luke had family nearby because they don't like to move you away from any family that has visitation rights."

"Yeah, that's why Katie said the agency is prioritizing Liam and his half sister over Luke, because this is closer to the prison where their father is currently."

"From what I remember, Luke doesn't have any known family, right?" Gigi popped a fry in her mouth.

"Not that I know of. His mother died in a car accident, and Katie told me no one knew who the father was."

"We could always try to find the dad," Gigi offered. "Or there could be an aunt or uncle or grandparent somewhere out there. The agencies are all too overwhelmed to really do thorough searches, especially if there's no father on the birth certificate."

"Okay, how do we do that?"

"There's a flip side to that too," Gigi warned him. "Maybe the mother didn't put the father on the birth certificate because she didn't want him knowing about the child. He could be a bad guy, maybe even dangerous."

Austin sat back in the booth and sighed. "I hadn't thought of that. If we poke around, do we have to tell anyone what we find? I don't want to put the kid in a worse situation."

It was sweet how much Austin clearly cared about Luke. Obviously, any sane person wanted to keep a child out of harm's way, but she could tell Luke was special to Austin. The worry was etched across his face.

"I've got a guy," she said. "He's discreet, but I can't be the one to hire him. It wouldn't be ethical for me to find out something and not report it to the agency."

"So I'll hire him," Austin said. "Shoot me his info."

"If you find something I shouldn't know, you can't tell me," Gigi said. "I'm just referring you to a private investigator. My involvement has to end there."

"Understood," Austin said. "But you'll help Katie with the license?"

Gigi had just taken a huge bite of her burger, so she only nodded.

Austin's food arrived and they chatted about the latest town gossip while they ate. Stanley Moore was going to run against his brother-in-law, Gil Chester, for one of the city council seats coming up for re-election. They both mused that Thanksgiving in their family would be fun this year, just a few short weeks after the election.

"Coach!" a little boy shouted as he ran up to their table.

"Hey, Owen," Austin said, reaching over to pat the boy on

the shoulder. "Good game tonight. You got yourself out of a tough situation on the mound."

"Thanks, Coach. I didn't realize being a pitcher was so stressful." He blew out a sigh.

The little boy said the last part as if the weight of the world was on his shoulders. Gigi smiled at him.

"Is this your girlfriend?" Owen asked, wiggling his eyebrows at Austin.

Austin laughed as he gestured at her. "No, this is my friend, Miss Gigi. We've known each other since we were even younger than you."

Owen's parents walked up, and Gigi realized she knew his mother. "Jordan Jeffries, is that you?"

"Jordan Adair now," she said, leaning down to hug Gigi. "This is my husband, Dean." She gestured to the man beside her.

"Nice to meet you," Dean said before getting interrupted by Owen asking for quarters to play the old-school pinball machine Mack kept at the back of the diner.

"I didn't know you'd moved back," Gigi said. Jordan had been a year behind Gigi and Callie in school. "Or gotten married and had a kid. We'll have to get together sometime and catch up."

"We just moved in time for Owen to start school. My parents are both having some health struggles, so I wanted to be nearby. Besides, what better place to raise a kid than Big Dune Island, right?"

She saw Jordan's eyes fall to Gigi's left hand that was resting on the table, and she realized the woman was checking for a wedding ring. Gigi bristled at the implication that she too should be married with children by now. She got enough of that from her mother.

"We certainly all had wonderful childhoods here," Gigi agreed.

Mack came over to tell them a booth had opened up in the back, and they all exchanged goodbyes and promises to get together soon.

"We all had wonderful childhoods here?" Austin asked her. "Which part was wonderful? The part where my dad yelled at me in front of all the other guys on my team on a weekly basis or the part where your mother shoved you in every beauty pageant on the East Coast and refused to let you play any sports lest you bruise and spoil your perfect skin?"

Gigi waved a hand. "It's not Big Dune Island's fault our parents were jerks when we were kids."

"Mine still is," he huffed, jabbing a fry in the puddle of ketchup on his plate. "He came to the game tonight so he could critique my coaching."

"Seriously?"

"I mean, technically, he came to watch Luke, but, of course, he had to point out every mistake my team was making."

"I'm confused. Why did he come to watch Luke?" Gigi sipped her thick strawberry milkshake through the straw, savoring the sweet treat she rarely allowed herself to have. She'd won at the city council meeting though, so she decided she deserved it.

Austin groaned. "He walks the park because his heart stops beating if he's too far from a baseball field, and he saw me teaching Luke how to bunt last week. Surprise, surprise, he had to come over and give his own instruction. And for reasons I'll never understand, Luke immediately wanted to please him and invited him to the game. The poor kid has probably been practicing that bunt around the clock, knowing my dad was going to come watch tonight."

"So, did he do it?"

"Do what?"

"Did the kid lay down a bunt in the game and win your father's approval?"

Austin rolled his eyes. "He put down a beautiful bunt, advanced the runner, and got on base, but, of course, that wasn't good enough for my dad. He had to come talk to Luke after the game about how he could have done it better."

"Was he right? Could the kid have done it better?"

"Were you listening? I said he advanced the runner and got on base. How does that get any better?"

Gigi shrugged. "Just because it worked this time doesn't mean it will next time, right? The kid is eight. I'm sure he could still work on his technique. It's good for a kid like Luke to have men in his life who show an interest. Your dad was always a good coach for other kids. Jesse loved him."

Austin grumbled, taking a big bite of his burger instead of replying to Gigi's comment, which she took to mean she was right. She didn't have the energy or will to rub it in though. She knew what it was like to have a complicated relationship with a parent.

Austin excused himself to go to the bathroom, and Gigi could see Owen catch him on the way back to the table and talk him into playing pinball. She watched him with the boy and could tell without hearing the conversation how much Owen liked his coach. Austin would make a good dad one day. She could see him being one of those hands-on fathers who got down on the floor to play with his kids after work. He was basically a big kid himself most of the time.

"Kid kicked my butt," Austin said when he slid back into the booth a few minutes later.

"Can you believe we have friends old enough to have kids that age?" She motioned toward Owen.

Gigi mostly found kids to be loud and messy—Why were their hands always so sticky?—and she'd never pictured herself with one of her own. Sure, some of their other friends from high school had kids by now, but she'd convinced herself she still wasn't old enough to seriously consider having children. Her law firm was her baby, and it still required constant attention.

"Crazy, right? I feel like we were just kids ourselves last week."

"Well, some of us still are," she said, raising an eyebrow.

"Growing old is mandatory, but growing up is optional." He shrugged. "Walt Disney said that, and I figure it worked out pretty well for him."

Gigi would never admit it to Austin, but she envied him a little. She'd been acting like a grown up since she was a little kid. Her mother didn't really like children either and, because of that, she'd never really let Gigi be one.

"Do you want kids one day?" she asked him.

His face lit up. "Definitely. Kids are the coolest. Every new thing they learn is like the most exciting thing that ever happened. And you can see it on their face when they do something they didn't think they could. It's the best feeling."

"You'll be a good dad," she said. "I don't really see myself as a mom. I didn't exactly have the best example."

"And I had a good example for a dad?" he scoffed. "That's half the reason I want to be a dad, so I can be the opposite of him. You'd be a great mom, G. You're always thinking about other people. You're one of the most selfless people I know."

Gigi considered his rationale. She understood the instinct, but she wondered if she really could be different from her mother. She didn't think she had the patience for baby talk and a tiny human incapable of acting rationally. She'd seen enough toddler meltdowns in the grocery store to know you couldn't always reason with them.

Then Gigi thought of the Carsons and the other families she'd helped with fostering and adoption. Maybe an older kid wouldn't be so bad. She could save herself the stretch marks, the baby talk, and the diapers. She wouldn't even have to find a man; she could do it on her own.

The next day at the office, Gigi spent half her day on Luke's foster situation. Katie called and relayed much of the same information Austin had given her the night before, which reminded her to send Mitch's information to Austin. She didn't share this with Katie though, as she didn't want to put her in the middle if the investigator found something Luke was better off not knowing.

The rest of the morning was spent calling the local agency and then the state to inquire about amending the Carsons' foster license. They referred her to the forms and the normal process, but she wanted to find someone willing to take a personal interest in this case and shepherd it through the red tape. They surely had more emotionally charged cases than they could keep up with, but she just needed one person who was willing to show this case a little extra attention. If she'd learned anything from her mother, it was how to charm someone into doing what she wanted. She finally got lucky with an older woman at the state office who promised to assign an evaluator as soon as she received the paperwork.

After lunch, Gigi started filling out everything she could on the forms for the Carsons. She was almost done when a call came in from Rebecca asking if she had time to stop by. Gigi told her she just needed to finish one thing, and then she'd head over.

Once the forms were complete and emailed to the Carsons, Gigi drove to the Salty Breeze. Rebecca only mentioned she had found something while going through Mrs. Cunningham's bedroom. They'd both agreed it was only prudent to double-check for any personal effects that might help them determine the rightful heirs. Gigi wasn't sure what to expect, but Rebecca had seemed unsettled on the call, insisting they talk in person.

When she arrived, Rebecca led Gigi down the hall to Mrs. Cunningham's bedroom. The bed was neatly made, but the closet doors were open, along with several drawers in her dresser.

"I found these in the bottom drawer under some sweaters," Rebecca said, picking up three leather-bound journals from where she'd left them on the top of the dresser. "They're old diaries."

Gigi stared at the journals as Rebecca held them out to her. What did Rebecca want her to do with them?

"Did you read them?" It felt a little invasive, but right now they didn't technically belong to anyone, and Rebecca was the person who has been closest to Margaret.

Rebecca looked down at the floor, chewing on her top lip, cradling the journals in her arm. "I may have taken a peek." Then she looked up to meet Gigi's eyes. "I didn't mean to, I just opened one to see what it was, and I read part of a page before I realized."

"That's okay," Gigi said. "You haven't done anything wrong."

"The thing is, I think maybe you should read them. I think she might have had a daughter. I stopped reading because it didn't feel right. I felt like I was invading her privacy. But what if she really does have a daughter out there somewhere?"

Gigi frowned. "The Cunninghams never mentioned any children, right?"

Rebecca shook her head.

"Maybe it was a goddaughter or a friend's child?" Gigi asked, thinking of the children's drawings she'd found.

"Maybe," Rebecca said. "It just seemed so personal. She was really worried about a girl named Grace."

Gigi gasped. "The name on the drawings."

Rebecca nodded. "You should read them," she said, thrusting the journals at Gigi as if they were too hot to hold any longer.

"Me? Why me? You knew her better. You should read them."

Rebecca shook her head. "You're an attorney. Don't you have attorney-client privilege or something like that? If I read them, I'm just being nosy, but if you read them, it's part of your job."

Gigi wasn't sure if attorney-client privilege applied here—Mrs. Cunningham had done a consult with her years ago, and now she represented the inn, but it was a bit of a gray area—still she had to admit she was curious. She took the journals from Rebecca, and she thought she could hear the woman audibly sigh with relief.

"I'll let you know if I find anything important," Gigi said, holding up the journals.

Gigi was so curious she would have sat in her car reading the journals right away, but she was running late. She'd promised to have dinner with a former colleague who was in town for a golf tournament at the island's big resort, so the journals would have to wait.

Chapter Fourteen

Austin

"Happy birthday, baby sis," Austin said, leaning down to hug his sister as he greeted her outside Dune & Brine, the fanciest restaurant on the island.

"Thanks, big bro," Chloe said, smiling up at him. "I think Mom and Dad are already here. Is that for me?" She pointed at the small, wrapped box he was holding.

"No, it's for the other birthday girl." He shook his head. "You can open it when we get to the table." He handed it to her.

She squealed in delight. "Looks like jewelry," she said, shaking the small box.

He shrugged as if he didn't know what was inside. "Guess you'll have to wait and see." He opened the door and motioned for his sister to enter.

Once inside, Chloe got sidetracked saying hi to a friend,

and he continued into the dining room to look for their parents. Austin silently prayed that his father would focus on Chloe's birthday and not spend the whole dinner breaking down the Little League game from the night before. One of Austin's biggest regrets about his childhood was the singular focus on him and his future baseball career. Chloe hadn't been interested in sports, and therefore their father hadn't been interested in her. Besides, he was too busy watching and orchestrating Austin's every move to pay attention to his daughter.

Their parents were seated in the back of the restaurant at a table that overlooked the marina through giant picture windows.

"Hey, Mom," he said, leaning down to kiss her cheek when he reached the table. "Dad." He nodded in Dan's direction.

"Happy birthday, little girl," Mrs. Beckett said, standing to hug Chloe as she came up behind Austin.

Their father stood and gave her a hug too. "Happy birthday, baby."

Chloe took the seat across from their father, and Austin settled in across from his mother. Mrs. Beckett lifted a wrapped box from the floor by her chair and handed it to Chloe.

"Presents." Chloe clapped. No one had more enthusiasm for life than his sister. He both loved that about her and got nervous about all the ways in which the world or a man might hurt her because she only saw the good in everyone.

"I know Austin's is jewelry," she said, ripping off the wrapping paper.

"I hope you're not disappointed when you find out what it really is," he joked.

Chloe opened the small white box to reveal a gold locket with an intricate pattern. Lindy, who owned the jewelry store on Main Street, told him Chloe had been eyeing it in the antique jewelry section for months.

Chloe squealed as she hugged him. "I love it! How did you know?"

"I had a little help from Lindy," he admitted. "I went in to buy you some earrings, but she said you'd been eyeing this."

Chloe flipped open the locket to the empty cavity. "Lindy told me it's Victorian. Doesn't it just make you wonder who used to own it and what they kept inside? It's so romantic." She held it to her chest.

"People wore them in mourning, so it probably meant someone died," their father said, ever the historian. When he wasn't watching baseball, he was usually reading books about war or historical figures.

"Dan," their mother said, frowning at him. "Let's not be depressing."

"I'm just being realistic." He huffed and took a sip of his scotch. "Aristocrats had tiny portraits commissioned of their loved ones or put a lock of hair in there to remember the deceased. It's a fact."

"Thank you for the history lesson, darling," she said, patting his arm.

The waiter came by to get drinks for Austin and Chloe before disappearing again. Chloe lifted the present from their parents and shook it.

"It's heavy," she said, knitting her brows. "And nothing is moving. I don't know what it could be."

"You definitely won't guess this one." Her mother smiled with a pride that said she'd thought of the perfect gift. She usually did.

Chloe tore through the paper, balling it up and placing it on the table. She'd revealed a thin cardboard box, but it had no text or markings to indicate what might be inside. She pried open one end and pulled out a flat wooden board with text engraved into it.

"Omigosh, this is the coolest thing I've ever seen," Chloe said, running her fingers over the text.

Austin could see enough to tell there was cursive handwriting all over the cutting board. Turning his head, he read the block letters on the side of the board: Grandma Sophie's Buttermilk Biscuits. Chloe handed him the board so he could see it better.

"That's Grandma Sophie's actual handwriting," Chloe said, pointing to the recipe written out across the board.

"I hope you like it, sweetheart," their mother said. "I saw it on Etsy and just had to get it for you. I know that's your favorite recipe."

Chloe always had a pile of buttermilk biscuits at the coffee shop, and they rarely lasted through lunch.

"I thought you could display it at the cafe," Mrs. Beckett said.

"It's perfect, Mom." Chloe took the board back from Austin. "I can't wait until everyone sees it. They're all going to want one with their own family recipes."

"You should talk to Teddy," Austin suggested. "He does some woodworking on the side for fun. I know he has one of those tools that can engrave wood. Might be a nice little side business for him."

"My little dynamic duo," their mother said. "I never imagined you'd grow up to run a cafe together, but it just warms my heart to see what a good team you make. Chloe, you've become such an integral part of Main Street and, Austin, you're doing such a wonderful job giving back by coaching Little League."

"You could be coaching at a much higher level," Mr. Beckett said, folding his arms across his chest.

His father just couldn't help himself. "Nothing I do is ever enough—"

Austin was cut off by his mother. "Boys," she hissed. "That's enough. It's Chloe's birthday."

Thankfully, the waiter returned with Austin and Chloe's drinks and took their order, diffusing the situation. His mother ordered the mahi with citrus salsa, his dad a ribeye, and Chloe the shrimp and grits. Austin had been planning to order the ribeye, but couldn't bring himself to do anything like his father, so he ordered the bone-in filet mignon instead. At least he could stick it to his dad's wallet.

"Michael," his sister suddenly called out, waving.

Michael Russo was one of the investors in Jesse's family's company, Thomas Construction. A New Yorker, he spent time on the island when he was purchasing land nearby or developing new projects. Austin got the feeling the island had grown on him and that he found excuses to be in town. Jesse could certainly handle things without him, but they'd become good working partners over the years.

Michael came to the table and greeted everyone, exchanging pleasantries. Austin could feel Chloe practically levitating next to him. Callie and Gigi had made him aware that his sister had a crush on Michael, who was nearly ten years her senior. He hadn't worried about it, because the two couldn't be more different, and Michael seemed as oblivious as Austin had been to his sister's interest in him.

"It's my birthday," Chloe told him, beaming.

"Well then, happy birthday," he said.

"Omigosh, Gigi is here too," Chloe said, looking beyond Michael and waving wildly. "Who's that guy she's with?"

Austin craned his neck to see around Michael, but he didn't recognize the man Gigi was with. He was wearing a navy blazer with a blue-and-white-checked shirt underneath and dark jeans with dress shoes. His thick, dark hair was styled perfectly, and even Austin had to admit the guy was objectively attractive.

"I have no idea," he told his sister.

Austin tensed as Gigi and the man made their way over. Gigi was wearing a black dress that hugged her body in all the right places, her lips in her signature shade of red. Had she worn that to work today, or was this more like a date? He bristled at the idea.

"Well, the gang's all here," Gigi said as she approached, bending down to give Mrs. Beckett a hug and nodding at Mr. Beckett before embracing Chloe, who'd stood.

"It's my birthday dinner," Chloe said. "And now I feel like it's a whole party."

"Happy birthday," Gigi said. "Sorry, where are my manners? This is a former colleague of mine from New York, Alexander Davis." She motioned to him. "He's in town for the golf tournament."

"Please, call me Xander," he said.

Xander? What kind of name was Xander? He sounded like a Marvel character.

Gigi introduced him to the table and then to Michael, who was standing next to them, and he shook each person's hand, wishing Chloe a happy birthday.

"Michael lives in New York too," Chloe offered.

"Small town. It's amazing we don't know each other already," Xander joked.

Was he taking a shot at Big Dune Island? Austin didn't like this guy. He was too tall, and his hair had too much product now that he could see it up close.

"Well, we won't interrupt your celebration," Gigi said. "I hope you have a wonderful birthday dinner, Chloe."

"I should get going too," Michael said. "I've got a working dinner." He nodded toward the mayor, who'd just entered the dining room.

After the visitors all left the table and were seated far enough away that they were out of earshot, Mrs. Beckett expressed her concerns about the future of the Salty Breeze. It was all the buzz on Big Dune Island this week. They talked about all the potential scenarios, from Simon keeping the inn and updating it, to the potential for disaster if it was sold and bulldozed to make way for something new.

Austin was thankful they stayed on safe topics for the duration of the meal. However, he was having trouble concentrating on his steak and the conversation. The host had sat Gigi and Xander four tables behind his parents, so Gigi was in his direct line of sight. She'd been laughing as if Xander was a standup comedian, and he'd seen them clink glasses when their wine arrived as if they were toasting to something special. Gigi kept tucking her hair behind one ear, a nervous tic she'd always had. It definitely looked like a date.

She caught Austin watching her at one point and had given him a small smile before he'd looked away and pretended to be watching a sailboat gliding by. The boat wasn't even out of view before he was watching her again.

His table was finishing up their entrees when the waiter brought over a bottle of champagne and four glasses for the table.

"Compliments of Mr. Russo for Miss Chloe's birthday," he said.

They all turned toward where Michael was seated across the restaurant with the mayor. He smiled at Chloe and gave a little nod.

Austin turned to see his sister blushing. Was there more going on between these two than he realized? His protective big brother instincts kicked in. He'd have to see what Jesse knew.

"Well, wasn't that nice of him," Mrs. Beckett said, turning to wave at Michael.

"Good bottle too," his dad said, sipping the champagne the waiter had poured. "How well do you know this Michael guy?" he asked his daughter.

She shrugged, her cheeks still flushed as she took a sip from her glass. "He comes into the cafe for espresso when he's in town."

His father drew his lips into a fine line. "So he's just a random customer and he's ordering a hundred-dollar bottle of champagne for your birthday?"

"Dan." Their mother placed a hand on her husband's arm. "It was a nice gesture. Let's just enjoy it."

They finished the champagne and the dessert the restaurant sent out for Chloe, back on safe topics like the Junior League's upcoming tour of homes and the new pizza place by Main Beach. As they stood to leave, Austin wanted to go by Gigi's table and say goodbye, hoping to catch some of her conversation with Xander. Unfortunately, his sister was chattering away about some maintenance issues with one of the tenants in their building, and he had to follow her toward the front of the restaurant. He caught Gigi's eye and gave a little wave. She raised a hand and wiggled her fingers at him before laughing at something Xander said.

The green monster of jealousy was firmly attached to Austin's back by the time his family got out to the valet stand. He told himself it was silly. Xander lived in New York and was probably only here for a few days. It wasn't like Gigi was going to move back to the city.

His parents' car arrived at the valet first, followed by his sister's. He'd parked his truck a couple of blocks over and walked, so he wished his sister a happy birthday before putting her in the car to go meet her friends and watching her pull off.

Michael came up beside him as he turned to leave.

"Thanks for the champagne, man," Austin said, reaching out a hand.

Michael clapped his hand to Austin's, patting him on the shoulder with the other. "Chloe's always waiting on me. Just wanted to give her something for a change. Good to see you guys."

"You too," Austin said, glancing at the restaurant one last time as he walked off. He was hoping to see Gigi leaving, ready for her night with Xander to be over. But all he saw was a closed door.

Chapter Fifteen

Gigi

She'd caught Austin watching her with Xander more than once during dinner. He'd been giving off the same protective big brother vibes she'd witnessed any time a guy showed interest in his sister.

Austin *had* been like a big brother in Atlanta. He was always checking in on her, even staying over the night Dalton had broken up with her, instead of proposing as she'd expected. He'd held her while she'd ranted and told her she was too good for Dalton. Which was part of why it had felt so weird that night in the hot tub. She'd always looked at Austin like an older brother. An annoying—and, yes, objectively attractive—older brother. But you didn't really think about your brother's rock-hard abs or sculpted biceps, did you? See, confusing.

"So, what are you working on these days?" Xander's question interrupted her thoughts. "I imagine the commercial real estate projects look a little different here."

Gigi laughed. "In fact, there are so few. I think I've only done one since I got back. I do mostly zoning and land use projects these days, with a little HOA work thrown in."

"HOAs?" he asked. "That sounds like a nightmare. I tried to represent my condo board one time and it was the most thankless job I've ever had. And I say that having worked for Ned the Nightmare," he joked, referring to the nickname of the most notoriously ruthless partner at their firm.

"Oh, I miss Ned," she said, sarcasm dripping from her voice. "How is he these days?"

"Still a nightmare." Xander shook his head as he refilled his wine glass with the bottle he'd ordered. "But, luckily, he only likes to pick on associates."

"Yes, congrats on making partner." She lifted her wine glass to clink against his. "That's quite the accomplishment."

"You know, I thought it would feel better than it did. Frankly, it was more of a relief than a celebration. I was just thinking how it must be nice for you to be your own boss and call your own shots."

"It is," she agreed. "I can mostly pick and choose the work I want to do, and I can say no to anyone who acts like a jerk."

"You must get to do some things that are more fulfilling here, right? It's such a small community. I bet you feel like you're actually making an impact."

"Yeah, but that can be stressful too when you feel like it's all on you to get the desired result." Gigi told him what she could about the Salty Breeze without breaking any ethical rules, covering Margaret dying without a will and the arrival of Simon, but not the discovery of the artwork or the diaries.

"That does sound like a lot on your shoulders. It's not like you can control who she's related to or what they decide to do with it."

"Yeah, tell that to my mother," she huffed.

"Ahh, yes. The infamous Ms. Myrtle lives here too. I bet that's a treat."

Gigi and Xander had been summer associates and then first-year associates on the same team at the firm. She'd only stayed there three years before moving back to Big Dune Island, but she'd regaled him with stories of her mother several times when explaining why Ned the Nightmare didn't actually scare her.

"You have no idea." She rolled her eyes.

"So an estranged heir showed up in town, but you don't know how he found out or if there are any more?"

"No, I'm waiting on the investigator. Hopefully he turns up something this week."

"Have you tried searching Ancestry.com?"

She shook her head. "I've been so busy with—" She caught herself before she mentioned the wedding. "—other matters that I didn't even think of it. I just delegated it to Mitch. He's excellent at tracking people, so I knew he could handle it."

"Tell me her name again," Xander said, pulling out his phone. "I helped my sister do our family tree last year as a gift for our grandfather, and I still have a subscription. Let's see what we find."

Xander clicked around on his phone while Gigi nervously sipped on her water, not wanting to drink any more wine.

"Aha!" Xander exclaimed, expanding something on the screen. "I bet this is how they found him. Someone on Margaret's side of the family—looks like a distant cousin—started putting together a family tree, and it's public so other people can add to it."

"Do you see any kids for Margaret?" Gigi thought about Grace.

His eyebrows knitted together as he concentrated on the

small screen. "No, doesn't look like it. If there was a birth record, it would be in something called a 'hint' attached to Margaret's profile here. I thought you said she didn't have any though."

"No, she didn't. At least not that we know of. Just checking."

"Looks like she had a sister named Carol," he said, passing the phone across the table to her. "They were the only two siblings, and her sister appears to have died without having any children."

Gigi navigated around the small screen, seeing what Xander was saying laid out in a visual family tree. That meant Margaret didn't have any nieces or nephews by blood. She handed the phone back to him.

"Okay, so how do we find her cousins?"

Xander tapped a few more times, studied the screen, then stood up. "I'll come sit next to you so we can look at this together."

When Xander sat next to her, she could smell his woodsy cologne, and the hair stood up on her neck when his arm brushed hers. They'd kissed one time many years ago when he'd walked her home after work. She'd been attracted to him from the first day she'd met him and, by that point, they'd been working alongside each other for nearly a year. They worked such long hours there was no time to meet anyone outside of the office, so they'd been shamelessly flirting for weeks.

Then he'd walked her home, and they'd stopped to look at Christmas lights on one of the streets lined with brownstones. He'd just leaned down and kissed her, catching her sleep-deprived brain off guard. It had been a nice kiss, but they'd decided the next day it was a mistake. The firm required anyone dating a colleague to register with HR, and they hadn't wanted to make it look as if they were distracted from their work. Their firm was known for making cuts after the first year, and neither of them wanted to be on the chopping block. So they'd cooled off the flirting and gone back to being just colleagues.

She'd be lying if she said she hadn't thought about that kiss when Xander told her he was in town. They stayed in touch a few times a year by email, but she hadn't seen him since she left New York. They weren't colleagues anymore though. And Xander was still really handsome, with his chiseled jaw and olive skin. He was tall with broad shoulders and a strong chest. He definitely knew how to fill out a suit. And tonight, she noticed, also a pair of jeans.

"—and there's Simon," he said, pointing at the screen.

She'd clearly missed something while distracted by his closeness. "I'm sorry. Run that by me one more time."

He scrolled up on the screen. "Margaret's mother had two sisters, Elizabeth and Beatrice. It looks like Beatrice had two children, one who died just after birth and one who died as a toddler."

"That's terrible," Gigi said.

"Her sister Elizabeth had three children, Anthony, Mark, and Jean. They all three predeceased Margaret, but see there." He pointed. "Jean had one son named Simon."

"Ahh, I see," she said. "So no first cousins remain on her mother's side, which gives Simon the best claim as her first cousin once removed."

"Yes, assuming this family tree is complete and they didn't omit any children of Anthony or Mark. I wouldn't take this as the gospel truth though. People start on these projects and never finish them, so it's likely not fully accurate. It just gives you a starting point." He scrolled back up and tapped a few things, making levels of the tree expand. "Unfortunately, whoever did this was only interested in that side of the family tree. There's nothing here for Margaret's father. She might still have cousins on that side who would inherit before Simon, or they could have children who would inherit equally with Simon."

"Honestly." Gigi shook her head. "I'll never understand why people are so reluctant to get a will. It would sure save me a lot of headaches."

"Do you have any idea who got in touch with this Simon guy and what their angle is?" Xander asked, putting his phone on the table and reaching across to get his wine glass.

"My money is on this shady real estate broker on the island who's about to get the listing for a big tract of land right next door to the inn. That parcel doesn't have any ocean frontage, so snagging this one would make both properties worth exponentially more. You could build quite the development there."

Gigi noted Xander hadn't moved back to sit on the other side of the table. She imagined what it would be like to kiss him again. It had been a long time ago, but she remembered him being a good kisser.

"Well, I hope it works out the way you want it to," Xander said. "If anyone can find a loophole or a creative solution, it's you. I still remember how you got Darlington International out of that commercial lease deal. They would have lost millions if you hadn't found that rezoning issue from a decade earlier."

She'd spent weeks pouring through city records that no one else had bothered to check. Instead of simply pursuing a breach of contract claim, she'd gotten their client out of the whole deal and even given the partner on the matter the ammunition to score them a substantial settlement.

"Geez, I'd forgotten all about that. It's like another lifetime ago." She couldn't believe he remembered it. He had to have worked on hundreds of transactions since then.

"Who forgets a major win like that?" he asked. "Honestly,

I'm glad you weren't there anymore when I came up for partner. You probably would have gotten it over me."

"Stop it." Gigi swatted at him playfully. "My head won't fit out the door when we leave if you keep it up."

They continued to chat about some of Xander's current deals while they ordered and ate dessert. Then she offered to drive him back to the resort instead of him riding the shuttle he'd taken over to meet her for dinner.

As they walked to her car over at her office a few blocks away, Xander asked if he could see where she worked now. After a quick tour of the historic-house-turned-office suite, she found herself standing with him in the front lobby that had once been a living room. The room was only illuminated by a Tiffany lamp on a side table that flipped off with the switch by the front door.

"This is really impressive, Gigi," he said, reaching out to touch her arm. "You've really built something for yourself here."

Gigi couldn't remember the last time a man had touched her, and her skin was on fire where his hand still lingered.

"It's not as fancy as your workplace," she said, remembering the firm's impressive five floors of impeccably designed office space on the top of a seventy-story skyscraper.

"I have to admit," Xander said, his warm brown eyes focused on hers, "I miss our late nights working together."

"Yeah, me too," she said, trying to steady her voice as her heart pounded in her chest. Was he going to kiss her? He looked like he was going to kiss her.

"But there is one advantage to us not working together. No HR forms to fill out."

She slowly shook her head as he took a step closer. "Nope. I don't even have an HR department."

Xander placed a finger under her chin and lifted it. He seemed to search her eyes for permission, which she gave by rising on her toes to reach him. Their lips met . . . and she felt nothing. Sure, she felt his lips against hers, but they didn't feel right. They were too soft. Too wet.

It was nothing like she remembered their first kiss. Had her memory failed her after all these years?

She pulled back, not meeting his eyes. Xander was objectively perfect on paper: successful lawyer, cultured, sophisticated. The kind of man Myrtle would love.

"That was. . ." Xander started, his voice warm with promise.

"Nice," Gigi finished quickly, taking a step back. The word fell flat between them, damning in its mediocrity. She forced a smile, hoping to soften the awkwardness.

The entire drive to the hotel was painful. She wanted to like Xander. Heck, she wanted to enjoy a good kiss after her recent drought. But that wasn't it.

"Thank you so much for the help with the ancestry stuff," Gigi said when she pulled up in front of the hotel.

"Of course," he said, disappointment still evident on his face. "It was good to see you again, Gigi."

"You too, Xander. Good luck with the golf tournament."

Although she was disappointed the evening hadn't ended on a romantic note, something good had come out of dinner with Xander. She hoped that Simon wouldn't be the only heir. He might be a perfectly nice guy, but his association with Neville and Phil didn't bode well for the Salty Breeze.

She hadn't started Margaret's journals yet. She wouldn't have time tonight either, as she still had a will and trust to draft before a client meeting in the morning, and it was already getting late. Besides, Xander said there weren't any hints for children under Margaret and Ron, so Grace had to be a goddaughter or a friend's child. She'd get to it later in the week when her schedule slowed down.

Austin and Gigi had agreed to meet at Island Coffee the next afternoon to go over some details for the joint bachelor-bachelorette party. The only weekend everyone could do it was just a little over a week away.

Gigi got there first, ordering an iced coconut latte and settling into her usual table near the back. She was scanning through emails on her phone when she saw Austin enter. He stopped to give Chloe a hug as she finished cleaning off a table near the door. Their relationship was really nice, and it made Gigi wish she'd had a sibling. It would have been nice to feel like someone was on her team growing up. Heck, even now.

"So, how was your date last night?" Austin asked as he settled in across from her.

She frowned. "It wasn't a date."

"It looked like a date."

"And what exactly does a date look like?"

"You, in a little black dress, your hair all done, red lipstick. Wine and candlelight by the water."

"You noticed what I was wearing?" She raised an eyebrow.

He looked like a little kid who'd gotten caught with his hand in a cookie jar before he glanced across the cafe toward his sister. "Chloe said she liked it."

"Mm-hm," Gigi said, sipping her latte. "It wasn't a date. He's just an old colleague."

"Kind of cozy for former colleagues."

She narrowed her eyes at him. "Why are you so concerned about my dinner?"

"I'm not." He looked away. "I was just curious if it went well. You haven't dated anyone in a while."

"Now you're keeping tabs on my dating history too?"

Iris came over to the table with a cold brew for Austin, interrupting their conversation.

"Thanks, Iris. And, might I add, you're looking lovely today." He flashed her an easy smile. It was as if flirting was his first language, even if the woman was in her sixties.

"New hairdo," Iris said, patting the ends of her short curls with one hand.

As she left the table, he turned to Gigi. "See, I notice things."

"Iris is single," Gigi teased. "She's pretty hot for a grandma."

"I don't know." Austin scratched his head. "Her grandson is on my team. I wouldn't want anyone to think I was playing favorites."

Chloe came over and dropped a small dessert plate in front of each of them. The pattern on Gigi's plate that day was brightly colored flowers over lace, and Austin's was bamboo with platinum plating around the rim. Gigi loved seeing all the different china patterns.

"I'm testing a new pumpkin cheesecake recipe for the fall," Chloe said. "Let me know what you think. The crust has a secret ingredient, but I want to see if you can guess."

"It's a tough job, but someone has to do it," Austin said, already digging into his slice with a fork.

"Seriously, Chloe. I think I've gained five pounds from the free desserts you give me every time I come in." Gigi put a small amount on her fork and tested it, groaning in delight at the flavors. "On second thought, it's worth it. I can just buy new clothes."

Chloe beamed. "Glad you like it."

"Speaking of not fitting into my clothes anymore, Austin said you liked my dress last night. I got it from Cori's," she said, referring to a boutique on Main Street.

Chloe looked confused, looking from her brother back to Gigi. "Oh, yeah. It was super cute. I'll go check it out."

The kid with the cookie jar look had returned to Austin's

face, and Gigi knew then that he had lied about why he'd noticed the dress. It was strangely satisfying to know he'd checked her out.

After Chloe returned to the counter, Gigi pulled the wedding binder from her bag, scooting the pie to the side of the table.

"Oh, no, it's the binder in all its bridal glory," Austin said in mock horror. "That must mean it's time to get down to business."

"We have ten days to pull off an epic bachelor-bachelorette weekend. I just want to make sure everything is perfect for Callie."

"I told you I had it under control," he said. "All you have to do is pack a bag and show up."

She frowned. "I'm going to need more details than that. When are we leaving? Who's driving? Do we need to take any food or drinks with us? And what about party favors?"

"Party favors? Like we got at birthday parties as kids?"

"Yes, bachelorette parties have party favors."

"Like straws in the shape of"—he lifted an eyebrow suggestively—"certain male body parts?"

She rolled her eyes. "No, we're not having phallic straws. That's just tacky."

"You sounded just like your mother there," Austin said, pointing his fork at her. "You should have heard yourself." He sat up taller, repeating what she said in a voice that was meant to sound like her mother.

"Shoot me now," she groaned. "If I'm turning into my mother, just put me out of my misery."

"I'll do it for you if you do it for me," he said, referencing his fear of turning into his father. "I think we're safe for now though. Phallic straws really don't seem like Callie's style."

"Agreed," she said. "I'll get the party favors for the ladies. Now, what are we eating and drinking?"

They hammered out the rest of the details for the weekend away, and Gigi was pleasantly surprised by how much thought Austin had put into it. It really did sound as if it would be a fun time away, and she could use a break from work. She hadn't had a vacation in nearly two years.

"Gigi, I'm so glad I ran into you." Patricia Tompkins came up to their table just as Gigi was putting away the wedding binder.

"Ms. Pat," Gigi said, standing to hug the older woman. "So good to see you."

"Hi, Austin," Pat said. "Nice to see you too."

"Ms. Pat," he said. "I love that color on you."

"Why thank you, dear," the older woman said. Ms. Pat ran the dance school on the island and was in the Junior League with both of their mothers.

"Gigi, Harold was going to call your office. There was someone over on the twenty acres today. Harold went over there, and he said he'd been hired to do soil testing. That means they're getting ready to build, doesn't it?" She was wringing her hands as she spoke.

"Not necessarily," Gigi said. "But I'm glad you told me. I'll call over to the permit office and make sure nothing has been filed yet. Gail promised Reagan she'd call her if anything came across her desk, so I don't think we should worry yet."

"I'm just so concerned," Pat said. "If someone got ahold of that and the Salty Breeze, they could put an entire resort there."

No doubt, that's exactly what someone would want to do if they could get ahold of both properties.

Gigi wasn't ready to admit it out loud, but she knew the Salty Breeze was living on borrowed time. And she had no idea how to save it.

Chapter Sixteen

Austin

Austin had reached out to his friend Mark Swisher a couple of nights before and invited him for a round of golf on Friday morning. Mark knew everyone in the real estate industry in Northeast Florida. Austin thought he might know something that could help Gigi on the twenty acres. He'd seen the worry etched on her face after they ran into Ms. Pat.

It seemed like a good idea when he'd sent Mark the text, but when Austin's alarm went off before the break of dawn that morning after he'd been out way too late at Casino Night, he wondered why he was getting involved. He told himself it was because he didn't want to see the island get overdeveloped, but he knew that wasn't the entire answer. After all, he'd never gotten involved in development debates on the island in the past. Something about the look in Gigi's eyes the week before when she talked about the twenty acres had moved him into action though.

"Boy, it's a hot one for September, huh?" Austin asked, attempting to steer the conversation away from the Gators' quarterback situation.

Mark wiped the sweat from his brow with his forearm. "Did I tell you we put in a pool this winter? I tried to tell Dana the beach is only a short drive, but apparently that's not good enough."

Austin laughed and shook his head to commiserate with his friend. Mark had been a star quarterback for the Gators who quickly washed out in the NFL, but remained a local legend. He lived along the banks of the St. John's River in the prestigious San Marco area of Jacksonville. His family had been in real estate in the area for three generations, and his father had been the top-selling agent in the city for decades. Mark joined the business after leaving the NFL, but he provided commentary on the Gators for the radio station on a regular basis. They'd become fast friends, easily able to relate to what the other had been through as a pro athlete.

"So I have to admit I had a bit of an ulterior motive for asking you to play today." Austin shifted his driver from one hand to the other.

"Shoot," Mark said, resting his club head on the ground and leaning on the handle.

"I know you don't do much up on the island, but have you heard anything about a developer coming in on the south end? There's a twenty-acre parcel of undeveloped land, and it's been a little bit of a controversial thing for the past year or so."

"Yeah, I remember reading about it in the paper last year. You wanting to get in on it?"

Austin shook his head. "No, definitely not. A friend of mine is an attorney on the island and has been trying to stop anything from being built. I guess the owner got sick, and even though he hadn't planned to ever develop, it sounds like maybe his kids have other ideas."

Mark let out a long whistle. "Man, it's prime land. There's no ocean frontage though, right?"

"No, that parcel is mostly cut off by a B&B on the beach, but there's a small access point between the B&B and the house next door."

"Still valuable, especially if they could ever snag the B&B for the frontage."

That's what Austin was afraid of, but he decided not to tell Mark about the B&B situation. He liked Mark, but he did invest in real estate sometimes and might decide he had his own plans.

"You know I'm friends with Callie Jackson, right?"

Mark nodded.

"She tried to buy it last year, but they wouldn't sell to her. She was going to donate it to conservation."

"It would command a premium for sure. If I remember correctly, the zoning already allows multi-story condos there."

Austin nodded in confirmation. "Yeah, that's what Gigi says."

"So, what can I do?"

"Can you ask around? Find out if anyone has immediate plans for it? Gigi thought she caught someone out there surveying recently, and it sounds like they were doing soil testing or something earlier this week. No one has filed any permits yet though."

"You bet. I'll see what I can find."

"Thanks, I owe you one."

"Shank one to the left here, and we'll call it even." Mark laughed, jerking his head toward the tee box.

"Nah, you'd never enjoy it if you won just because I tanked it." Austin smiled as he lined up to make his drive and watched it go sailing down the middle of the greenway into a near perfect position.

"Ouch. Come on, I thought you were going to play nice."

Austin shrugged. "You know what they say. A bad day on the golf course beats a good one at work."

"Yeah, yeah. Move out of the way, hotshot. I'll show you what a real drive looks like."

Austin watched Mark line up to take his shot. If anyone could find out what was going on with the twenty acres, it would be Mark. Even if he hadn't been in real estate, he knew everyone important in town. His family was always hosting fundraisers and charity galas. They were one of the most well-connected families in Jacksonville. Austin practically patted himself on the back for having such a good idea and the relationship to make it happen.

He thought about what Gigi would think when she found out he'd gotten to the bottom of things. Would she throw her arms around him? Kiss him on the cheek? Okay, that sounded more like something he'd enjoy, not something she'd actually do. She wasn't one for public displays of affection.

"You coming?"

Austin was so lost in thought he hadn't even noticed Mark had walked over to the golf cart, where he stood now waving for Austin to hurry up.

"What are you in such a hurry for?" Austin teased his friend. "Rushing home to get in that pool of yours and float around? I can just picture you on one of those giant flamingo floats."

"Shut up and get in the cart. One day, you'll meet a woman who'll have you building pools and buying flamingo floats and doing whatever else it takes to keep her from realizing you've out kicked your coverage."

Austin laughed, knowing his friend was right. They might

even have you playing golf in eighty-five-degree heat and playing amateur detective.

As Austin was driving home after his radio show on Thursday, he passed the twenty acres and silently hoped Mark would get to the bottom of what was going on there. He was just imagining all the trees being clear cut to make way for the development when Mitch, Gigi's investigator, called him. Had he found something about Luke's family already? And was that good or bad news?

"Hey, Mitch," he said, answering over the truck's Bluetooth speaker.

"Hey, Austin. I've got something. I'm not sure quite what it is yet, but I wanted to keep you updated."

"Okay, what is it?"

"It looks like Luke's mom changed her name about twenty years ago. First and last. I'm waiting for the court to answer my records request, so that's all I know right now. It could be something, or maybe nothing."

Luke was eight, so he wasn't sure how his mother changing her name twenty years ago would make any difference when it came to him.

"It might mean she has family that doesn't even know she had a kid," Mitch said as if sensing his question.

That could be good news. Or bad. Surely she had a good reason for changing her name.

"How long before you get the records?" Austin asked.

"Could be a day. Could be a week. She did it in a small town in Ohio that hasn't digitized its records that far back. I'll let you know when I have them though."

"Thanks, Mitch," he said, pushing the button to end the call.

His first instinct was to call and tell Gigi. She was the only one who knew he was doing this, but she'd also asked him not to tell her what she found. And, besides, it's not like he really knew anything yet.

The rest of the drive home, he second-guessed the entire decision to hire Mitch. This all started because he wanted Luke to be able to stay with the Carsons. If they found family, however, he could get shipped off anywhere in the country. Heck, maybe not even in this country. It could upend his whole life.

There was a reason his mother had changed her name. What if she'd been abused? What if she was in witness protection?

He watched too much television. There was probably a perfectly reasonable explanation.

He hoped so for Luke's sake.

Chapter Seventeen

Gigi

Gigi had to go with a client to court on Friday morning over a disputed easement, and she decided to try Mitch on her way back to the office. She'd emailed over the family tree on Ancestry.com after her dinner with Xander, so she hoped it had helped him get somewhere with his search for more heirs.

"Sorry, Gigi," Mitch said after they'd exchanged pleasantries. "I haven't found anyone else yet. The Ancestry.com stuff helped, but so far everyone I've found is already deceased. Margaret's father only had one brother, and it appears his only child died while in the army. It does look like the woman he was married to had a daughter, but I can only see her year of birth. It is possible she's his child, but it's also possible she's someone else's. I'm trying to get ahold of the birth certificate, but it'll probably take a few days for the county to process."

"You haven't run into anyone named Grace, have you?"

"Grace," he said, pausing to think. "No, I don't think so."

"It's probably nothing." Gigi told him what she'd found among Margaret's papers.

"Adoptions are usually sealed, but I'll dig around in case they had an adopted daughter."

"Thanks, Mitch. Let me know anything you find. I'm pretty sure Simon has already filed to open probate."

Pretty sure turned to official confirmation when Gigi walked into her office.

"You were right," Reagan said as Gigi stopped by her desk on the way into the office. "Simon opened probate. I'm emailing the filing over to you now."

Once she was at her desk, Gigi scanned the filing. Picking up the phone, she dialed Neville.

"Gigi Franklin," he said in his slow Southern drawl when his assistant Amy transferred her call to his desk. "To what do I owe the pleasure?"

"I see you've opened probate for Margaret Cunningham on behalf of Simon Frazier. I wanted to let you know I've been retained to represent the Salty Breeze."

"Well, that seems unnecessary. Margaret was the sole owner, so it'll be taken care of in the probate."

"We just want to make sure *all* the heirs are found and notified. Rebecca thought it was prudent if the interest of the inn was represented during this process."

"I assure you we intend to follow the letter of the law. I have done one of these before," Neville said in a condescending tone.

Yeah, she remembered another probate where he'd conveniently missed an heir who had a superior claim to his client. They'd done the bare minimum search and concluded his client was the sole heir to a sizeable estate. The true heir was admittedly difficult to find, but Mitch had found her, and

Gigi had been able to intervene in the case and ensure it went to the correct person.

Simon would likely get appointed as administrator of Margaret's estate since he was currently the only known heir, which would leave finding anyone else up to him and Neville. They were about as likely to find another heir as she was to join the circus alongside Myrtle for a mother-daughter act.

Gigi almost told Neville she'd already hired Mitch to track down any missing relatives, but she decided to keep that information to herself for now. The only thing worse than him not bothering to look for any other heirs was him getting to them first and pushing his and Phil's agenda.

"Say," she drawled in a sickly sweet voice, "how did you find Simon anyway? He showed up pretty quickly for someone who didn't even know Margaret existed."

Neville was quiet for a moment, no doubt deciding how much he wanted to reveal. "Amy is a whiz on the internet. We just wanted to make sure there'd be family at that dear woman's funeral."

"Well, aren't you just a sweetheart," Gigi said. "Who knew you were such a teddy bear underneath all that seersucker?" Neville was known for wearing his seersucker suits and white Panama hat year-round.

"You know how much I love this community," he said without a hint of irony.

Yeah, love to sell it for its parts. She knew how he operated.

Lucky for her, she had Margaret's journals. She'd thought she might have a chance to start going through them before she was due to meet Austin at her house. They were riding out to the lake together to decorate before the rest of the group arrived. After ending the call with Neville, she pulled the first journal from her purse. The first two entries detailed a new recipe Mrs. Cunningham was experimenting with and a fight with her sister. It was pretty run-of-the-mill. It was the third entry where Gigi finally found mention of Grace.

July 12, 1984

Sweet little Grace had me in stitches today! She insisted on "helping" me bake for my annual cookie swap with my friends. The kitchen looked like a flour bomb had gone off, but I couldn't bring myself to care, not with those big brown eyes looking up at me explaining that the cookies needed "extra sprinkles for the fairies."

She's such a determined little thing. When she couldn't reach the counter, she dragged over Ron's footstool from his reading chair, completely ignoring my offers to lift her up. She assured me she could do it all by herself.

I've been trying to teach her to garden, just like my mother taught me. Today she proudly showed me the little row of marigolds she's been tending. Half of them were actually weeds, but she was so proud I didn't have the heart to tell her. She named each one. Now I have a garden full of flowers named after storybook princesses.

She is the embodiment of pure joy. Ron says she gets her spirited nature from her mother, and I can see it in the way she throws her whole heart into everything she does.

When she finally wore herself out, she curled up in my lap on the porch swing, smelling of sunshine and cookies, and asked me to tell her stories about when I was a little girl. My heart feels so full on days like these.

Gigi sank back in her office chair. Grace wasn't Margaret's daughter. It did, however, sound like Ron had some sort of connection to her mother. So maybe Gigi had been right about Grace being a goddaughter or a friend's child. Unfortunately, that would mean she was a dead end as far as the inheritance went.

Reagan came in with some documents for her to sign, so she stuffed the journal back in her bag. She'd read more later in case Grace turned out to be some other sort of relative.

―――

LATER THAT AFTERNOON, GIGI PACKED THE LAST OF her bags for the bachelor-bachelorette weekend and double-checked her list to ensure she'd remembered everything. Austin would be at her house any minute to pick her up.

When he arrived and rang the bell, she answered the door breathless from carrying everything from her bedroom to the front hallway.

"All that stuff over there goes," she said, pointing to her suitcase and a pile of large tote bags filled to the brim with decorations and party favors.

"You do know we're just going for two nights, right?" he said as he surveyed it.

"It's not all for me." She frowned.

As Austin began loading everything in his truck, Gigi went back to the kitchen to fill her water bottle.

"You forgot to add 'fun' to this," he said, pointing at the checklist she'd left on the counter.

"I thought you said you were bringing that." She smirked at him while she screwed the lid on her bottle.

"Oh, man," he said, smacking his forehead. "I knew I forgot something."

"That's okay. I've got some classic bachelorette party games for us to play."

His smile turned mischievous. "Is that like pin the pe—"

"Don't even say it," she warned, laughing. "Not that kind of game."

After fighting over who got to control the radio on the trip—which Gigi won thanks to her superior negotiation skills—they started the two-hour drive inland to the lake.

"So tell me about these games. How ridiculous are they?" Austin asked once they were on the state highway.

"There's a two-legged race down the aisle. I want to make sure Sienna and Teddy end up paired together for that one." Gigi wiggled her eyebrows. Everyone knew Teddy had a crush on Sienna, but he was too shy to do anything about it. She'd just have to push his hand.

"I think Piper and Wyatt might hit it off too," Austin said.

"I guess that leaves the two of us," she said, realizing for the first time that everyone could end up coupled off, leaving her and Austin together. Her mind went back to Mary Catherine's wedding and that night in the hot tub.

He turned to look at her as he slowed to a stop at a red light, and she felt exposed. She wondered if he was thinking about the same night.

Luckily, the light changed and he turned his attention back to the road. Clearing her throat, Gigi tried to think of the other games.

"I brought my computer so we can hook it up to the TV for karaoke roulette. I found a bunch of wedding-themed songs we can load up."

Austin shot her a sideways glance. "Wasn't singing your pageant talent?"

She tucked a strand of her brunette hair behind one ear. "Yeah, but like seventy-five percent of the girls in pageants sing."

"Mm-hm," he said. "What else?"

"Then there's 'Who Knows the Couple Better.' I ordered these cards online and they have all these fill-in-the-blanks about the couple we all complete and then see who gets the most right, which obviously either you or I are going to win."

He laughed. "So you rigged it to win all the games is what you're telling me?"

Mouth wide open, she mocked surprise. "How dare you accuse me of such a thing."

"You're the most competitive person I know. Of course you made sure you'd win all the games."

"I don't know what you're talking about." Gigi tried not to smile as she looked out the window at the farmland they'd hit just beyond the metro Jacksonville area.

"It's fine," he said. "As long as I get to be on your team for everything."

She snuck a look at him, and he shot a smile at her.

All this time they'd been spending together for the wedding had her remembering how much fun she'd always had with Austin. Sure, they loved to get in a good dig on one another, but wasn't that basically just childish flirtation?

Gigi had never really stopped to picture herself with Austin. She did it now as she looked out the window at the massive oak trees dotting the fields of horses and cows they passed on their way into the more rural part of Northern Florida. As much as he might look like a ladies' man from the outside, she knew he rarely let things get past a few dates. Not because he was callously using women and tossing them aside, but because he didn't let many people get close. Had he ever even said "I love you" to any of those women? She doubted it. She couldn't even remember one that had lasted beyond weeks into months.

"Have you ever been in love?" she turned to ask him.

He looked at her and then back to the road. "That's random. Why are you asking me that?"

She shrugged. "Just curious. I was thinking about all those women you used to date in Atlanta. Were you ever in love with any of them?"

He pressed his lips together as he continued staring out the windshield. "No, I don't think so," he finally said.

"If you don't think so, the answer is no," she said. "You know when you're in love."

"What about you?" he asked.

"I was in love with Dalton, but we know how that worked out." She hadn't meant it to sound like an accusation, but she saw Austin's jaw flinch.

"Think we'll ever find people who make us feel like Jesse and Callie do?" he asked, turning to look at her, but she couldn't read his expression behind his sunglasses.

She thought about it for a minute. They were only in their early thirties. There was still plenty of time to fall in love.

"Maybe?" Gigi hadn't pictured herself getting married in a long time. Not until she'd had to pull out that wedding binder. "We're still relatively young, so I guess we've got time."

They rode in silence the rest of the way to the two-lane county road that would take them to the lake. She thought about the kind of woman Austin might one day fall in love with. She was sure most of the women he'd been with thought he was the stereotypical jock, manly and tough with just enough sense to throw a ball.

That wasn't Austin at all though. He may have kidded and joked his way through school, but he could have gone to college almost anywhere—outside of maybe the Ivy League—on a baseball scholarship because he actually had good enough grades to get into most places. And the bravado on the outside hid a sensitive little boy who'd spent his whole life trying to make a man proud who only ever tore him down.

The woman who won Austin's heart would have to be sure of herself. She couldn't be someone who would back down from a challenge or get her feelings hurt if she had to say things first. She'd need to be patient and kind. Tell him she was proud of him and make him feel valued.

And she'd have to get through Gigi first because she wasn't going to let just anyone be with her friend.

Chapter Eighteen

Austin

Relationships. One more thing he hadn't been good enough at. Austin didn't know why Gigi had asked him that question about being in love. He knew it only reinforced her idea that he was a womanizer.

His hands had clenched around the steering wheel when she'd confirmed she'd been in love with Dalton. That little weasel hadn't deserved her on his best day. And she would know it if he'd told her the whole story back then, but he'd been trying to protect her. All she knew was that Austin saw or heard something and pushed Dalton into breaking up with her. That had come out the week after Mary Catherine's wedding. Austin had been vague about what it was, so he wasn't sure what she thought happened. Cheating seemed like the usual suspect, but what he actually witnessed was arguably even worse.

She'd been upset with Austin for meddling in her relationship instead of bringing it to her to handle, and that had turned to fury when Austin refused to share more details, only telling her she deserved someone better. Their fight and the rehab assignment that had sent him to the Mississippi Braves minor league team had ushered in a long break in their friendship. It lasted until they'd both moved back to Big Dune Island several years later and slowly repaired it, mostly thanks to Jesse and Callie. She'd never asked him about that time again, and he would like it to stay that way.

As they pulled into the driveway of his uncle's lake house, Austin hoped he'd remembered everything for the weekend. He wanted to show Gigi she'd been right to put her trust in him to plan the party, and he definitely wanted everything to be perfect for Jesse and Callie. They were two of the best people in the world, and seeing them happy made him happy. He just hoped that one day he'd find the person who made him feel like that too.

After unloading the truck, he asked Gigi if she needed help with anything. When she said she had it under control, he went outside to make sure the firewood delivery he'd ordered had been put out by the fire pit. He'd get up in the morning to get the jet skis, kayaks, and canoes out for the full day of activities he had planned, but tonight they would eat dinner, play games, and relax by the fire.

After confirming the firewood delivery was there, Austin went over to the hot tub. Images of the night of Mary Catherine's wedding flashed through his mind as he slid off the cover and stored it under the deck.

They'd stayed up half the night just talking. At first, it was all about their high school friends and acquaintances. Who'd already dropped out of college, who was dating who, and who had moved back home to live with their parents. Then it had moved to their parents. His helicopter father and her overbearing mother. They were like two peas in a pod.

Except Gigi wasn't having it. She was forging her own path, doing exactly what she wanted. She'd just found out she got into Emory's law school, and she wasn't even afraid to tell Ms. Myrtle. She was looking forward to it. She wanted to do it in person so she could see the look on her face.

Meanwhile, he was doing extra workouts with the hitting coach to try to make the major league roster for a team he didn't even want to be on. All so he could finally make his dad proud.

Austin knew now how that had gone. He'd made the roster, but it still wasn't good enough. His batting average was too low. He wasn't hitting enough home runs. He'd made a fielding error. The list never ended. Unless he went back and reinvented himself as a pitcher and pitched a perfect game, he'd never have an accomplishment his father couldn't pick apart.

"Hey, I need a hand," he heard Gigi call out from the deck above him.

"Be right there," he told her, heading for the stairs. As he entered the house, he caught her stretching up on her tiptoes, trying to reach above the doorway between the kitchen and living room. The late-afternoon sun streaming through the windows caught her hair, turning her dark waves to honey-gold at the edges.

"I want to hang this across here," she said, holding up a string of letters under the opening between the kitchen and living room. "Can you reach it?"

The opening was about eight feet wide by eight feet tall, and his six-foot-two height allowed him to easily reach where she was pointing to, so he took one end from her. As he reached up, Austin was acutely aware of how close they were standing, her shoulder brushing against his chest as she steadied herself.

Gigi pulled the tape from the counter, tore off a piece and

handed it to him. "I bought the kind that doesn't peel the paint," she assured him.

Her fingers lingered for just a moment as she passed him the tape, and he found himself missing the brief contact when she pulled away.

Once he hung the other end, he stood back to read it: Camp Bach. There were even little pine trees on either end of the words. The satisfaction on Gigi's face made him smile. She always did throw herself completely into any project she took on.

"Summer camp theme?" he turned to ask her, admiring how her eyes lit up with excitement.

"I even got us all shirts," she said, smiling big. "I'll get yours!"

That smile of hers would be his undoing. He loved seeing her this happy.

Austin watched her practically bounce away to retrieve the shirts. These moments when she let her guard down, showing the playful side beneath her tough lawyer exterior, were becoming his favorite part of this whole wedding planning adventure.

Gigi returned with a shirt in each hand. She passed him a dark green one and held up a tan one in front of her. Both said "Camp Bach" on the front in the log-style letters. She turned hers around to reveal words across the top on the back: "Counselor." Austin turned his around and realized it said the same.

"So we're the camp counselors this weekend?"

"Exactly," she said. "Isn't it so cute? Callie always wanted to go to summer camp as a kid, but she never got to go. So I figured it's never too late. Wait until you see everything I got!"

She started pulling things out of her bag with the enthusiasm of Santa Claus. There were koozies, water bottles, and hats with the same camp logo, tote bags for the ladies filled with beauty products they would use the next night during the slumber party portion of the weekend, and more signs and banners to hang, including a giant one with retractable poles she wanted him to install at the top of the driveway before everyone arrived.

She'd thought of everything. But that was Gigi. She could be a party planner if she wasn't a successful lawyer. There was no doubt in his mind, Gigi could be anything she wanted to be.

"Let's change," she said, throwing the T-shirt over her shoulder. "I'll meet you back in here in ten and we can finish decorating."

He did as he was told, taking the bedroom he and Jesse would share on the second floor while she wheeled her suitcase into the master bedroom on the first floor beyond the living room.

When Austin came back out, he couldn't believe how cute Gigi looked in her T-shirt and jeans. She was stuffing the tote bags with T-shirts, water bottles, and other items at the kitchen table. The jeans hugged her subtle curves. Her T-shirt was secured in a knot on one side, and her hair tucked behind her ears with the hat on top.

"How do I look?" she said, turning to face him. "Like a camp counselor?"

"Not at any camp I ever went to," Austin mumbled, thinking of the all-boys baseball camp he'd gone to every summer.

Gigi never wore jeans. She was always dressed up as if she had a meeting or a fancy dinner. Even in high school and college, she hadn't been the T-shirt and jeans kind of girl. It looked good on her though. As if she'd finally let herself relax. Gotten off the hamster wheel of trying to prove she could be so much more than a pageant queen, wife, and mother.

"What'd you say?" she asked.

"Yep, camp counselor. Nailed it," he said, stuffing his hands in his pockets.

She looked at her watch. "They'll be here in less than an hour. Can you go put that big sign up by the road? I'll keep working on the rest in here."

"Sure," he said, grabbing the banner and retractable poles from where she'd left them.

By the time they heard the crunch of tires on gravel out in the driveway an hour later, the lake house had been transformed into a summer camp.

"Let's go," Gigi said, practically skipping to the side door that led out onto the driveway.

Jesse, Callie, Sienna, and Piper were in Jesse's four-door truck, and Teddy and Wyatt pulled up beside them in Teddy's truck. Callie practically leaped from the truck before it had come to a full stop, running to Gigi. The two of them jumped up and down while they hugged, and Austin could remember them doing the same thing as kids. Neither had a sibling, but they were sisters in all the ways that mattered. It made him miss his own sister, but she couldn't be trusted to keep a secret, so she didn't get to be in on any of the wedding festivities.

"Is it a summer camp theme?" Callie squealed. "It is, isn't it?"

"Welcome to Camp Bach," Gigi said, pointing toward the door. "New camper orientation is about to begin."

The two of them went inside, more squealing from Callie coming once she saw the interior. Austin helped Jesse, Teddy, and Wyatt get everyone's luggage while Sienna and Piper went in to see what all the fuss was about. Teddy practically knocked over Austin in his effort to get Sienna's bag first. Man, that guy had it bad.

"Coed camp," Wyatt said as he hauled a bag out of the back of the truck. "Now that's what I'm talking about."

"Right? A far cry from that baseball camp we used to go to," Austin said as he carried two bags from Jesse's truck toward the house.

"You mean baseball boot camp?" Wyatt joked, referring to it as they had back then.

"Definitely would have been better with girls there," Jesse agreed.

Once everyone was inside and had properly shown their appreciation for Gigi's efforts to transform the lake house, she sent them off to their rooms to change into their camp T-shirts. She wanted to get a photo of everyone on the back deck overlooking the lake before they got too busy with dinner and games and forgot.

Austin was just thinking she probably had an itinerary for the entire weekend—despite the fact she'd pretended to let him plan the party—when she started passing out cards. Printed in all caps below the Camp Bach logo, he read, CAMP SCHEDULE, followed by time slots for dinner, games, sleep, breakfast, water activities, showers, Saturday night dinner, and the ladies' slumber party with "guy time" for the men following.

All he could do was shake his head and smile.

Chapter Nineteen

Gigi

Despite their eight-inch height difference, Austin and Gigi won the three-legged race down the aisle by several feet. Callie was hopelessly clumsy when it came to athletic endeavors, and Sienna wasn't much better. Combine that with Teddy's awkwardness about having his leg attached to Sienna's and the two were lucky they'd stumbled halfway down the aisle. Piper and Wyatt were the only ones keeping pace with Austin and Gigi in the beginning, but Piper tripped and took them both out in the final stretch. Judging by the way they were rolling around in the grass laughing though, those two were hitting it off, as expected.

Gigi was pleasantly surprised when dinner arrived via a catering van. Austin had ordered quite the spread of pulled pork, ribs, and brisket. She hadn't even told him about the camp theme, just to keep things casual, and he'd ordered the perfect meal for the occasion. After dinner, they all grabbed drinks and headed for the fire pit to play the fill-in-the-blank game to determine who knew the couple best.

"Oh, come on," Piper said as Gigi passed out the cards. "Obviously you're going to win, Gigi."

"Why Gigi?" Austin asked, feigning hurt. "I've known them just as long as she has."

"Because I'm more detail-oriented," Gigi said.

"No, because you made up the game." He frowned.

"I did not," she said. "I bought these cards pre-made. And Jesse and Callie have to fill it out together, so I have no idea what their answers will be."

"Let's settle it on the field," he said, challenging her. "Loser has to make breakfast in the morning."

"Deal," she said.

"Are they always like this?" Sienna asked Callie.

"Worse," Callie said, laughing. "They make more bets than a bookie in Vegas."

In the end, Austin and Gigi tied.

"Guess you two are making breakfast together," Callie said.

"Can either of them actually cook?" Wyatt asked. "Or is this more of a cereal situation?"

"Cereal," Jesse and Callie said in unison.

"Do you feel ganged up on?" Austin asked Gigi. "I feel ganged up on."

"I know. Who needs enemies with friends like this?" she joked.

"Let's play truth or dare," Piper said. "Some of us are outsiders to your little childhood foursome, so let's get to know each other."

Everyone agreed, and Piper started with Wyatt. "Truth or dare?"

"Truth," he said, leaning forward in the Adirondack chair to put his elbows on his knees.

Piper looked at him and smiled. "What are three qualities you look for in a woman?"

Wow, Piper wasn't holding back. Gigi knew she could be direct, but she might as well have rigged spin the bottle to land on Wyatt.

"I like a smart woman. One of us has to be," he poked at himself. Then he looked around the women in the group. "Oh, and a woman who can cook breakfast."

"Oh, so I'm out?" Gigi laughed.

"I'd make an exception for you." He winked, joking.

"That's only two," Piper teased.

"Oh, and I love redheads," he said, taking a swig of his beer as he sat back in his chair. Piper was the only redhead in the group.

"Whew," Sienna said, fanning her face. "It's getting hot out here."

The group laughed.

Wyatt chose Teddy next, who picked dare. Wyatt dared him to sing a verse of one of Callie's songs, and Teddy's face turned as red as a ripe tomato.

"What's the alternative?" Teddy asked.

Wyatt thought about it for a minute. "You have to streak down to the lake."

He was only kidding, but Teddy managed to turn an even darker shade of red in the firelight.

"No, he doesn't," Callie said. "No one is streaking out here." She turned to Teddy. "I'll sing it with you."

"No way," Wyatt said. "That's not fair."

"It's my bachelorette party, and I make up the rules," Callie said. "Come on, Teddy. What are we singing?"

He named one of her most popular songs, and together they sang the chorus.

"Come on, that deserves a bow," Callie said, walking over to him and tugging him out of his chair before putting her arm around him and bowing.

"You actually have a really nice voice," Sienna said to him as he sat back down, instantly turning his cheeks into tomatoes again.

Teddy chose Callie next, and when she picked truth, he asked her what was the most embarrassing thing that ever happened to her on stage.

"I know the answer to this one," Gigi said, taking a sip of her wine.

Austin held up a hand. "We aren't playing fill-in-the-blank anymore. You don't get any more points for this."

"Fine," Gigi said. "I'll let her tell the story."

Callie proceeded to tell the group about the time she came out on stage and said the wrong city name in her introduction. She'd done four cities in five nights in the middle of a three-month tour and didn't even know where she was anymore.

She buried her head in her hands after she finished the story. "I was mortified. I recovered and made a joke out of it, but my heart was pounding out of my chest. I was sure I'd get canceled."

Callie picked Sienna next, who chose truth.

"If you weren't a soon-to-be-famous recording artist, what would you be?"

Sienna laughed nervously. "I don't know about the soon-to-be-famous part."

"Oh, with me as your publicist, you're going to be famous," Piper promised her.

Sienna blushed, looking down at her hands and twisting a ring around her finger. "Hmm, what would I be if I wasn't a singer? Gosh, I don't know. It's all I've ever wanted to do. I took one of those aptitude tests in eighth grade though, and one of the things it said was veterinarian. I love horses, so maybe a horse vet." She shrugged.

"Sure, why not," Callie said. "You could have been a horse vet. Too bad you're going to be a famous recording artist instead."

Eager to get the attention off her, Sienna looked around at who was left. Gigi thought she'd choose her, but she chose Austin instead. "Austin, I don't know much about you except that you're Jesse's best friend. Let me think." She looked off into the distance as she thought of a question.

"If you could switch lives with anyone here for a day, who would it be and why?"

Gigi knew Austin envied Jesse's relationship with his father. And who didn't want to be Callie Jackson? When he said her name instead, she jerked her head to look at him.

"Me?" she asked. "Why would you want to be me?"

"You're the smartest and bravest person I know," he said, taking a sip of his beer. "You always know exactly what you want, and you go after it without caring what anyone thinks. I've always wanted to be more like you."

The circle grew hushed at his serious tone. It was the nicest thing anyone had ever said to Gigi, and she had no idea how to respond. Thankfully, Callie broke the tension.

"She is a total baddie," Callie said, holding up her wine glass to Gigi.

Gigi could feel herself blushing, or was it just the heat from the flames? Either way, it was the first time in her life she'd ever been uncomfortable being the center of attention. Is this what it felt like to really feel seen?

"Truth or dare?" Austin asked Jesse, finally taking the focus off her.

Jesse proceeded to do a dare that involved acting out a scene from his favorite movie without speaking. Absolutely none of them came even close to getting it right through their hysterical fits of laughter as Jesse leaped back and forth, apparently trying to play two roles from *Die Hard*.

That left Gigi, who Jesse let off easy with a truth question involving which reality show she'd most want to be on, to which she answered *Shark Tank*.

"What would you be pitching to the sharks?" Sienna asked.

"Oh, I don't want to go pitch anything. I want to be one of the sharks," Gigi said, smiling as she sat back in her chair and steepled her hands together before playfully wiggling her fingers like a Disney villain.

Jesse laughed. "Yep, that checks out."

In lieu of another round of truth or dare, they told stories about Jesse and Callie dating as teenagers, about Wyatt, Jesse, and Austin, and some of the pranks they used to play on each other when they traveled for baseball games, and other fun stories about childhood on Big Dune Island. Piper shared some of her favorite stories about celebrities misbehaving, and they all tried to guess who they were.

An hour or so later, Sienna yawned, saying she might go ahead and turn in after having an early-morning recording session. Callie agreed, and Jesse followed her in so they could watch TV together until she fell asleep. Teddy and Wyatt wanted to go inside to play a gaming system they'd spotted in the living room, and Piper said she'd go watch, leaving Austin and Gigi alone by the fire.

"Should I put a few more logs on?" Austin asked her.

"Sure," Gigi said. She was a bit of a night owl, so she wasn't tired yet. She watched as he fed the fire, moving the new logs into place with a metal poker. His biceps flexed under the tight sleeves of his T-shirt, and she was glad she hadn't guessed a size up when she ordered it.

When Austin sat back in his chair, he plopped down as if he had the weight of the world on his shoulders.

"Is there any word yet on getting the Carsons' license extended so Luke can stay with them?" he asked.

Gigi shook her head. "Nothing yet, but that doesn't mean anything. It's a government office. They're notoriously slow."

"How much time do you think we have before they move Luke?"

"Luckily, they'll be slow on that too. So hopefully it'll all work out."

Austin ran a hand through his floppy blond hair, sighing. She could tell the situation weighed heavily on him.

"I've been thinking," he said, pausing as if he wasn't sure he wanted to say whatever it was out loud. "What would it take for me to get approved to foster? Could I get Luke placed with me?"

Gigi was even more shocked than she had been when he'd answered the truth-or-dare question. "Wow, you really care about this kid, huh?"

"Yeah." He smiled. "He's just such a great kid. He's happy all the time, despite having every reason to be mad at the world. It's kind of inspiring actually. I'd just hate to see him ripped away from all the friends he's made here and the team, his teachers, all of it. It doesn't seem fair to make him start all over again somewhere new."

Gigi remembered her own thoughts recently on fostering. It wasn't something she was ready to do yet, so she was impressed that Austin was ready to just jump in headfirst.

"You can probably get approved in six to eight weeks if you're serious," she told him. "There's a shortage, and you'd look great on paper. You're financially secure, have a solid work history, and own a home with plenty of room. I don't think you'd have any problems getting approved."

"They won't care I'm not married?" Austin asked.

"Nope. That doesn't matter at all. They do like to know that you have a backup sitter for times when you can't be home, but you could put down Chloe. You could put me too," she said. She surprised herself with the suggestion, but she realized she meant it. If Austin wanted to foster Luke and needed her help, she'd be there.

He looked at her, his green eyes serious. "You'd do that?"

She shrugged as if it was no big deal. "Of course I would. I mean, obviously, I'm not going to bake cookies with him or anything. I wouldn't want to burn down your kitchen." She laughed.

"Yeah, maybe just order pizza and watch a movie," he said. "Keep it safe." Then his tone turned serious again. "I want to do it. On Monday when we get back. Can you help me start the process?"

"Just like that? You're ready to do it?"

"I am," he said.

Gigi could see in the way his jaw was set that he'd made his decision. "Well, look who's brave now," she said, smiling at him.

Maybe it was her who should be wishing she was a little more like Austin.

THE FIRE DIED DOWN AS GIGI EXPLAINED MORE TO Austin about the process for getting approved to foster. There was a lot of paperwork, an orientation class, a home visit, and then a home inspection. Gigi was confident he'd ultimately be approved. Then there would be more calls to try to get Luke placed with him. Foster parents didn't get to choose children, but if he was the only open home nearby—and she already knew he would be—chances are they'd put Luke in his care, especially since they already had a relationship.

"I think I'm going to hit the sack," Austin said, throwing some sand from a nearby pile on top of the remaining embers in the fire pit.

Gigi followed him back to the house, but she wasn't the least bit tired. She'd packed Margaret's journals and decided to read a little before bed on the off chance Grace was revealed to be some sort of relative. Tiptoeing into the bedroom she was sharing with Callie so she wouldn't wake her, Gigi got the journals from her suitcase and took them back into the living room. Settling in on the couch, she started to read.

There were a few more mentions of Grace as the entries spanned the mid-80s. It did seem as if Grace was at the house quite a bit, but there were no additional clues as to her exact relationship with the Cunninghams. Maybe she was a neighbor's child they watched often?

She picked up another journal, expecting it to start in 1987, where the last one had left off, but it jumped to 1995. Thinking they were out of order, she grabbed the third journal, but the first entry in it was in 1997.

Were there more journals somewhere in Margaret's room? She'd have to ask Rebecca if she'd been through everything yet. Gigi decided to go ahead and start reading the 1995 entries. The first two recorded some recipe experimenting and a detailed account of what Margaret had planted in the garden that spring, but as she turned the page to the third entry, her eyes were immediately drawn to Grace's name.

April 15, 1995

It's been another trying day with Grace. I don't know where we went wrong. We've given her everything—a loving home, the best education, all the opportunities a young lady could want. Yet lately, it feels like we're losing her.

Today, I caught her sneaking out again. When I confronted her, she lashed out, saying we could never understand her. Most hurtful of all, however, was when she reminded me that I'm not her real mother. I felt like she'd slapped me in the face.

There's a rebelliousness in her that I can't comprehend. She's been distant, secretive. I've noticed her school grades slipping, and she's been hanging around with a crowd I don't approve of. Ron says it's just typical teenage behavior, but I can't shake the feeling that it's something more.

I only hope we can find a way to reach her before it's too late. The thought of losing our little girl, of her walking away from everything we've built together, is almost too much to bear. But if we can't mend this rift soon, I'm afraid that's exactly what might happen.

Gigi sat back, stunned, even though her gut had been telling her that Grace was someone important to Mrs. Cunningham ever since she found that file folder full of drawings. It sounded as if maybe the Cunninghams had adopted Grace. So where was she now?

Gigi kept reading, each entry expressing more and more

concern for Grace. And then she found the entry that answered, at least in part, what had become of the girl.

March 15, 1996

I can barely hold the pen as I write this my hand is shaking so much. Grace is gone. My sweet, stubborn, beautiful girl has left us, and I fear it's for good this time.

It started as just another argument. Grace came home late again, smelling of cigarette smoke and alcohol. I was worried sick, imagining all sorts of terrible scenarios. When she stumbled through the door, I lost my temper. I demanded to know where she'd been, who she was with. I was scared, and that fear came out as anger.

Grace shouted back, accusing us of suffocating her, of trying to control every aspect of her life. I made a terrible mistake then. In my frustration, I snapped, "Fine! Go ahead and throw away the life we've built for you. See how well you do on your own!"

The moment those cruel words left my mouth, I wanted to take them back. The hurt in Grace's eyes was unbearable. For a moment, she fell quiet, and in that silence I saw the chasm I'd just carved between us.

Then she exploded. All the pain, all the confusion she'd been holding in, came pouring out.

She railed against the pressure we'd put on her to be perfect, to fit into the mold we'd created. And then she told us she was pregnant.

Ron and I were stunned. Before we could even process this revelation, Grace spat out that she'd rather raise her baby alone than subject it to the same suffocating expectations she'd endured.

I tried to backpedal, to apologize, to tell her we loved her and would support her no matter what. But it was too late. The damage was done. Grace ran upstairs and started throwing clothes into a bag. Ron tried to stop her, but she pushed past him.

The last thing she said before slamming the door was that she'd make her own family.

And just like that, she was gone. Into the night, carrying our grandchild with her.

I've spent hours by the phone, praying it will ring. I've called all her friends, but no one knows where she's gone. Or if they do, they won't tell me.

My heart is breaking, knowing she's out there somewhere, alone and scared, thinking we don't love her.

Tears stung Gigi's eyes. Mrs. Cunningham's anguish was palpable. Gigi herself had said plenty of things in the heat of the moment to Myrtle, but she hadn't meant most of them.

Sure, she was a control freak with outdated notions of the woman Gigi should grow up to be, but Gigi never doubted that her mother loved her. And although she could identify with the feeling of being suffocated that Grace expressed, she'd never once thought of running away. But she'd never been a pregnant teenager either, and she couldn't even begin to imagine how Ms. Myrtle would have reacted to that.

More of the puzzle was starting to come together. Either Grace was adopted or maybe she was a child from a previous marriage of Ron's? There was definitely some sort of lead here now that she knew Margaret wasn't Grace's biological mother, but that Margaret had called the child she was carrying her grandchild.

The next several entries were more of the same, and they were almost too heartbreaking to read. Gigi stopped to fire off an email to Mitch with enough details to help him search for Grace and her child. They had to be out there somewhere. If it turned out she was adopted, she'd inherit the estate just as a biological child would. However, if she was only Ron's biological child and had never been adopted by Margaret, she wouldn't inherit. But at least they had something to go on. She was confident Mitch could track her down.

Gigi's eyes were beginning to feel heavy, but she couldn't stop reading. She had to know if they'd eventually found Grace, although she feared she knew the answer based on the fact that no one on Big Dune Island even knew the Cunninghams had a child.

September 3, 1996

It's been six months since Grace left, and the ache in my heart hasn't subsided. I find myself wandering into her room, touching her things, desperately hoping for some connection to my little girl. The house feels so empty without her voice and her footsteps down the hall.

I keep replaying our last conversation in my mind, wishing I had said things differently. If only I had listened more and lectured less. If only I had told her how much I loved her, how proud I was of her strength and spirit, instead of focusing on my disappointment and fear.

I realize now that in my attempts to protect Grace, to give her the perfect life I thought she deserved, I sometimes forgot to see her for who she truly was. I was so focused on the daughter I imagined that I missed the remarkable young woman standing right in front of me.

Oh, how I long for a chance to tell her that I understand now. That being a mother doesn't mean being perfect. It means loving unconditionally, even when it's hard. Especially when it's hard. I would give anything to hold her once more, to tell her that no matter what she's going through, no matter what mistakes she thinks she's made, she will always have a home here. Always have a mother who loves her.

I've been thinking a lot about my own mother lately. We had our share of disagreements, but she never gave up on me. Even when I thought

I knew better, even when I pushed her away, she was always there, waiting with open arms. I see now the strength it must have taken, the love that fueled her patience.

If Grace ever reads this, I want her to know: You are loved. You are missed. And you will always be my daughter, no matter where life takes you. I'm sorry for the times I made you feel less than the amazing person you are. I'm here, I'm listening, and I'm ready to start again whenever you are.

And to myself, a promise: If I'm ever blessed with a chance to mend this relationship, I won't waste it. I'll listen more than I speak. I'll support more than I direct. I'll love without condition or expectation. Because that's what mothers do. That's what Grace deserves. That's what I should have done all along.

Tears were free-falling down Gigi's face now. Had Mrs. Cunningham really never seen Grace again? It was too much to bear.

Gigi had the strongest urge to hug her mother. Could she even remember the last time she'd done that? The last time she'd really hugged her, not just a perfunctory one-arm gesture she did because it was expected?

Entering the bedroom quietly, she put the journals back in

her suitcase before crawling in bed next to Callie. Poor, sweet Callie, who hadn't even been able to tell her mother goodbye.

Callie stirred next to her. "You okay? It's late."

"I'm okay," Gigi whispered. She reached for Callie's hand under the sheet, holding it like they used to when they were little girls and couldn't sleep after watching a scary movie. "I just had a bad dream."

Callie squeezed her hand before her breathing evened out again, and she was back asleep. Gigi resolved to be nicer to Ms. Myrtle the next time she saw her. And she made a silent promise to Mrs. Cunningham that she'd find Grace.

Chapter Twenty

Austin

Austin had been thinking about applying to be a foster parent ever since Mrs. Carson told him about Luke's situation. He'd tried to be patient to see how the Carsons' situation was going to play out, but the more he'd thought on it, the more he pictured the little boy living with him and all the fun they'd have together.

He and Luke had had such a great time the day he'd picked him up after school, from practicing at the field to video games, pizza, and even doing homework. Austin wasn't naive enough to believe things would always be as easy, but Luke was a joy to be around. He deserved more than life had given him so far.

He hadn't planned on blurting it out to Gigi last night, but he couldn't keep it in any longer. The prospect of it excited him, and he wanted to get the process going as soon as possible. He wondered if Luke had ever been in a canoe or a kayak. His uncle would let them come out to the lake house anytime they wanted. And on the island there was surfing and fishing and maybe even windsurfing. Was Luke a good swimmer?

In Austin's mind, Luke was already living with him. He couldn't wait.

Austin had been thankful when Jesse had volunteered to cook the eggs and bacon that had been delivered in the grocery order the day before. They were the first two up, so he left Jesse in the kitchen and went out to the shed to pull out the canoes and kayaks for the big day ahead. Once he had them all lined up on the shore, he went back inside to find everyone was starting to stumble into the kitchen, thanks to the delicious smell of bacon and coffee. Gigi seemed uncharacteristically quiet, but he chalked it up to her not being a morning person.

The day was a flurry of nonstop activity from there. What was supposed to be a leisurely caravan in the canoes and kayaks over to an island in the middle of the lake turned into a race to see who could get there fastest. This time, Wyatt and Piper edged out Austin and Gigi, claiming victory.

Back at the lake house they played badminton on the lawn with equipment they'd found in the shed, but no one was all that knowledgeable about the rules, so they didn't keep score. They made sandwiches for lunch, eating out on the deck overlooking the lake. A song of Callie's written about Jesse came on the radio over the outdoor speakers and they all sang along, making her blush.

After lunch, the guys decided to take out the jet skis while the ladies lounged in chairs on the deck to gossip and catch some rays. Gigi made sure everyone knew what time they were supposed to be showered and dressed for dinner, putting Austin and Wyatt in charge of grilling the steaks.

Dinner was followed by the official splitting of the group.

The men were going to the lower level in the game room to play poker while the ladies had a slumber party in Gigi and Callie's room. They were putting on face masks and painting each other's nails or whatever it was women did at a slumber party while watching an old rom-com.

After the movie was over, the women wandered downstairs to check on the guys. Austin sent Wyatt and Teddy up for the provisions for s'mores while he and Jesse went out to get the fire pit going. The group played another round of truth or dare around the fire pit before the women decided they'd rather get in the hot tub than play the karaoke game Gigi had planned. Who wanted to compete against two professional singers anyway?

Although it was an oversized hot tub, it was cozy with all eight of them in it. They ended up paired off on each of the four sides of the bench that ran around the interior. Piper and Wyatt had been flirting hard all day, and Teddy had practically tripped over the side of the tub, trying to get in next to Sienna. That left Austin next to Gigi, not that he minded.

He tried to ignore each time her leg brushed against his, her smooth skin like silk against him. Each time it happened, she scooted away. Obviously, she wasn't thinking the same thing he was.

That time in the hot tub after Mary Catherine's wedding wasn't the first time he'd wanted to kiss her. Back when they were in high school, they'd ended up on the beach alone one night when Jesse and Callie had gone for a walk down the shore. They'd had a nice chat, dropping their usual banter to commiserate about their parents and the pressure he felt about the upcoming MLB draft. Neither of them was dating anyone at the time, and when he'd walked her to her car in the dark parking lot, she'd gone up on her toes as if she was going to kiss him. He'd started leaning down, welcoming the opportunity, but she'd gone left of his mouth and kissed him on the cheek instead.

She'd friend-zoned him. She couldn't see herself with someone like him. So he'd settled for being her friend.

Austin was so distracted by her closeness that he didn't hear everyone deciding to head back inside, suddenly noticing they were all standing up. As he rose to leave, Gigi grabbed his arm.

"Stay?" She looked at the others wrapping towels around themselves, seemingly checking to see if they were listening. "I want to tell you about something."

He'd basically do anything Gigi asked, so he sat back down in the corner closest to her.

"We're going to stay a little bit longer," Gigi said when Callie turned back to look for her. "Be up in just a bit."

"Okay," Callie said, raising an eyebrow as she looked back and forth between them as if they were stealing away for a private rendezvous.

Gigi rolled her eyes. "It's not like that."

Of course it wasn't. Once you got friend-zoned, women never looked at you any other way. Not that it happened to him with many women. Any other women, really. Just the one that mattered.

Gigi waited until they'd heard everyone's footsteps recede, the back door on the deck finally closing.

"Top secret wedding plans?" he guessed.

"No." She frowned. "Although please tell me you already had the guys get measured for their suits and got them ordered."

She'd trusted him with exactly three wedding-related tasks: this weekend at the lake house, getting suits ordered, and making a suggested playlist for the band. And by trusted, he meant assigned him tasks and reminded him regularly. But he felt confident he'd aced this weekend. Everyone was having a great time.

"Everyone's measured and ordered," he said, drawing a check mark in the air. He and Teddy had gone one day in Jacksonville, and Wyatt had gone to the local seamstress claiming to need to order a suit for a college buddy's wedding. Jesse already had a tux he'd bought to wear to awards shows with Callie. Operation secret wedding was on track.

"You know how I told you I went to see Rebecca?" Gigi asked, changing subjects.

"Yeah," he said. "I assume it had something to do with the estate?"

She chewed on her bottom lip. "It does. I really need to talk this out with someone, but I can't break confidentiality now that the inn is a client." She smiled. "However, if you were an employee of Franklin Law, then I could tell you. So I'd like to hire you for a contract position as my probate assistant."

"Do I get healthcare?" he joked. "A 401(k)?"

"No, but you can put it on your résumé so it looks like you've had one real job in your life." She smirked.

He shrugged. "I always wanted to work in a law firm. I'll take it."

Gigi held out her hand, and he reached across the hot tub to shake on it. When she slid her hand inside his, every muscle in his body told him to use it to pull her closer to him and kiss her.

No, that was the two beers he'd had that evening talking. This was business, not pleasure.

"Okay, now that you're my probate assistant, I can tell you that I think there might be another heir to the Salty Breeze. Someone with a better claim than Simon." She told him about the journals and what she'd read the night before.

"Think Mitch can find her with what you know now?" he asked.

"Yeah, it'll just take him some time," she said. "I emailed him about it last night."

"Potentially good news though, right?"

She explained to him how it could still be a dead end if Margaret hadn't adopted Grace and was only related by blood to Ron.

"So she just packed a bag and left one day, never to be heard of again?" he asked. "Wow. Even I never hated my dad that much."

"I don't think she hated them. She just felt misunderstood and like she didn't fit in. She probably felt trapped by her pregnancy. Like it somehow proved they'd been right about her."

He considered this. He'd certainly felt trapped in the life of a baseball player, as if he'd been born into a role and given no other choice. Then he thought of Luke. Was that what it was like to try to raise someone else's child? He had already imagined adopting Luke if their foster situation went well. Gigi had explained the program was called "foster-to-adopt," meaning he intended to adopt Luke if everything went well. But he didn't want to make any promises to Luke upfront that he couldn't keep. Then again, what if it was Luke who didn't want to stay with *him*? What if Austin could never truly relate to everything he'd been through and made Luke feel as if he didn't belong anywhere?

"I'm going to go see Myrtle when I get back," Gigi said. "Reading what Mrs. Cunningham wrote made me realize that maybe she and Myrtle have some things in common. Myrtle just wants my life to be perfect. She's just never been able to reconcile that her version of a perfect life and mine aren't the same. But our problem has never been a lack of love. I know she loves me." Gigi rolled her eyes. "Loves to drive me crazy, but loves me."

He thought of his relationship with his father, which he'd so often compared to Gigi's with Ms. Myrtle. It didn't feel the same though. He did question if his father loved him. If anything he did would ever be enough.

"Your dad loves you too," Gigi said quietly, as if she could read his mind. When he didn't reply right away, she pushed further. "He needs some serious therapy to resolve his stuff with his own dad, don't get me wrong. But that's not about you. It's about him."

She wasn't wrong. His mind drifted back to Luke. How could he be any kind of father figure to him when he had issues with his own dad? He might just be repeating the cycle.

"Think that means I need to heal my own stuff before I try to take on a kid like Luke?" Austin asked her, genuinely interested in her opinion. She'd seemed supportive the night before, but had she just gotten caught up in the excitement of solving Luke's imminent relocation?

"No," Gigi said. "I think you've had a pretty good playbook for what not to do. Do you still see that mindset coach?"

She was referring to Jed, the psychologist he'd met while playing for the Braves. Jed used the title "mental performance coach" to make it more accessible to guys who would never agree to see a psychologist or therapist. He'd helped him sort through a lot of his issues with his father and with baseball, but Austin wasn't arrogant enough to think he'd done all the work. He could tell by the way his father still got under his skin so easily. So he still had calls with Jed when he felt he needed to vent.

"Yeah, we talk every few months."

"Have you talked to him about Luke and the plan to apply for fostering?"

He ran his hand over the bubbles that gurgled to the surface of the hot tub in front of him. "No, but I guess I should."

"Don't say it like it's a punishment," she teased. "It's just a chance to sort through all your feelings on it, confirm you're committed and doing it for the right reasons, and go into the situation confident about what you have to offer Luke."

"Maybe he can help me come up with some boundaries for my dad too," Austin said. "He's already showing more interest in Luke than I'd like. I don't need him thinking this gives him license to play grandpa and treat Luke like he did me."

"That's the spirit," Gigi said. "Very healthy. See, you'll make a great foster parent and one day a great dad, whether that's to Luke or someone you haven't even met yet."

"Thanks, G," he said. "That means a lot."

They sat in silence for a minute, each sipping their drinks and enjoying the sound of the crickets and cicadas serenading them.

"Do you think you would have been ready to do this if the Luke situation hadn't come up?" Gigi asked him, studying his face.

"I mean, I've always wanted kids. I just hadn't really thought about fostering or adopting. I figured it would happen the more traditional way one day when I found the right woman and settled down."

She raised an eyebrow. "I can't wait to see what she's like. This woman who can tie you down and make you fall in love with her."

"You and me both," he joked, but the truth was he had a pretty good idea who she was, and she was sitting right across from him. He'd always felt drawn to her, but these past few weeks working on the wedding together had only made the pull stronger.

Maybe it was the beer talking, but he wanted to test the waters. See if she'd pick up on the hints.

"I think she'd be kind of like you," he said, locking eyes

with her. He saw the surprise in her green eyes, the water reflecting in them, making them dance. "She'd be smart and funny, and she'd call me out when I was being dumb. She wouldn't need me, but she'd let me take care of her every once in a while. And, of course, she'd be insanely good-looking."

When Gigi didn't break eye contact, he scooted over on the bench closer to her. Not close enough to touch, but close enough to see if she'd back away. If she'd find an excuse to get out.

She didn't move, so he decided to make his.

"G, why do you think we never dated?"

She opened her mouth and then closed it again, and he couldn't stop looking at her lips, imagining what they'd feel like against his.

"Because we're friends," she finally said, but her eyes were on his again, and he could swear they were begging him to counter her argument.

He scooted closer until he was next to her again like he had been when the rest of the group was there. "But isn't that the basis of the best relationships? Friendship?"

Her eyes searched his, as if she wanted to ask him where this was coming from. But she couldn't be that surprised, could she? She had to know he'd always had it bad for her.

"But what if it didn't work? Jesse and Callie are our best friends. What if we couldn't even stand to be in the same room together?"

"What if it did work? What if we couldn't stand to be apart?" Austin reached for her hand under the water, holding it tightly in his. When she didn't resist, he reached his other hand up and ran it along the right side of her jaw, tracing it before lifting her chin. When he saw her eyes drop to his lips, he knew exactly what she was thinking, because he was thinking it too.

And then he stopped thinking. He stopped listening to

the voice in his head that told him he was in the friend zone and lucky to be there, to be in any part of her life, and he lowered his lips to hers.

They were every bit as soft as he'd imagined, and she was kissing him back. She scooted closer, turning into him until their knees were touching, electricity racing through his entire body, so aware of every place their bodies were meeting.

He forced himself to pull back. He wanted to look into her eyes, to see if she thought this was a mistake. That's not what he saw in her eyes though. Gigi wasn't looking at him as if he was just a friend anymore.

"I've wanted to do that for almost fifteen years," Austin said, reaching over to tuck a strand of hair that had escaped her ponytail behind her ear.

Her laughter filled the night air. "Oh, please. You were making out with half my class back then. Never once did you try to kiss me."

He shrugged. "Doesn't mean I didn't want to."

"Honestly, I thought you were going to kiss me in the hot tub after Mary Catherine's wedding, but then you didn't."

"I didn't think you wanted me to. I thought you'd friend-zoned me."

"Pretty hard to get out of the friend zone when you've never even asked me out on a date."

"Dinner then. Tuesday night."

"Okay," Gigi said, smiling as she pulled him closer for a kiss that wasn't nearly as long as he wanted it to be. "Tuesday night. Pick me up at eight." Then she took her hand from his, stood up, and walked out of the hot tub.

All he could do was watch her walk away and wonder why he'd wasted the last fifteen years not kissing Gigi Franklin.

Chapter Twenty-One

Gigi

Callie had already gone downstairs by the time Gigi woke up the next morning. She was grateful because she needed a minute alone before seeing Austin again. Would he have told Jesse when he got back to his room last night? Callie had been sound asleep, and Gigi wasn't ready to tell anyone anyway.

What surprised her most was that she didn't regret it. Quite the opposite. But her biggest fear was that Austin would. She knew he hadn't consumed enough beers to be drunk, but the combination of even a couple with a hot tub could leave you feeling a little uninhibited.

She blushed, remembering the kiss. It had been a toe-curling, insides-melting, fireworks-overhead kind of kiss. Of course, he'd had plenty of practice.

No, she had to stop thinking of him like that. She'd spent too many years giving him a hard time about the women he dated when she knew the real him and the very valid reason he had for not getting close to anyone. He was a grown man who was ready to turn his entire life upside down to keep a little boy from having to leave the community he'd come to call home. If Austin had avoided serious relationships, it wasn't because he only wanted to have fun; it was because he had such a big heart, and it was already half broken thanks to his childhood.

As she got dressed, Gigi tried not to care that her hair was curling around her face from the humidity of the hot tub the night before or that her nose was a little pink from being out in the sun. If she put on a full face of makeup, everyone would comment. Their time at the lake had been very casual, and there was no need for makeup today just to eat breakfast and drive back home.

Well, maybe just some tinted moisturizer and mascara. No one would really notice that.

Her heart was pounding in her ears as she descended the stairs. It sounded as if everyone had already convened in the kitchen for breakfast. She had no idea how Austin would act in front of everyone else. She had no idea how she should act.

Austin turned as she entered the kitchen, where everyone was in various stages of putting bacon, eggs, and biscuits onto their plates. His lips curled into a smile when he saw her, giving her a little wink before he turned back to scooping eggs from the skillet.

"Morning," Callie said in her usual cheerful voice. "I never even heard you come in last night. How late did you guys stay up?"

Did Callie know? Was that a leading question or was she just making conversation?

"I didn't hear Austin come in either," Jesse said. "I was wiped from yesterday."

Why was everyone so obsessed with how late they stayed

up? She'd stayed up much later the night before reading the journals.

She knew she was just being paranoid, so she busied herself with putting food on her plate and pouring a giant mug of coffee to help her wake up.

Once they were all around the table out on the deck, conversation turned to the wedding and how surprised everyone was going to be when they found out they weren't at the Franklins' anniversary vow renewal, but instead Jesse and Callie's wedding.

"I still need you to decide if you want to offer the official photos to *People* or *Vogue*," Piper said between bites of bacon. "I'm sure they'd both jump at the opportunity for an exclusive. That dress totally begs to be on the pages of *Vogue*, but *People* is a little less showy, more your style, Callie."

"*Vogue*," Gigi said at the same time as Callie said, "*People*."

"Oh, good, there's a consensus," Piper joked.

"Do we get to be in it too?" Wyatt asked. "Like the whole wedding party? Because that would be killer."

"Maybe," Piper said. "I'll send them a bunch of early edits from the photographer—all approved by Callie, of course—and then they'll make the ultimate decision. I'll see what I can do though," she said, tossing a flirty smile Wyatt's way.

Gigi snuck a glance at Austin, who sat diagonally across the table. His eyes were already on her, and she felt self-conscious, wondering how long he'd been watching her eat. No one looked good stuffing their face. He flashed a quick smile before turning to answer a question from Jesse about the song list they'd been working on for the band. She glanced around the group to see if anyone had noticed, but everyone was chatting and eating, completely oblivious to anything happening between them.

She couldn't believe they were going on a date on Tuesday. What was it like to go on a date with someone you already knew so well? All the usual first-date conversation starters about work and family could be skipped. So, what would they talk about? The wedding? The inn? They already talked about those things, so would this just feel like a normal meal together like the dozens they'd shared over the years?

Then she thought about the end of the date and the potential for another one of those kisses. Gigi could still feel the way he had traced his fingers along her jaw before tilting her chin up. How everything had gone quiet, and his lips had met hers in a moment she could still see in slow motion in her mind.

It hadn't been anything like she'd imagined kissing Austin would be when she'd thought back on that missed opportunity all those years ago. Instead of their usual competitiveness, there had been a gentleness that made her chest ache. The kind of kiss that felt like a beginning.

"You coming?" Callie asked her, already standing next to the table.

"Yeah, sorry. My caffeine hasn't kicked in yet." She stood to follow the group inside, noticing that Austin was hanging back, waiting on her. They were the last two lining up to file through the door, and she felt his finger graze hers. When she looked up, he smiled at her, his long lashes framing his deep green eyes. She let her free hand linger by his, a little thrill running up her spine, knowing they were flirting right under their friends' noses.

The boys were heading out to fish before going back to the island. Callie and Sienna needed to get back into the studio in the afternoon though, so the ladies were planning to leave after they ate breakfast and cleaned up the house. Gigi was a little bummed she wouldn't have the ride alone with Austin like they'd had on the way to the lake, but part of her was also relieved. She had no idea how to talk to him now they were exploring something beyond friendship. Suddenly, everything they knew about each other made her feel vulnerable. He knew some of her deepest fears, her biggest insecurities. Things that could be weaponized against her if their relationship went south down the road.

Gigi shook the thought from her head as she packed up her bag. They weren't in a relationship. They'd shared one kiss. Okay, two.

As the women hugged the guys goodbye, the house returned to its previous condition, she and Austin fumbled to find the right placement for their arms. She was considerably shorter than him, but she'd tried to go up on her toes and put her arms around his neck when she should have gone under his arms. This resulted in their arms tangling and then rearranging.

"Bye, G," he said before leaning down to whisper in her ear, "I'll see you Tuesday."

His warm breath had all the hairs on her neck and arms standing up despite the late-summer temperatures outside. And as she pulled back so no one would notice they were hugging way too long, Gigi could hardly wait for Tuesday.

―――

Margaret's words in the journals about her relationship with Grace had stayed with Gigi through Sunday and into Monday. Gigi had thought she'd accepted her relationship with Myrtle for what it was, but Margaret had her wondering if it had to be that way.

She could tell Myrtle was surprised when she called and asked her to have lunch on Tuesday.

"I have to say, Georgia, I was surprised you wanted to have lunch," her mother said as she transferred the takeout salads from their to-go containers to her everyday china. "You usually treat dining with me like a chore." She suddenly stopped what she was doing and turned to Gigi. "You aren't sick, are you? Is something wrong?"

Gigi gave a little smile and shook her head. "No, I'm fine. But I did want to talk about some things."

Ms. Myrtle raised an eyebrow. "You're not pregnant, are you?"

"No, I'm not pregnant either. I'm not even dating anyone." Her mind went to Austin and their date that evening, but she wasn't ready to tell her mother about that.

"That's a whole separate problem we need to discuss," Ms. Myrtle said, pointing a fork at her. "Mary Louise's son just got divorced. It's not an ideal situation, but he's handsome and recently made partner at his firm. At least have dinner with him."

Gigi took one of the salads, topped with shrimp, from the counter, shaking her head as she followed Ms. Myrtle into the dining room.

"I'm not going on a date with Mason Cartwright. The ink isn't even dry on his divorce, and I hear it was his infidelity that caused it."

"That's just gossip," Ms. Myrtle said as she placed her salad and ice water at the head of the table and pulled out her chair. "Jennifer started those rumors so she could get more alimony out of him."

"Regardless, I'm not interested in Mason," Gigi said, taking her seat. "As a matter of fact, I already have a date tonight."

"With who?"

She wasn't ready to tell her mother who it was with, because she wasn't really sure whether Myrtle would approve. After all, Austin wasn't a doctor or a lawyer, and Myrtle still talked to him as if he was a child half the time. Besides, the whole point of this lunch was to start rebuilding their relationship.

"I promise to let you know if it goes well. Let's give it a date or two."

Ms. Myrtle narrowed her eyes while she chewed. "This all sounds very mysterious. It's a small town. You know I'll find out who it is."

"I'm sure you will." Gigi laughed. "And when you do, we'll talk about it, but that's not what I wanted to discuss."

Her mother waved her fork in her hand for Gigi to continue. "Okay, so what did you want to speak with me about?"

Gigi couldn't reveal any of the confidential details to her mother, so she kept things vague. It wasn't hard to do, because she didn't know the whole story anyway.

"I recently did some work with a woman whose daughter ran away. The daughter was only in her teens and ended up pregnant. Their relationship was already strained, and she assumed her parents wouldn't approve, so she just packed a bag and left."

Her mother clutched at her heart. "Have they found her yet?"

Gigi shook her head. "No, it's been a long time now, and they haven't seen or heard from her."

"So they hired you to help find her?"

"Something like that."

"Teenage pregnancy isn't what any mother wants for their child, but it's so much different than it was back in my day. There was this girl from my prep school who got pregnant, and her family shipped her off to Nebraska to live with an aunt and uncle until she had the baby and gave it up for adoption. Then she just came back to Charleston and pretended she'd gone to help them on their farm for six months. Like a debutante from Charleston knew anything about farming," she said, shaking her head. "But we all pretended we didn't know what happened, because those kinds of things simply weren't discussed. Today, it's just all out in the open. They even made that awful reality show glamorizing teen pregnancy." She waved her hand in the air then furrowed her brow. "But why are you telling me all this if you're not pregnant?"

"I'm telling you because I got to know the mother." It wasn't exactly true, but she had read her diaries, which made her feel as if she had. "And it made me realize that even though her daughter thought her mother didn't understand her, and felt some pressure to live up to the idea her mother had in her head about who she was supposed to be, she didn't really give her mom a chance to try by being open with her."

Gigi paused because the next part was going to be hard to say. Her mother had one perfectly shaped eyebrow raised, and she'd put down her fork.

"I'm not pregnant, but I have always felt pressured to live up to some sort of ideal you have about who I'm supposed to be."

Her mother was immediately defensive, sitting up straighter in her chair and putting both hands on the dining room table as if she might push back from it and leave the room at any second. It was exactly the sort of dramatic thing she was prone to do.

"You have always done exactly what you've wanted, Georgia Franklin. If you're not happy with your life, don't put that on me."

Gigi reached over and put her hand over one of her mother's. "Mom." Tears sprung to her eyes as she used the word she hadn't said in years. "I *am* happy with my life. That's what I'm trying to tell you. I know I didn't do things the way you would have had me do them, but I'm very happy with my choices. I just wish seeing me happy made you happy."

Gigi half expected her mother to jerk her hand out from under hers, but she felt it relax. Her mother stared at her for a long minute, and Gigi braced for what she might say next.

"That's all I've ever wanted for you," her mother said. "I guess I just don't understand it. For me, happiness is you and your father." She shrugged. "And I want that for you. To find a man who loves and supports you. To have a child"—she gave her a little smile—"who brings you such joy when she isn't driving you completely mad."

Gigi felt a single tear escape her eye and roll down her cheek. She waited for her mom to lecture her about crying and how all it does is make your eyes puffy, but her mother's eyes were full of tears too.

Ms. Myrtle turned her hand over under Gigi's so they were holding hands. "I'm so proud of you, my beautiful girl. Even if I don't always understand you. I give you a hard time because pressure makes diamonds. And you, my dear, were born to sparkle."

Now the tears were flowing freely down both their faces.

"I would still like for you to find a husband though," her mother said after dabbing at her face with her linen napkin. When Gigi opened her mouth to retort, her mother held up her other hand to stop her. "Not because you need one, but because you want one. Your father is my best friend, and I hope one day you find yours. And that you have beautiful babies together." She laughed as she squeezed Gigi's hand. "But they're not calling me grandma. I'll never look old enough to be a grandma."

"No," Gigi assured her mother. "Certainly not."

Gigi wasn't naive enough to think they'd never have another disagreement, or that her mother would ever truly understand her choices. However, she did think maybe they'd finally found a way to start respecting each other's differences.

When Gigi climbed into her car after lunch, she realized she'd missed a call from Mitch. Her mother didn't allow phones at the table, so it had been in the kitchen in her purse. His voicemail said he'd found something, so she was anxious to hear what it was. She dialed from her car's Bluetooth before pulling out of the driveway to head back to the office.

After they exchanged greetings, Gigi told Mitch how surprised she was he'd found something already.

"You're not going to believe this," he said. "Are you sitting down?"

"Yeah, I'm driving. What is it?" Possibilities swirled through her mind. Had he found her? Was she nearby?

"I think that kid Luke is the Cunninghams' grandson."

"What?" She jerked her car into a parking lot so she could stop and pay attention. Luke's mother was dead. Luke's mother was Grace?

"I'd already been trying to track down that kid's mother's real name. I found out last week that she changed it about twenty years ago, but it took me a few days to get copies of the filing. Then I saw her birth name, Grace Marie Cunningham. You'd just sent me the info from those journals, and I realized all the pieces fit together. I didn't want to tell you until I was sure, but I got more records requests back this morning, and Ron was definitely her father. Her mother, Ron's ex-wife, died when Grace was seven. Annnnd," he drew out the word, pausing for dramatic effect. "Margaret adopted her on her tenth birthday."

"Are you sure?" Gigi was still putting the puzzle together in her mind. "Luke isn't old enough. Grace was pregnant in the mid-nineties."

"I'm pretty sure," he said. "Unfortunately, I think she must have lost that first baby. I can't find any birth records under either of her names except for Luke. I'm still tracing things, but it looks like she bounced around the Midwest for years. I found a few misdemeanor drug charges and a DUI. Then eight years ago, she had a son: Lucas David Washburn. One month before she died, she moved to a little town between Big Dune Island and Jacksonville. That's how he ended up in foster care here."

It couldn't be a coincidence she had moved so close to Mrs. Cunningham. Had they reunited and Margaret never told anyone? Gigi really hoped they had. She knew from Luke's file that he never remembered meeting any grandparents or aunts or uncles, but he'd only been six when his mother passed.

"If that's all true, then Luke would inherit Mrs. Cunningham's estate," she said, still connecting all the dots in her head. "Not Simon."

"I'll leave the legal stuff to you," Mitch said. "Can you email me over what you found? On Luke and Simon?"

"Sure thing," he said.

The few miles drive to her office felt as if it took hours. Gigi was so excited she was practically buzzing. It sounded crazy, but the inn was safer in the hands of an eight-year-old than it was with Simon, especially if Austin was going to be his guardian.

An hour later, she'd reviewed all the documents Mitch sent over. She was as convinced as he was that Luke was Mrs. Cunningham's grandson. She had plenty she could take before a judge.

Assuming the boy did inherit the estate, it would be placed in trust until he was eighteen, and she'd need to petition the court to appoint a trustee. Her mind went back to Austin. His plans to foster Luke just got a lot more complicated.

Chapter Twenty-Two

Austin

Austin felt his phone vibrate in his pocket during practice, but he was in the middle of hitting fly balls into the outfield for the boys, so he ignored it. As the boys jogged in to put their equipment away at the end of practice, he looked to see who had called.

It was Mark. Maybe he'd found out something about the twenty acres next to the inn.

Luke came into the dugout, so he stuffed his phone back in his pocket. "Good job out there," he told the boy, nodding toward the outfield. Luke had caught every fly ball he'd hit him.

Luke reached out his hand to do the secret handshake they'd devised during their sleepover. He gently slapped the little boy's hand palm-to-palm, then back-to-back, before fist bumping him and making an exploding gesture.

It took everything in Austin to keep him from telling Luke that he'd filled out the foster-parent application the day before. As far as he knew, the Carsons hadn't shared with the boy that he might have to relocate in the hopes they could figure out a solution before then. He'd gone to see them the night before to tell them about his idea, and they'd been fully supportive of his plan, saying they couldn't think of a better situation for Luke.

Austin had been a little afraid they'd prefer to try to keep Luke with them, but they admitted their hands would be pretty full with three children, and Liam's younger sister needed a lot of attention since it was her first foster home. They'd been excited that he'd still be nearby and could stay in the same class and participate in the same activities, plus he and Liam had grown very close.

"Are you coming for dinner again tonight?" Luke asked him now.

"Sorry, buddy. Not tonight. I have a date."

"Ooh, Coach has a girlfriend," Sam teased from where he was putting his bat away in his bag nearby.

"She's not my girlfriend," he corrected. In his head he added *yet*. "I'm just taking her to dinner."

"Are you going to kiss her?" another kid teased.

He sure planned to, but that wasn't an appropriate conversation with young boys. Austin wasn't really sure what was appropriate. He was going to have to read some parenting books or something. Having Luke with him full-time was going to be really different from just being his coach.

"I'm going to be a perfect gentleman," Austin assured him. "Now you go home and work on those pop-ups. We've got a big game on Saturday."

Austin was anxious to get the rest of the kids packed up and safely with their parents so he could leave. He needed to get home and take a shower before picking up Gigi for their late dinner.

On the way home, he returned Mark's call.

"Your instinct was right," Mark said after they exchanged greetings. "The kids do want to sell. I called, acting like I was interested, and they shuffled me off to their broker, some guy named Phil. He let me know they already have an offer in hand from a developer."

"Do you know who it is?"

"Some outfit from Atlanta I'm not familiar with. I did a quick search though, and it looks like they build a lot of resorts and large hotel complexes."

"Of course they do," Austin groaned.

"This Phil guy said something else interesting you might not have heard yet. Are you familiar with the piece of property next door, the bed and breakfast?"

"Yeah," Austin said, not revealing anything more.

"Sounds like the owner died recently—you probably know that—and the guy who's inheriting it from her is planning to sell. Phil bragged about how he was the one who tracked the guy down, some distant cousin who didn't even know he was related to the lady. Anyway, Phil is trying to package the properties together to drive up the sale price of both."

"That sounds like Phil," Austin confirmed. "Real peach of a guy."

"I kind of got that vibe. Don't worry, man. I told him I wasn't interested. Too rich for my blood."

"Appreciate you. Next round of golf is on me."

"Anytime. See ya."

He couldn't wait to tell Gigi she'd been right about Phil being involved.

After his shower, Austin changed his clothes three times

before settling on a dark pair of jeans and a sage-green button-down his sister had once told him matched his eyes. That was a good thing, right? He rolled the sleeves up to look a little more casual before tucking in the shirt and untucking it again. He wanted to look as if he was trying, but not like he was trying too hard.

Satisfied he'd hit the mark, Austin grabbed the calla lilies he'd picked up on his way home from work earlier and hopped in his truck to go pick up Gigi. The woman at the florist had assured him they'd be perfect for the woman he'd described, and Austin had to admit they looked classic and elegant, just like Gigi. Cranking the radio, he sang along with The Rolling Stones on the way over to keep from overthinking the date he'd wanted since he was a teenager.

When Gigi opened her front door, his heart did a little skip. She was wearing a navy dress that made her look as if she'd just come home from work, her feet bare and her hair piled on top of her head in a bun. The casual elegance of it made him want to reach out and pull her close.

"These are for you," he said, holding out the bouquet of white flowers.

Her face lit up as she took them, bringing them to her nose. "They're beautiful. Thank you." She stepped back, gesturing for him to come in. "I just need to get these in water, and then I have some exciting news to tell you."

"Really? I have some news to tell you too," he said, following her into the kitchen. He settled onto one of the barstools at the kitchen island, watching as she pulled a vase from under the sink and filled it with water.

There was something different about her tonight—a lightness to her movements, a sparkle in her eye when she glanced his way. He found himself leaning forward on his elbows on the gray marbled countertop, drawn to her energy.

Gigi took her time arranging the flowers, humming softly

to herself. When she finally set the vase on the counter to his right, she came around to take the barstool next to his, swiveling on it to face him.

"So," they both said at the same time, then laughed.

"You first," Austin offered.

"No, you go ahead," Gigi insisted. "I want to hear your news."

"You know Mark Swisher?"

"The football-player-turned-real-estate mogul in Jacksonville? Yes."

"I asked him to look into the twenty acres. You know, just poke around and see if the kids really are putting it up for sale and whether they have anyone interested." He could see her face dropping, so he rushed to get to the good part. "And you were right! The kids put Mark in touch with Phil, and he told Mark he already has an offer in hand, *and* he told him about the inn and how he'd helped find an heir who wants to sell it as a package deal with the twenty acres."

Gigi blinked back at him, a line forming between her eyes.

"You were right, G," he said, reaching out to grab her arm for emphasis. "Phil has been manipulating all of this behind the scenes. I can't wait to see his face if you're right and Margaret had a daughter who should really inherit it. Hopefully she won't be as eager to sell."

"Why did you call Mark?" Her voice was carefully controlled, but he could hear an edge beneath it.

"I thought. . ." He trailed off as she pulled her arm away from his touch. "I was trying to help."

"Help?" She slid off the barstool, putting distance between them. "By going behind my back to just step in and solve my problems? Like you did with Dalton?"

"G, that's not—"

"No, let me finish." She wrapped her arms around herself, pacing the kitchen. "My whole life my mother has been convinced she could run my life better than I could. I finally convinced her that's not true, and now I have to worry about you stepping in and taking her place?"

"Why do you insist on doing everything yourself? Why can't you let anyone help you? I was trying to protect you. How many times have we hashed this out? I thought we put the Dalton stuff to bed."

"We did, but then you went and did it again. You learned nothing." She threw her hands up in the air before tightly crossing her arms across her chest.

He opened his mouth to fight back against her accusations, but closed it for a second to think. Was there any merit to what she was saying? Had he done the same thing again? In his mind the situations were totally different.

"This is completely different from Dalton," he said.

"Is it? Because from where I'm standing, it looks exactly the same. You decided something needed to be done, and instead of talking to me about it, you went and did it yourself."

Austin stood up, running a hand through his hair in frustration. "You want to know what really happened with Dalton? I've kept quiet about it for years because I thought I was protecting you, but maybe it's time you knew the whole story."

She stopped pacing, turning to face him. "What do you mean, the whole story?"

After convincing her to sit back down, he told her everything he'd hidden from her. How Dalton had been divulging information he'd obtained from Gigi's computer about a big project she'd been working on as an intern at a law firm. She'd told Austin about the project being adverse to Dalton's father's firm, but she'd thought they could keep business separate from personal. Then Dalton had revealed himself to be the self-interested prick Austin had always thought he was when he overheard him in the parking lot of Gigi's apartment complex one night telling his father what he'd just seen on Gigi's computer.

Austin confronted him and told Dalton he could break up with Gigi on his own, and Austin wouldn't file an ethics complaint with the bar against his father. Austin didn't want to tell Gigi the truth, because he knew she'd beat herself up over it. She'd probably even have to report it to her boss, which might put her in a bad position for allowing Dalton to so easily access the confidential information. She'd told him how important the internship was, and Austin didn't want her to be punished because Dalton was a jerk.

Gigi sat in silence for a long moment, processing everything he'd told her. When she finally spoke, her voice was quiet but steady. "You should have told me."

"I was trying to protect you."

"That wasn't your call to make." She met his eyes. "I thought you'd caught him cheating on me and were just sparing me the humiliating details. I questioned everything about myself after that. My judgment. My ability to balance my personal and professional life. I wondered if I'd done something wrong, if I wasn't good enough." She took a shaky breath. "And all this time, you knew the real reason."

"G, I—"

"Let me finish." Her voice softened. "I understand why you did it. But, Austin, I'm a big girl. I'm smart, and I'm resourceful. Yes, it would have been awful to report it. Yes, it might have affected my internship. But those were my choices to make."

He leaned forward, elbows on his knees. "I didn't want you to have to make those choices. Not when I could handle it."

"But that's exactly what I'm trying to tell you. When you make decisions for me—even with the best intentions—you're taking away my agency. Just like my mother does when she tries to plan my life for me." She reached out and touched his hand. "I need a partner, not a protector."

"I never thought about it that way," he said quietly.

"With Mark, with Dalton . . . you saw problems you could fix. But Austin, I need you to trust that I can fix my own problems. That doesn't mean we can't work together, but you have to talk to me first."

She said *we*. She wasn't closing the door. He could show her that he could step up. That he heard what she was saying.

It reminded him of the thing that had struck him most when he'd confronted Dalton all those years ago. He hadn't fought Austin on it at all. He'd just let Gigi go. She deserved someone who was not only trustworthy, but who also recognized what a lucky man he was and fought for her.

Him, he was that man.

"I'll promise to talk to you first, if you promise to accept my help every once in a while. You don't have to face everything alone, you know."

Her face softened. "I'll take it under advisement." A small smile tugged at the corners of her lips. "I hear that's what good partners do. They trust each other to handle things, and then they're there to support each other through the fallout."

He took her hands in his. "I get it now. I promise. Remember what I said the other night during truth or dare? You're the bravest and smartest person I know. You don't need me to fight your battles. You need me to stand beside you while you fight them yourself. I see that now."

She squeezed his hands. "What if we compromise?" she asked. "You can protect me if there's a ball flying at my face or a rabid-looking dog lunging at me or something like that. Physical threats only. Anything else, you bring to me and we discuss. Deal?"

Austin nodded. "Deal. So maybe we can start over with

this Mark thing? You tell me what you need from me, and I promise to actually listen this time."

A slow smile spread across her face. "Actually, that brings me to my news. I think I found something in Margaret's papers today that's going to make Mark's intel completely irrelevant. Let's order in instead of going out. You're going to have to sit down for this part."

After they ordered delivery from a local Chinese restaurant, they went out on Gigi's back deck overlooking the ocean with a couple glasses of wine. She flipped a switch and globe lights strung in a crisscross design above her deck turned on. They settled into side-by-side Adirondack chairs facing the waves crashing in the darkness in the distance, and Gigi told him about Mitch's discovery that the girl in Mrs. Cunningham's journal was Luke's mom.

"Whoa," Austin said, running his hand through his hair. "You weren't kidding about needing to sit down. That's crazy."

"It's kind of sad," Gigi said, looking down at the white wine she was swirling in her glass. "She must have moved here to be near Mrs. Cunningham, but there's no evidence to suggest they ever saw each other again or that Mrs. Cunningham knew she had a grandson. Surely she would have gotten a will done if she'd known, if they'd reconciled. Or Luke would remember meeting his grandmother."

"So, what happens now?"

"Mitch sent me all the court documents he found, and I think it's enough to take to the judge to have Luke confirmed as the heir to Mrs. Cunningham's estate."

"That would make Simon what? Luke's cousin?"

"Very distant cousin, yes."

Panic raced through Austin's body, making him sit on the edge of his chair and turn to Gigi. "Does that mean he'd get custody of Luke? Because he's family?"

"He could file for custody if he wanted to, but I don't think that'll be an issue..."

"But what if he wanted Luke to get to the B&B?"

"Honestly, I hadn't thought about that," she said, pausing for a moment to reflect. "But he'd be taking on raising a child for the next ten years. Sure, he could get appointed as the trustee for what Luke would inherit. And he could try to get permission to sell or develop the land under the guise of raising funds needed for Luke's health and education, but he'd still be committing to raising a child. I just don't think he'd take it that far. Plus, you could always hire someone to fight the custody. Just because he's a cousin—a very distant cousin, at that—doesn't make his case a slam dunk. They've never even met each other. Plus, you can keep Luke in the community where he is, and you actually want to foster him. The Carsons would testify on your behalf. I just don't think it'll come to that."

He relaxed a little, sitting back in his chair. It was all a lot to take in.

"Okay, so let's say he doesn't want custody of Luke. What happens to the B&B?"

"Anything Luke inherits would be placed into a trust by the court, to be held until his eighteenth birthday. The court will appoint a trustee to protect the assets, using them only when necessary to support his health, education, maintenance, and support." She turned to him. "You could petition to be the trustee. If he were placed with you for fostering, you'd be his legal guardian."

"So, what? I'd run the B&B?" That sounded like a little more than he'd signed up for.

Gigi shrugged. "What's to run? Rebecca oversees the day-to-day. You'd just have to make major decisions on things like renovations or budget changes. Your financial advisor could help you. I'll help you."

If I'd Have Known

The whole situation felt overwhelming. Austin was a single guy with very few responsibilities, and now he was talking about not only fostering Luke, but also being in charge of everything he would inherit from Mrs. Cunningham, including a B&B. Was he biting off more than he could chew?

Chapter Twenty-Three

Gigi

Gigi asked Neville Long if she could meet him on Wednesday morning. She wanted to break the news about Luke and the inheritance in person to see the look on his face when she did, and his office was only a couple of blocks from hers.

Neville's office was in one of the historic buildings on Main Street that had been converted into office suites. He had half of the first floor with room for two offices, a conference room, a reception area, and a break room with a small kitchenette. She'd been there many times before for real estate closings.

"Good morning," Neville's assistant, Amy, greeted her as she entered his office. "Can I get you a coffee?"

"Please," Gigi said. "I haven't fully caffeinated yet this morning."

She'd stayed up late after Austin left, drafting up the documents to file with the court to declare Luke the sole beneficiary of the Cunningham estate. After she told Simon and Neville, she'd head over to the B&B and share the news with Rebecca, and then she would meet with the Carsons to decide how to tell Luke.

Austin had been really rattled by the news about Luke's inheritance. It had shifted their date to more of a business meeting with a side of therapy, but she was glad she was able to be there for him to talk it all out. Fostering had felt like a small step to him, one that could be temporary if it didn't work. However, stepping in as Luke's trustee and making more decisions for his future, along with managing the trust's ownership of the B&B, felt like a heavier responsibility. Gigi had assured him there were other options for trustees, such as professional companies that managed trusts, but she could tell it had him rethinking the whole situation, and she wanted to give him space to sleep on it.

Amy returned from the kitchen with a steaming mug of coffee and said she could show Gigi back to Neville's conference room.

Neville stood from the table to shake her hand as she entered. He was wearing one of his trademark seersucker suits, this one in a pale blue and white-striped pattern. She towered over his small stature in her heels.

"We've got Mr. Frazier on with us as well," he said, nodding toward the phone speaker in the center of the large mahogany table.

"Good morning, Mr. Frazier," Gigi said pleasantly as she sat in one of the black leather chairs to the side of where Neville occupied the head of the table. She only wished she'd be able to see Simon's face too. She'd wanted to wipe that smug look off it since the first day she met him at Margaret's celebration of life.

"I expect we'll have the signed order back any day now

appointing Mr. Frazier as administrator." Neville took a sip of his coffee. "You mentioned you had some news about the inn you wanted to share with us?"

"Actually," Gigi said, leaning her elbows on the table to make sure Simon could hear this part, "the news is about the estate proceedings, but—yes—it does affect the inn. Its ownership, specifically."

She paused, taking in Neville's reaction. If he was concerned, it didn't show. He was leaning back in his chair, hands folded over his midsection.

"Mr. Frazier, I'm not exactly sure how to tell you this, so I'm just going to come out with it," she said, pretending to be concerned about his feelings. "New information has come to light, and I don't think you're the legal heir to Mrs. Cunningham's estate."

Neville sat up in his chair abruptly, and Gigi was afraid it might catapult his small frame across the table.

"What heir? We've done a thorough search, and no one has a better claim than Mr. Frazier here."

Gigi resisted the urge to say something sarcastic about his "thorough search," instead keeping her delivery professional. "I'm afraid that's not true. We've discovered evidence that Ron Cunningham had a child from a prior marriage, a daughter named Grace. When Grace's mother passed, Margaret Cunningham adopted Grace at age ten. Unfortunately, she became estranged from the Cunninghams, going so far as to change her name, which is why no one here had any knowledge of her."

Neville shook his head. "I want to see whatever evidence you have that this woman—who you just admitted had no relationship with them and wasn't even Margaret's biological child—is the rightful heir."

"I brought a copy of all the court records my investigator found," Gigi said, removing a folder from her purse and sliding it across the table to Neville. "There's a very clear paper trail showing her adoption, then a name change, and then the birth of her only legal child. Unfortunately, she passed in an accident two years ago, so it's actually her minor child who appears to be the sole heir."

Simon was silent on the speaker phone, making her wish again she could see his face. She'd have to settle for Neville's however, which was now pinched as he scanned the first few pages of the file.

"I'll review these and get back to you," Neville said, shutting the folder and standing, clearly dismissing her.

Gigi took a long sip of her coffee before standing. "Good seeing you, Neville. Hope you gentlemen both have a good day."

And good riddance, Simon Frazier, she thought as she left the room.

GIGI'S NEXT STOP WAS THE SALTY BREEZE. SHE'D told Rebecca she'd be over after breakfast service.

Once they'd settled into rocking chairs on the back porch, Gigi told Rebecca what she'd found in the journals and the subsequent details Mitch uncovered, adding that the little boy was in foster care on the island.

"Wow, so he was right here under our noses?" Rebecca asked.

"It can't be a coincidence Grace moved back so close. But it breaks my heart to think she didn't reach out to Mrs. Cunningham before the accident."

"Maybe she wanted to get on her feet first?" Rebecca guessed. "Margaret rarely left the property after Ron died. I think I would have known if she'd gone somewhere to meet her or if she'd come here. I guess it's possible she kept it from me, but I doubt it."

"Maybe it's why she was always so hesitant to do her will," Gigi said, watching a family with a toddler trying to fly a kite down on the beach. "She didn't want to write Grace out because she still had hope she'd find her again, but she couldn't leave it to her not knowing what had become of her."

Rebecca shook her head. "It's all just so sad."

"The little boy is great though; wait until you meet him. She would have loved him."

"You've met him?"

"No, but he's on the baseball team Austin coaches, and Austin says he's a smart, happy, and funny boy. In fact, Austin recently applied to foster him because he may have to move out of his current situation. Austin is also open to adopting him in a year or two if everything goes well." Gigi didn't mention his hesitations the night before because she was sure he wasn't going to waver once he had time to digest it all.

"So my boss is going to be an eight-year-old?" Rebecca laughed.

"Hey, they always say to bring in young, fresh minds if you want to innovate." Gigi shrugged her shoulders, smiling.

"Honestly, I'd trust him more than I did that Simon guy."

"Right?" Gigi said, lifting her coffee mug to Rebecca's to toast. "Long live the Salty Breeze."

Gigi might not have been able to reunite Grace and Mrs. Cunningham in life, but she knew she'd found the right person to entrust the Salty Breeze and carry on Mrs. Cunningham's traditions. Now, she just hoped Austin believed he could be that person.

Chapter Twenty-Four

Austin

Austin had been distracted at his team's game that evening. He'd sent a runner to second when he should have held him. He'd left the pitcher in one batter too long, allowing what ended up being the winning run to score before replacing him.

He wasn't mad that his team had lost. He was mad at himself for putting the kids in bad positions where their confidence could take a hit. In his chat with the team after the game, he tried to make sure they knew it was on him. He'd made the mistakes, not them.

Gabe, the pitcher he'd left in too long, was kicking at a rock in the dirt with his toe, but the rest of the kids were pretty unfazed when he scanned their faces. No one liked to lose, but they seemed to be taking it in stride.

As the kids started to scatter toward their parents, he called Gabe over. Patting him on the shoulder, he said, "Hey, you pitched a great game. That's on me. You were in trouble, and I should have gotten you out of it. Next time, if you want out, you wave at me, and I'll come get you. Only you know when your arm is tired."

"Nah, Coach. It's my fault. I did a push-up challenge with my friend Caleb last night, and my arm was sore today. I shouldn't do stuff like that during baseball season."

Austin shook his head. "No way, dude. You're a kid. Have fun. Play with your friends. Baseball can't be your whole life."

What Austin would have given for someone to say that to him as a kid.

"You'll get 'em next time," he said, patting Gabe on the head.

"Thanks, Coach," Gabe said before trotting off to meet his folks, who were talking to another set of parents up near the parking lot.

"Left him in too long," Austin's father said as he came up behind him. He'd come to watch Luke again.

"I'm aware," Austin said, walking back into the dugout to start stuffing his gear in his bag.

"You need to work on Luke's stance too," his father said, talking to Austin through the chain-link of the dugout. "He's not bending his knees enough."

"Dad, not now," he snapped. "Luke has bigger problems than his batting stance."

"What do you mean?"

"I'm not discussing this with you." Austin jammed his glove into the top of his bag before zipping it shut.

"Sounds like you need to discuss it with someone."

Austin whipped around as he put the bag on his shoulder. "And why would that someone be you?"

"I don't know. Maybe because I've raised two kids." When Austin rolled his eyes, he continued in a gentler tone. "Besides, two heads are better than one. What's the problem with the kid?" His dad came into the dugout and sat on the bench.

Austin was already in what his mental performance coach would call a spiral of self-doubt, so why not just let his dad pour gasoline on the fire? He sat on the bench in the dugout and told Dan about Luke's situation with the Carsons and his decision to apply as a foster parent so he could take Luke in.

Instead of telling him it was another of his dumb ideas, his dad simply asked, "So, what's the problem?"

He looked up and stared at his father for a minute. "You have nothing to say about me deciding to foster a kid all on my own?"

"What's there to say? The kid needs a home, and you obviously have a special relationship with him. I see it when you're with him out on the field. Although, you probably shouldn't play favorites."

He frowned at his father, who held up his hands in surrender before continuing. "You have plenty of room, and you have the resources. The kid needs someone to take an interest in him, and you clearly have. So I'll ask you again. What's the problem?"

"It's not that simple." He told his dad the rest of the story about the inheritance and potentially becoming the trustee.

"Don't you have a money manager or something? It's not like you have to make financial decisions on your own. You've got Gigi for the legal stuff, and you're no idiot yourself. You're in a much better position to become a parent than most people are. Certainly better than I was."

Austin stared at his father again. He'd never heard him comment on his parenting before. All he knew was that his father and mother had Austin after it was clear Dan's dreams of making it to the majors were over. Being a dad had always seemed sort of like a consolation prize he accepted only to try to live out his dreams through someone else.

"Look, I know I was hard on you." Austin scoffed before his dad continued. "Okay, probably too hard. But it was only because I saw so much potential in you. I didn't want you to waste it like I did and have regrets."

"What do you mean 'waste it'?" His dad never talked much about why he hadn't made it to the majors, just that he hadn't.

His dad waved a hand. "We didn't have sports psychologists and whatever back then. You were either clutch or you weren't. As I got closer and closer to making it, the pressure started to get to me. I began to get a reputation among the scouts for choking in critical situations. I overheard two of them talking about me one night after returning to the dugout, and that was it. I fell apart after that. Couldn't get out of my own head. My stats just got worse and worse, and eventually I had to admit I was never getting called up and came out with my tail between my legs."

Austin wasn't sure what to say. His dad had never been vulnerable with him in his entire life. The only reason he knew what an alcoholic jerk his grandfather had been was because Austin's mother had told him every time she was trying to make excuses for his father's behavior.

"There's no doubt in my mind that I had the physical talent to make it to the Big Show, but I never had the mental toughness," his dad said, pointing to his head. "And, yeah, maybe I was too hard on you sometimes, but you didn't suffer from that same problem, did you? I was so hard on you there was no room for you to be hard on yourself."

Austin frowned. "I'm not sure that's exactly what happened, but I get that's what you tell yourself."

"You made it, didn't you?"

"Yeah, maybe I was mentally tough on the field, but not off it. I've never felt good enough to make you proud. I just finally got old enough to realize it was an unobtainable goal I should stop chasing."

His dad gently smacked him in the shoulder. "Why would you think I'm not proud of you? You made it to the majors. You come back here; you help your sister live out her dreams. You're coaching these boys when you could be drinking beer with your friends or playing a round of golf. Of course I'm proud of you."

Austin shook his head. "You criticize everything I do. You roll your eyes about me owning the cafe with Chloe. You come to the games and tell me everything I'm doing wrong as a coach."

His dad shrugged. "Okay, so maybe I was hoping you'd play longer or move on to being a coach at the professional level, but I can let that go. You've carved out a nice life for yourself here, and I know you can give that kid a good life too."

As Austin quieted to try to digest the weird turn the evening had taken, his dad patted him on the back.

"What's the number one rule?" he asked Austin.

"Practice makes perfect," he recited.

His dad nodded. "Can't become a good dad if you don't practice. So might as well get on with it. I will if you will."

They sat in silence for a few minutes, just staring out at the empty baseball field. All their problems had started here, so maybe they could start to be solved here too.

Chapter Twenty-Five

Gigi

With only a week to go before Jesse and Callie's wedding, Gigi had invited Austin over to her house for dinner Saturday night so they could go over the final details without the fear of being overheard in a restaurant. Since their failed date earlier in the week, they hadn't been able to see each other. Austin had a Little League game and a Thursday Night Football game for the Jaguars, and she'd had a night meeting with one of her HOA clients and a zoning board meeting.

It was finally Saturday, and she was beginning to get nervous about the wedding, both pulling off the surprise with the guests and giving Callie the magical day she deserved. Gigi was also anxious to learn how Austin was adjusting to the news of Luke's inheritance and the added responsibility that might come with fostering him.

When she answered her door to find Austin on the other side, she instantly relaxed at the sight of him. He had his hands tucked into the pockets of his jeans and was wearing a navy Braves T-shirt, his floppy blond hair still partially wet from a shower. He was just the friendly, familiar face she needed to see after a long week.

"Hey, stranger," she said, reaching out for a hug.

He slipped his arms around her, and she gladly settled her head on his strong chest. Taking in a deep breath of clean, soapy scent, she finally forced herself to pull away. The warmth of his embrace lingered, making her wish she hadn't.

"That was nice. What was that for?"

As she stepped back and invited him in, she shrugged. "I just needed a hug."

Austin raised an eyebrow. "Something wrong?"

"I'm getting stressed about the wedding. I just want everything to be perfect."

"Get your checklist," he said, smiling. "We'll go over every single item and make sure all the i's are dotted and t's are crossed." His smile turned teasing. "Though knowing you, G, you probably have backup plans for your backup plans."

She swatted his arm playfully. "Mock all you want, but my obsessive planning is exactly why Jesse and Callie are getting their dream wedding."

"True," he conceded, following her into the kitchen. "Though I still say the guitar-shaped ice sculpture is overkill."

"It's not an ice sculpture. It's an ice luge for the signature cocktails," she corrected, unable to hide her smile at their familiar bickering. "And it's going to be amazing."

"I'm sure it will be," he said. "Show me what's left on the list. We'll divide and conquer."

"It's on the kitchen table," she said, walking over to sit down in her usual seat. "The pizza should be here soon."

Austin scooted a chair over next to hers, close enough that their shoulders brushed when he leaned in to look at the list. The casual contact sent a flutter through her stomach that she tried to ignore.

They flipped to her master checklist and started going down it. She'd already called Hannah at Whispering Palms the day before to answer final questions, and she'd confirmed with the florist and photographer. Reagan had called all the outstanding RSVPs to get the final headcount and then confirmed it with the caterer. Piper had secured people she trusted to do Callie's hair, makeup, and nails, and Gigi would join her to get ready over at her house. Callie, Gigi, Piper, and Sienna's dresses were all in and had been tried on. Austin assured her Jesse's tux was pressed and the groomsmen's suits were all scheduled to arrive on time the following week. Gigi had purchased a guest book, cake topper, and cake knife, along with some other wedding-day goodies for Callie. Austin and Jesse had finished the playlist for the band, and he'd sent it over and confirmed their arrival time.

The pizza arrived just as they finished checking off every item on the list. Austin insisted on paying for dinner, waving off her protests with an easy, "You can get the next one."

The casual assumption of future dinners together made her heart skip.

"I had no idea of all the planning that goes into a wedding," Austin said as he waited for Gigi to put a slice on her plate before he took one.

The gentlemanly gesture wasn't lost on her—another glimpse of the thoughtful man beneath the teasing exterior.

"I thought I knew, but there are so many little details you take for granted when you're just a guest. I have a newfound respect for Myrtle and all those events she plans," Gigi said.

Austin raised an eyebrow. "Did you just say something nice about your mother?"

"I did." Gigi smiled and then told him about her lunch with her mom the week before.

"Must be something in the air," he said. "I had a similar conversation with my dad the other night after the Little League game."

"Really?" She couldn't hide her surprise.

"Yeah, he actually talked me off the ledge about fostering Luke and being the trustee for his inheritance."

"Do tell," she said, putting down her pizza and leaning forward so she could give him her full attention. Their knees touched under the table, but neither moved away.

Austin told her about the conversation with his father and his renewed commitment to fostering Luke and stepping in however he was needed to help manage his inheritance and the Salty Breeze. As he spoke, Gigi found herself watching his face, struck by how his whole expression softened when he talked about Luke.

"Wow, I never thought I'd see the day," she said when he finished. "I don't even know which was less likely, Myrtle and me finding common ground or you two."

"I know. Who are we going to blame for all our problems now?" he joked.

"Oh, I'm certain Myrtle will still do something to irritate me before too long. There's no chance we'll get through this wedding weekend without her trying to make something all about her."

"Yeah, we've got two games this week, so plenty of time for my dad to come by and tell me everything I'm doing wrong."

"So, speaking of fostering Luke, you passed your background check, as expected, and you've been cleared for a home study. You just need to complete the orientation class."

"Two steps ahead of you. I'm going to one tomorrow afternoon."

She sat back in her chair. "I'm impressed, Beckett."

"I also bought some sort of course online about running a successful B&B." He smiled like a little boy who'd just spelled a word correctly in front of the whole class.

The earnestness of his expression made her heart flutter.

"So you're up to the challenge?"

"Of course I am. I intend to make the Salty Breeze the number-one ranked B&B in the entire Southeast."

That was the competitive spirit she'd always been drawn to in Austin. She had no doubt he'd achieve any goals he set with the B&B.

"Luke doesn't even know he just saved the oldest B&B on the island simply by existing," she said.

"Yeah, that's going to be a lot for an eight-year-old to try to understand." His confident facade cracked slightly, showing genuine vulnerability.

She smiled at him. "Good thing I know just the guy to explain it to him."

"I barely understand it myself." He laughed. "I just hope I'm up for this. Being responsible for a kid, a business. . ."

Gigi reached across the table and squeezed his hand. "Hey. You're not alone in this."

He turned his hand to lace their fingers together, his thumb brushing over her knuckles. "I know. That's probably the only reason I'm not completely freaking out. You're going to help me tell him though, right?"

"Of course," she said, walking over to where he was still sitting at the table. She leaned down and kissed him softly on the lips, running her hand through his hair. "I'm going to be right there with you every step of the way."

He pulled back slightly, his eyes searching hers. "You know, you're making some pretty big commitments here too, G."

She felt her cheeks flush, but held his gaze. "Maybe I'm realizing some things are worth the risk."

His answering smile was soft and genuine, without a trace of his usual smirk. He stood, pulling her closer. "Keep talking like that, and I might start thinking you actually like me."

"Don't push your luck, Beckett," Gigi murmured, but she was smiling as she pulled him down for another kiss.

Chapter Twenty-Six

Austin

The next week flew by in a flurry of radio shows, baseball games, foster-parent orientation, and wedding errands. It was finally the day before the big event. Austin had taken the day off to play golf with Jesse, Teddy, and Wyatt before the rehearsal dinner at Ms. Myrtle's house.

Jesse met him ahead of their tee time so they could get in a few swings at the driving range.

"Are you ready for the big day?" Austin clapped Jesse on the shoulder as he walked up behind him in the pro shop.

"I've been ready for this since the day I met her," Jesse said, beaming.

They got buckets of balls and started out toward the driving range.

"Speaking of things that are a long time coming," Jesse

said, "it looked like maybe you and Gigi were flirting a little more than usual at the lake house."

Austin and Gigi hadn't discussed letting their friends in on their budding relationship, but he was pretty sure she hadn't told Callie yet. He'd seen Callie twice since the lake house, and he was fairly certain she didn't know anything. He was bursting at the seams to tell Jesse now though. He wanted to twirl Gigi around the dance floor tomorrow night for all to see. He finally had a real shot with the girl of his dreams, and he wanted to scream it from the rooftops.

"There might be something happening there," he said as they claimed two spots side-by-side at the range.

"Wait, seriously?" Jesse asked, turning to face Austin and leaning on his golf club. "I was mostly kidding."

Austin couldn't hold back the smile pulling at the corners of his mouth. "We still haven't managed to go out on a real date yet, but I've been over at her place a couple of nights for dinner."

"It's about time. Callie and I have been waiting on you two to figure out you're perfect for each other since high school. She is going to die when she finds out," Jesse said. "I'm happy for you, man."

The two started hitting through their buckets of balls, talking between swings about the timeline for the rest of the weekend.

As they headed back to the pro shop to meet up with Wyatt and Teddy, Austin stopped, deciding to tell Jesse one more thing. He'd already told him what Mitch found about Luke being Mrs. Cunningham's grandson, but he hadn't shared his plans to foster yet. He'd wanted to wait until he was sure he was moving forward with it.

"You know how the Carsons were trying to amend their foster license so they could keep Luke?"

"Yeah. Did something happen with that?"

"No, they're still waiting, but it might not matter. I've applied to become a foster parent, and the plan is for me to foster Luke and become the trustee for his inheritance. Gigi's been helping me with the whole process."

"Wow," Jesse said. "That's not what I expected you to say."

Austin frowned. "You think it's a bad idea?"

"No," Jesse said, patting him on the shoulder. "Not at all, man. I think it's awesome. He's a great kid, and you're so good with him. In fact, I think maybe you both have what the other one needs."

Austin hadn't looked at it like that, but Jesse was right. He needed Luke as much as the kid needed him. Maybe the only way to move past his issues with his father was to become the kind of father he wished he'd had for a deserving kid.

THE REHEARSAL DINNER THAT EVENING WAS HOSTED at the Franklins' house. Their backyard was secluded enough that they'd been able to rehearse the wedding ceremony outside and then have dinner on the back deck.

There were tables covered in pale blue cloths, expensive-looking china and silverware arranged so perfectly he imagined Ms. Myrtle standing over someone as they used a ruler to get it all perfectly straight. In the middle of the table were low centerpieces full of white and blue hydrangeas, the latter being Callie's favorite flower, and small candles scattered around them.

Gigi was seated across from Austin at the rehearsal dinner, with him sitting next to Jesse and her next to Callie, the rest of the wedding party filling out the remainder of the table. The only other people in attendance were Jesse's parents, Uncle

If I'd Have Known

Lonnie, and Jacqueline, who were eating inside at the dining room table with the Franklins.

Every time Gigi looked up at him, Austin knew he got a goofy grin on his face, and he wondered if anyone else noticed. Callie clearly had because she kept leaning over to whisper to Gigi and giggle, both of their eyes firmly on him. He'd asked Gigi before the rehearsal started if they should pretend as if there was nothing going on between them, assuming she wouldn't be ready to tell everyone, but she'd said there was no need to make a formal announcement. They'd just act however they wanted, and everyone else could figure it out.

She was completely fearless. But not him. He was terrified of Ms. Myrtle and what she would think.

"She's always wanted me to marry someone rich, from a good family who she can brag to her friends about. You're a former professional athlete, for heaven's sake, and you have plenty of money. She likes your parents, and she's happy for me to stay here on Big Dune Island," Gigi had assured him. "It might not look like what she pictured in her mind, but you do actually check off most of the boxes on her list."

"As long as she doesn't throw her clipboard at me," he joked, nodding to where Ms. Myrtle had grabbed one from Piper's event coordinator and was jabbing her finger at something on the list.

Piper clinked a glass and asked everyone to come join the parents and families for toasts. They all went inside and found seats in the living room adjoining the dining room, where those who ate inside remained seated.

He'd been disappointed when it appeared Gigi was going to sit next to Callie, but she ushered Jesse over and told him to sit in the chair next to his bride. Then she came to the loveseat where Austin was seated alone, and it took everything in him not to put a hand on her leg or put his arm around her shoulders. Now that he could touch her, it was all he ever wanted to do when she was near.

When the toe of her high heel brushed his pant leg, he looked over to find her smiling at him. He scooted an inch closer to her, and Gigi did the same toward him, their hips and shoulders meeting in the middle as the cushions sagged. A casual observer might not even notice how close they were sitting, but he did. He could feel the heat coming off her, and he loosened his tie so he could breathe.

Jesse's father rose to give the first toast, thanking the Franklins for hosting the event at their home.

"Jesse, I am so proud of the man you've become. I'm not sure I say that enough, but your commitment and loyalty are unmatched, and I know you'll bring those same qualities into your marriage. I hope your mother and I have set a good example of what a loving relationship looks like"—he turned to Ms. Thomas and smiled at her—"but I can't take all the credit for the man you've become. Callie, many years ago you did a very unselfish thing by forcing my boy to stay home and help save the family business. I'll be forever in your debt, even if I would have told you back then that I didn't need his help. Son, I would have never asked you to make the sacrifices that you did, but the fact that you did so without being asked just speaks to the kind of man you are."

Mr. Thomas's eyes were welling with tears now as he continued. "Callie, I know we could never replace your parents, and you have your own family with Lonnie and now Jacqueline," he said, turning to raise his glass to the older couple. "But I hope you know that we've always considered you part of our family, so tomorrow is just a formality. I'd be so proud to have you call me Dad."

Callie jumped from her seat, tears streaming down her face, and ran to Mr. Thomas, hugging him. "I'd be so honored to call you Dad," she said.

Austin caught a tear of his own with his knuckle and felt Gigi slide her hand over his hand that was resting on his leg. She sniffed next to him, and he was surprised to turn and see tears glimmering in her eyes as well. As he looked around the room, he realized there wasn't a dry eye in the house. Even Ms. Myrtle was dabbing at her face with a napkin.

"Well, I don't know how I'm supposed to follow that." Uncle Lonnie chuckled as he rose from the table. "Jesse, you already call me Uncle Lonnie, so I'm not sure I have much to offer you." His smile turned serious. "Except that's not true. I'm offering you the most precious thing in my life: my dear, sweet Callie. I know I don't have to tell you how special she is, and that's why I'm willing to let her go. Because I've watched the way you've looked at her since you were teenagers—and I don't mean *that* way." He let out a hearty laugh as Jesse's face blushed. "I know fathers are biased when it comes to their children, but your father was right, Jesse. You've grown into an impressive man who's honest and kind and loyal. I'm trusting you with the most important person in my life, and I know I've placed my trust in the right man. You two are going to have a beautiful life, and I'm thankful to be here to witness it."

Everyone raised their glasses, and Austin turned to clink with Gigi as Jesse worked his way around the table to where Uncle Lonnie stood and embraced him.

"Now I know how she writes such beautiful songs about this place and the people here," Piper said from her chair next to the loveseat, wiping a tear from her face. "I should have worn waterproof mascara."

"You just wait. We'll have you convinced to move here next," Gigi told her. "The people here are pretty special."

When she turned to look at Austin, he was certain his heart literally skipped a beat. Somehow, he was finally living the life he chose, and it was even better than he'd imagined.

Chapter Twenty-Seven

Gigi

Gigi peeked out the windows of the house at Whispering Palms. She was with Callie, Piper, and Sienna at one end of the house, while Jesse, Austin, Wyatt, and Teddy waited at the other end so Jesse wouldn't see Callie yet. Nearly every chair on either side of the aisle outside on the lawn was filled. It had worked. No one in town had wanted to miss the Franklins' vow renewal.

Her father and the minister stood under a giant live oak. Spanish moss dripped from its branches and chandeliers were hung strategically from them, giving a soft, romantic glow in the pre-dusk hour. The plan was for her mother to walk down the aisle as if it were the vow renewal. Then, once she was in place alongside her husband, the minister would announce that everyone was really in attendance for Jesse and Callie's wedding.

Gigi had turned to give Callie's hair a final look when she suddenly heard her mother's voice over the speakers through the open windows.

"Good grief, who gave that woman a mic?" She rolled her eyes.

"I wanted to take a moment to thank you all for coming out this evening," Ms. Myrtle began. "Elliott and I are so touched that you'd take time out of your busy schedules for us. But I'm afraid I have some bad news. . ." She let her voice trail off.

Hushed whispers swept through the crowd, and Gigi could tell from the satisfied look on her mother's face that she was loving every minute of it. Gigi shook her head. Her mother was such a drama queen.

"Elliott and I will not be renewing our vows this evening."

The whispers grew louder—like a shock wave traveling through the gathering.

Her mother motioned for the guests to quiet down. "Don't worry. Elliott and I are still happily married. But today isn't really about us. It was just an excuse to get you all out here to celebrate another couple." She paused for dramatic effect. "Welcome to the wedding of Jesse Thomas and Callie Jackson!"

Gasps, clapping, and a few excited cheers erupted throughout the crowd.

Ms. Myrtle spoke over the noise, quieting them again. "Now, I know we all want to protect Callie and give her the wedding of her dreams. So, please, we ask that you refrain from taking and sharing any photos or news of the festivities ahead of the official release coming from her team tomorrow. After all, I didn't go to all this trouble to plan a secret wedding for you all to let the cat out of the bag. For tonight, let's keep Callie and Jesse to ourselves."

"She planned the wedding?" Gigi asked, rolling her eyes as she watched everyone in the crowd nodding, phones going back into purses and suit pockets.

"We couldn't have done it without her," Callie said. "I'll always be so appreciative to her and to all of you."

Gigi, Piper, and Sienna gathered around Callie for a group hug.

"Can we get our groom out here?" Ms. Myrtle asked before turning the mic back over to the officiant.

With that, music began to play, and Jesse made his way up the aisle. Gigi gave Callie a final hug as Uncle Lonnie entered the room to escort her.

"You're the most beautiful bride I've ever seen," she told her best friend before giving her a kiss on the cheek.

"Only until you get married," Callie retorted, winking at her.

Austin sprung immediately to mind, and for a second she could see him in a tux on the beach waiting for her to walk through the sand to him. They still hadn't even been on a real date yet, but Gigi knew more about him than someone she'd been on ten dates with. She knew there was real potential that one day he might really be that man waiting at the altar for her.

For now, she'd settle for walking down the aisle with him to watch their best friends get married.

When the bridesmaids met up with the groomsmen outside the back door to line up to walk down the aisle, Gigi instantly relaxed at the sight of Austin. He was handsome as ever in his perfectly tailored suit, his green eyes dancing as he looked her up and down.

"You look beautiful," he leaned down to whisper in her ear as they lined up at the back of the group. His warm breath and deep voice made the hair on her neck and arms stand up.

"Not so bad yourself," she shot back at him, looking him

up and down as he pulled away. She slipped her arm through his, ready to walk down the aisle and watch their best friends marry each other.

The wedding was beautiful and went off without a hitch. Sienna sang "Me and You Someday," Callie's first hit song, which she'd written about Jesse as a teenager. Callie and Jesse exchanged the traditional wedding vows. When the minister told Jesse he could kiss his bride, he tipped her back in a dip and gave her a long, sweet kiss to an explosion of applause from the crowd.

The wedding party took photos while the guests enjoyed passed appetizers and the open bar. Then everyone sat for a plated meal. Austin was seated next to Gigi, holding her hand or putting his arm around her as they waited between courses.

They'd decided not to hide their relationship tonight. Let everyone talk, including her mother.

Then it was time for the best man and maid of honor to give speeches. Austin went first.

"As I think you all know, I'm Jesse's best man, Austin Beckett, and apparently the guy he trusts not to embarrass him in front of all of you tonight. No promises there, buddy." He shrugged at Jesse, who stood a few feet away with Callie next to the incredible four-tier wedding cake Chloe had crafted.

"Jesse and I go all the way back to T-ball when I had to show him which way to run when he finally hit the ball. But that doesn't matter today, because Jesse has hit the biggest home run of his life by marrying his high school sweetheart, Callie Jackson.

"Jesse, I think you know you're not just my best friend. You're my brother. If I ever wonder how I should act or what I should do, I look to you. I know one day when I become a husband"—he caught Gigi's eye for just a second, and her stomach fluttered—"I'll be able to follow your example and have a happy marriage of my own.

"Planning this secret wedding has been quite an adventure, and I've got to give a shout out to Callie's incredible maid of honor, Gigi Franklin, for doing the majority of the work and letting me take half the credit." Austin laughed as he caught Gigi's eye again and nodded in her direction.

"To Jesse and Callie," he said, raising his champagne glass. "Here's to a lifetime of happiness, laughter, and hit songs."

Everyone toasted the couple as Gigi came up to take the mic from Austin. When their fingers met as he passed it to her, a jolt of electricity shot through her body. She couldn't wait to get out on the dance floor with him later.

"Good evening, everyone. I'm sorry we got you all the way out here tonight under false pretenses, but I hope you're having a wonderful time. It meant a lot to Callie to be able to get married in her hometown, surrounded by all the people she loves, and, as her best friend, I wanted to make all her dreams come true. So thank you to my parents for agreeing to this ruse and to Austin for just doing what I told him and not messing anything up." She laughed as she raised her champagne glass to him. He nodded and smiled back at her.

"Like Jesse and Austin, Callie and I go all the way back to elementary school. And like most of you know, Callie is still the same woman today she was back then. She's every bit as kind and caring as she is talented and beautiful.

"And today, she married her second-best friend," Gigi joked. "Okay fine, we can settle for a tie," she said, raising her glass to Jesse, who smiled and raised his back at her. "Jesse, I know I don't have to tell you to treat her well, but do remember that I'm not just her best friend. I'm also her lawyer. But don't worry, Cal, I'm not billing you for this." She'd been a little worried her joke wouldn't land, but laughter rippled across the crowd.

"In all seriousness, watching you two together over the last year or so has been inspiring, the way you support each other's dreams while building a life together. It's truly magical, and I wish you every happiness.

"To Jesse and Callie," she said, raising her glass as the crowd repeated her and raised their own.

From there, everyone went outside, where a dance floor had been set up under strings of globe lights. Jesse danced to "Landslide" by Fleetwood Mac with his mother, followed by Callie dancing with Uncle Lonnie to "Love Without End, Amen" by George Strait. There wasn't a dry eye in the house after watching Uncle Lonnie sway with Callie's head on his shoulder, followed by Jesse and Callie dancing to "Annie's Song" by John Denver.

The band kicked it up from there, inviting everyone out to the dance floor as they started Austin and Jesse's playlist. It kicked off with "Signed, Sealed, Delivered (I'm Yours)" by Stevie Wonder, and it wasn't long before the dance floor was full.

The first couple of songs saw all the bridesmaids gathered around Callie, singing along and dancing to the upbeat tunes. Then the band slowed it down and started their rendition of Etta James's "At Last" and Jesse stepped in to take Callie's hand. Piper spotted Wyatt on the edge of the dance floor and dragged him out with her, nodding her head as he shook his and pretended to resist.

Gigi felt a tap on her shoulder then and turned to see Austin with one hand out. She placed hers inside his, and he pulled her close, one hand on her lower back and the other still holding hers.

"I put this one on the list," he leaned down and said in her ear before pulling back to look in her eyes. He was searching them, and Gigi knew he wanted to know that she felt the same.

She smiled up at him. "I like it."

Austin was a better dancer than she ever would have imagined.

"Where'd you learn to dance like this?"

"I was Macy Roberts 'deb's delight,' remember?" he said, referring to what the dates of debutantes were nicknamed.

It was then she spotted her mother watching them closely from where she stood at a nearby high-top table with two of the League ladies. She raised an eyebrow in question when she caught Gigi's eye. It wasn't disappointment on her face, just curiosity.

"We've been spotted," Gigi said, rotating them so Austin could see where she'd just been looking.

"Do you think she suspects anything? She looks like she suspects something."

"Well, then let's solve the mystery for her," Gigi said, reaching a hand up behind his head to pull his face down to hers. She kissed him long enough to make her point, but also because she didn't want the kiss to end.

When she pulled back and glanced over toward her mother again, she was surprised to see a small smile on her lips. Her mother nodded at her and then turned back to the women at her table as if nothing had happened.

"I think we just got her blessing," Gigi told him.

"Really?"

"Okay, so it's probably not that simple, but she didn't jerk me off the dance floor by the ear either, so I think it's progress."

Halfway through the reception, all their friends had figured out they'd become something more. Gigi saw Wyatt high-five Austin at one point, and Piper had winked at her and said, "I knew he was taken."

Austin pulled her closer as another slow song started. "You know what I was thinking about?"

"What's that?"

"That first day we sat down to plan this wedding you had that giant binder, and that look on your face like you were preparing for battle."

Gigi laughed against his chest. "I was. I thought working with you was going to be torture."

"And now?"

"Now I think it might have been the best thing that ever happened to me." She felt his arms tighten around her. "Don't let that go to your head though."

"Too late." He grinned down at her.

The music shifted, and they watched as Jesse spun Callie across the dance floor, her dress twirling like a cloud around her.

"They look happy," Austin said softly.

"They do."

Gigi thought about how much her perspective had changed since they'd started planning this wedding. When she'd first pulled out the wedding binder to take to Callie, she'd flipped through her own pages of the book, thinking about what the little girl version of Gigi had thought love would look like. Less than a month ago, she'd thought it was about giving something up—her dreams, her identity, herself. She'd watched her mom pour everything into being a wife and mother, and swore she'd never do the same.

She'd watched Jesse and Callie over the past year though, noting how they made each other stronger instead of smaller. Now, here in Austin's arms, she understood something her younger self couldn't have known: The right person didn't ask you to be less. They helped you become more.

"What's going on in that brilliant mind of yours?" Austin asked, his thumb tracing circles on her lower back.

"I was just thinking about how wrong I've been about some things." She looked up at him. "You know, I used to think caring about someone meant losing a piece of yourself. But that's not it at all, is it?"

"No?" His eyes were searching hers again.

"No. It's about finding the pieces you didn't even know were missing."

As "(I've Had) The Time of My Life" filled the cool night air and Austin twirled her around the dance floor, she truly was having the time of her life.

Chapter Twenty-Eight

Austin

It had been a month since the wedding, but it was the biggest day in Austin's life. He hadn't been this nervous when he'd waited to see where he'd go in the MLB draft.

Today, Austin was going to tell Luke he could come live with him. He'd received his foster license permission for a foster-to-adopt arrangement with Luke, meaning he was taking Luke on with the intent to adopt him if things worked out. The social worker was coming to discuss it with Luke tomorrow, but Austin had talked with the Carsons and they thought Austin should be the first to tell him.

"You ready?" Gigi squeezed his hand before they got out of his truck.

He'd asked her to come along to help him explain the situation to Luke. She'd been there the previous week to tell him about his inheritance and explain his mother's relationship to Mrs. Cunningham, at least what they thought an eight-year-old could understand about it. They'd both agreed they'd share more with him as he got older, including Mrs. Cunningham's diaries eventually.

The boy had been confused at first, but upon learning he owned a B&B, he replied, "Cool! Can I live there?"

Now, it was time to talk to him about where he really could live.

The Carsons had arranged for Liam and his sister, Leah, to play at a neighbor's house, and Austin could see on Luke's face that he was nervous when he realized the adults were all sitting him down alone.

Katie started. "Luke, I hope you know how much Mr. Carson and I love having you live with us. You're such a good brother to Liam, and you've been so wonderful with Leah. I know it was a lot to ask you to move into Liam's room and give up your own for Leah. We're so proud of you for doing that for her."

The little boy looked from Katie to her husband, then to Austin and Gigi, clearly confused about where this was going.

"Did I do something wrong?" Luke's face was panic stricken, and Austin wondered if they were doing this the right way. He wanted it to be an exciting day, not an upsetting one.

"No, not at all, sweetheart," Katie said, moving from the couch where she'd been sitting with her husband to the loveseat next to Luke. "A while back, I went to Coach Austin and told him something I was worried about. You see, when we get approved to be foster parents, they tell us how many kids we can have in our house at one time, and we were only approved for two. I was worried when Leah came to live with us that they might not let us keep all three of you, but Miss Gigi has been helping us with that."

Luke looked at Gigi and back at Katie, too scared to ask any questions.

"But Coach Austin also wanted to help, so he decided to apply to be a foster parent."

When she paused, Luke looked over to Austin, who smiled at him to try to ease the tension.

"Buddy, how would you feel about coming to live with me?"

Luke looked from Austin to Katie, who smiled and nodded, and then back to Austin.

"Like all the time?"

"Yep, all the time. We didn't want to tell you until we knew everyone said it was okay, but your social worker is coming tomorrow to tell you that you can move in with me. That is, if you want to. You don't have to."

Luke looked back to Katie, and for a minute, panic rose in Austin's throat. He'd never considered that Luke might not want to come live with him.

"It's okay, Luke," Katie told him, rubbing his back as Jared came to sit on the other side of the boy. "Mr. Carson and I love you so much, but we always knew this wouldn't be your forever home. Remember we talked about that? And this way, we can still see you anytime we want. You'll be just down the street, and you can still go to the same school and play on the baseball team. And you can come over here anytime you want. You just pick up the phone and call us."

"Would I get to live with you forever?" Luke asked Austin as he turned back to him. "Or will I just have to move again one day when there's no more room for me?"

Austin's heart nearly shattered. He couldn't imagine what it must feel like for Luke to have lost his mother and now to be told he was leaving the only other family he'd ever had.

"What I asked to do is something called foster-to-adopt," Austin explained. "That means that I told the social worker that if you like living with me, I would adopt you, and you could live with me as long as you want. I wouldn't be fostering anyone else. I did this just because I wanted me and you to become a family."

Gigi reached over from the chair next to Austin and grabbed his hand, giving it a squeeze.

"So you'd be like my dad?" Luke asked, something that sounded like hope in his small voice.

"You don't have to call me that, if you don't want to. You can call me Austin. But I'd be what's called your legal guardian. You'd live with me, and I'd get to make all the sorts of decisions a dad would make for you until you're old enough to make them for yourself."

"Would I get my own room?"

"You sure would. Remember that room you stayed in when you spent the night at my house that time?" When the boy nodded, he continued. "It's all yours. We can even redecorate it however you want."

Luke looked at Katie again. "Can Liam come over and spend the night sometimes?"

"Sure, buddy," Katie said, squeezing him. "And you can come have a sleepover here sometimes too."

Luke nodded, his forehead furrowed, lips in a fine line as if he'd made a tough decision. "Okay, let's do it. I'm going to go pack." He was already leaping off the couch when Jared stopped him, laughing.

"Don't be in such a hurry to get out of here," Jared said. "You have to meet with your social worker tomorrow, and then you can move in with Austin next weekend, okay?"

"Okay." Luke shrugged, returning to the couch. "That works too."

They all laughed at his enthusiasm, and Austin felt as if he'd taken off one of those weight vests he used to run in for cardio training. Luke was just as excited about coming to live with him as he was, and he felt just like a little kid himself, counting down the days until it became a reality.

Austin had so many plans for the two of them already, from weekends at the lake house to surf lessons. He had also arranged with Rebecca for them to stay at the B&B one weekend so Luke could find out more about the Cunninghams and the inn he would one day own. He wanted them to spend time there on a regular basis so Luke could learn little by little what it took to run an inn, but Austin never wanted him to feel pressured to be involved in the day-to-day. His number two goal as a parent was to encourage Luke to be anything he wanted to be when he grew up.

His first goal was to make him feel loved. Every single day. And with Gigi by his side, he knew Luke was going to get everything he deserved.

Epilogue
One Year Later

Callie

"I think I'm more excited than when you proposed to me," Callie said to Jesse.

Austin had come to Callie the previous week and asked her to help him plan the perfect proposal for Gigi, and she knew exactly what to do. After all, they'd each planned their perfect proposals in the infamous wedding binder. And yes, of course, there was a tab for that.

"Omigosh, I see them coming down the beach now," Callie said, punching Jesse in the arm where he was sitting on the steps that led from Gigi's deck down to the sand.

While Austin and Luke took Gigi on a walk, Callie and Jesse had spelled out "Will you be my mom?" with seashells in the sand. In the wedding binder, it said, "Marry me?" but just this once, Callie didn't think Gigi would mind an adjustment.

Callie got the zoom lens ready, sitting down on the stairs next to Jesse so Gigi wouldn't spot them and get suspicious.

They were pretty well hidden by the dunes, but Callie had a straight shot down the path that led to the beach where they'd set up the message.

It seemed as if it took them an hour to get the fifty yards to the message in the sand, but it was probably only a minute or two. Callie was just so excited she could hardly sit still.

As she engaged the zoom lens, Jesse leaned over to peer at the screen with her. Gigi had stopped at the shells. Although Callie and Jesse couldn't hear anything, they could see the look on Gigi's face when she read the whole message and looked first to Luke, clutching her chest.

By the time Gigi turned around to Austin, he was down on one knee. Callie had been clicking as fast as her finger could push the button ever since Gigi had first started reading the message in the sand.

Gigi leaped into Austin's arms, nearly toppling him over as she hugged him. Callie could hear it when she shrieked, "Yes!"

Gigi didn't even pay attention to the ring as she picked up Luke and swung him around in a big circle. Luke made a face when she kissed his cheek—he was in that phase where public affection from your parents is embarrassing, despite the beach being practically empty—but he was all smiles. When she put Luke down, Austin wrapped them both in a big hug, still holding the ring box in his hand. Finally, they parted, and he put the ring on her finger.

Satisfied they had all the candid moments, Callie handed Jesse the camera and took off down the short path to the beach, yelling, "Congratulations!"

As the women ran into each other's embrace, Gigi said, "I thought you were in Nashville! You knew about this?"

"Who do you think put the message in the sand?"

"Hey, I helped too," Jesse said, coming up from behind and hugging Austin. "Congrats, man."

"Now we get to be moms together," Gigi said, putting her

hand on the bump that was just beginning to show through Callie's maxi dress.

"Yeah, except you're skipping the morning sickness." Callie laughed. The first trimester was a little rough, but she knew it would all be worth it when their little one arrived. "And the stretch marks."

"Can I babysit, Aunt Callie?" Luke asked. "Babies really like me."

Liam and Leah's father had gotten out early on parole for his white-collar crime, and they'd been able to go back to living with him. The Carsons now had a one-year-old boy they were fostering, and Luke loved playing on the floor with him when he went to visit.

"I'm not sure if you're quite old enough to babysit, but you can come visit the baby any time you like," Callie said.

Luke put his hands on his hips. "I'm old enough to own a B&B. Next week, I'm even going to give Miss Rebecca and Miss Josephine a raise."

They all laughed. Luke loved telling people he owned the Salty Breeze, and Austin took him over there to work on little maintenance projects on a regular basis. Gigi had told Callie about how they'd done the financials recently, and the inn was doing so well after Austin invested some of his own money into renovations that they had decided to give Rebecca and Josephine raises. They thought it would be fun to let Luke be the one to tell them as they tried to teach him about how important it was to take care of other people.

"You know if you babysit, you have to change the baby's diapers, right?" Callie asked him.

Luke scrunched up his nose. "I don't do that. Dad can do that, and I'll just play with the baby when it's a little bigger."

Luke had been calling Austin "Dad" for a few months, and Austin still smiled and puffed out his chest every time he heard it. Now Luke would have a new mom too, and Callie knew Gigi would be a great one.

Callie had had no idea when she came back home two and a half years ago, that it would change not just the course of her life, but also that of her best friends and this sweet little boy. If she had known that, she would have come home a long time ago.

A Letter from Savannah Carlisle

Hello!

Thank you so much for picking up my novel, *If I'd Have Known*. I hope you enjoyed being whisked away on a mental vacation to beautiful Big Dune Island!

If you'd like to know when my next book is out, you can sign up for new Harpeth Road release alerts for my novels here:

www.harpethroad.com/savannah-carlisle-newsletter-signup

I won't share your information with anyone else, and I'll only email you a quick message whenever new books come out or go on sale.

If you did enjoy *If I'd Have Known*, I'd be so thankful if you'd write a review online. Getting feedback from readers helps to persuade others to pick up my book for the first time. It's one of the biggest gifts you could give me.

Until next time,
    Savannah

Acknowledgments

Dear reader, thank you! If you've made it here, that probably means you've read my book. You have no idea how much that means to me!

I'd like to start out with a big thank you to Jenny Hale at Harpeth Road for continuing to believe in me and allowing me to continue the story on Big Dune Island with a second book set there. To my Harpeth Road editors—Karli Jackson, Lara Simpson, Lauren Finger, and Lottie Hayes-Clemens—thank you for helping make this book shine! Karli, thank you for helping me fine-tune my idea so Austin and Gigi could get the happy ending they deserved.

I have some of the best author friends a woman could ask for! Thank you to my author bestie, Lindsay Gibson, for always being just a text away, and to my Kiss Pitch 2022 group for their continued advice, cheerleading, and support.

To Olivia, my author assistant, I can't imagine doing this without you! Thank you for reading the very first draft of this book and ensuring I didn't turn in a mess.

I had a big assist on this one from two of my favorite lawyers, Teresa and Kristin. Thanks for eating chips and salsa with me until we figured out the B&B's succession issues!

So many of my other friends offer constant cheerleading and support through each and every one of my books. Shout out to Maggie, Stephanie/Twinny, Michelle, Scarlett, Allyse, Noreen, and Zoe! And to Austyn who helped keep me sane the final week of writing this while I hid out on a solo writing retreat in Breckenridge!

I have the best family. Thank you to my parents, my brother, Bo, and his wife, Nickki, and all my aunts, uncles, and cousins for always believing in and encouraging me. I have some of the most amazing aunts: Shug, Luder Belle, Nank, Mary Ann, and Judy. Also my adopted aunts Nancy, Gail, and Vicky!

I also married into the best family! Jane, Scott, Tonya, James, and Julie—I'm so lucky to have all of you!

To my husband, Chadd, thank you for always believing in me and giving me the time, space, and support to make my dreams come true. Love on!

And last, but certainly not least, to my readers and reviewers. I appreciate every email, social post, and review. I couldn't do what I love without you!